THE BEST
BRITISH FANTASY 2014

Also by Steve Haynes

The Best British Fantasy 2013

THE BEST BRITISH FANTASY 2014

SERIES EDITOR
STEVE HAYNES

CROMER

PUBLISHED BY SALT PUBLISHING
12 Norwich Road, Cromer, Norfolk NR27 0AX

All rights reserved

Selection and introduction © Steve Haynes, 2014
Individual contributions © the contributors, 2014

The right of Steve Haynes to be identified as the editor of this work has been asserted by
him in accordance with Section 77 of the Copyright, Designs and Patents Act 1988.

This book is in copyright. Subject to statutory exception and to provisions of relevant
collective licensing agreements, no reproduction of any part may take place without the
written permission of Salt Publishing.

First published by Salt Publishing, 2014

Printed in Great Britain by Clays Ltd, St Ives plc

Typeset in Paperback 9/12

*This book is sold subject to the conditions that it shall not, by way of trade or otherwise, be lent,
re-sold, hired out, or otherwise circulated without the publisher's prior consent in any form
of binding or cover other than that in which it is published and without a similar condition
including this condition being imposed on the subsequent purchaser.*

ISBN 978 1 907773 66 2 paperback

1 3 5 7 9 8 6 4 2

CONTENTS

STEVE HAYNES
Introduction   vii

PRIYA SHARMA
Thesea and Astaurius   1

JESS HYSLOP
Triolet   19

GEORGINA BRUCE
Cat World   35

TIM MAUGHAN
Zero Hours   50

DAVID TURNBULL
Aspects of Aries   57

HELEN JACKSON
Build Guide   74

E. J. SWIFT
Saga's Children   96

CAROLE JOHNSTONE
Ad Astra   110

JIM HAWKINS
Sky Leap – Earth Flame   132

GUY HALEY
  iRobot 165

CHRIS BUTLER
  The Animator 169

V. H. LESLIE
  The Cloud Cartographer 198

SARAH BROOKS
  Trans-Siberia:
  An Account of a Journey 223

NINA ALLAN
  Higher Up 237

  Contributors' Biographies 271
  Acknowledgements 275

STEVE HAYNES

INTRODUCTION

Those of you who read my introduction to Salt's previous *Best of British Fantasy* collection will know that I have a fluid definition of my favourite genre. British writers inherit a tradition that sees a blurring of the boundaries between rigid definitions of Sci-Fi and Fantasy, and that's the approach I have continued to take with *Best of British Fantasy 2014*. You will find in these pages an eclectic collection of Sci-Fi and Fantasy as well as stories that could sit in either, or both, camps.

I make no apology for this. In the year in which all these stories were published, there was a cultural event for an institution recognised by the wider public as very British Fantasy. I refer, of course, to the fiftieth anniversary of *Doctor Who*. For me, this Saturday evening TV programme, watched by millions around the world, is the inheritor of a particularly British approach to Fantasy and Sci-Fi. Make no mistake, I know the programme has its limitations, but I salute two separate dramatic scenes in the two TV specials commissioned to celebrate this show's half-century.

Towards the end of 'An Adventure in Space and Time', David Bradley's William Hartnell (as the Doctor) looks across his central console for the last time and sees Matt Smith (also as the Doctor). In 'The Day of the Doctor', Matt Smith's Doctor meets Tom Baker's Curator. In these two beautifully balanced moments, we have an elegant meta-collision that subverts traditional 'realistic drama' and reflects the on-going meeting of Sci-Fi and Fantasy pervading our genre traditions.

My recognition of this vibrant mix of Fantasy and Sci-Fi influences this anthology. I've purposely grouped stories into particular traditions, but my definition of the two genres is more complex than a simple 'half-and-half' division.

While one story might explore a mythical fantasy from a very particular perspective, another mixes a contemporary setting with poetry spouting flowers. Another takes us into a fantasy world and yet explores a very current real danger that many young girls face. (As I write this the news is full of international condemnation at the kidnapping of over 200 girls in a crime that is as old as humanity.)

The collection shifts suddenly into near-future political comment on a very current trend, while another story takes us into a British dystopia based on the most arcane of human divisions and prejudice. There are stories that explore 'classic' sci-fi territory (yes, you will find spaceships and robots in these pages), but through a lens of psychological complexity.

Finally, the anthology again moves into an uncertain territory, where politics and technology mix with fantasy worlds; where spores represent emotions and the adventurer can literally be lost in the clouds.

The collection finishes with two stories that challenge our assumptions of genre, one exploring an experience of something alien, on several levels, and another that grounds us in the fears and politics of the modern age while weaving a disturbing fantasy thread through both personal and world events.

Finally, for all my praising of *Doctor Who*, I recognise that there is a disturbing lack of women writers represented in such a major genre TV programme. It's a situation that has been recognised in the wider world of Fantasy and Sci-Fi publishing, and debated at some length during the last twelve months. I'd just like to point out that nobody could ever say that about the *Best of British Fantasy 2014*.

THE BEST
BRITISH
FANTASY
2014

PRIYA SHARMA

THESEA AND ASTAURIUS

'Daddy, you're telling it wrong.'

'Am I?'

Thesea looks up at her husband and daughter.

'You tell it then,' he says to the child.

'King Minos prayed to Poseidon, who sent him a magic bull but Minos didn't sacrifice it like he was supposed to, so Aphrodite made Minos' wife fall in love with it.'

Only the gods inflict love as a punishment, Thesea thinks.

'The bull and the queen made a baby called the Minotaur.' Thesea's glad that she's too young to be concerned with the details. She bares her teeth and draws her fingers into claws. 'It was a monster.'

'The Minotaur had a bull's head on a man's body.' Their son; older, placid, lacking his sibling's drama.

'I'm telling it. Minos made Daedalus, his inventor, build the labyrinth to hold the Minotaur. He fed it human sacrifices sent from Athens.'

'Really?' her father asks.

'Yes, then Athens sent a prince called Theseus who was so handsome that Ariadne, Minos' daughter, gave him a sword to kill the Minotaur and string to find his way out of the maze.'

The girl has no interest in being Ariadne. She leaps about pretending to be Theseus, imaginary sword in hand.

'Calm down,' Thesea puts an arm around her and draws her in. 'You've all got it wrong. Listen and I'll tell you what really happened.'

Athens. Thesea is eleven. The other children are paddling in the shallows, splashing one another. The fisherman's son follows her along the shore. He won't leave her alone.

'My mother said you're going to be sent to Crete to die.' He tries to grab her hand to stop her walking away.

Thesea runs into the sea and dives into the advancing wave. She holds her breath and twists about so that she can look at the churning surf from underneath.

So what she's heard is true. She's not meant for this world. Perhaps that's why she's always felt outside it. There are only these moments then. She resolves to make them last.

Thesea at seventeen. She stands apart from the cargo of weeping foundlings, looking ahead. As they approach Crete, blue is divided by yellow sand into sea and sky. The ship navigates the coast to where Minos and his men have gathered on the dock to greet the fresh meat.

The boat's close enough for Thesea to see their faces. They look like salivating dogs. She can read Minos with a glance; his smile is a yawning hole that could swallow her.

He wants the entire world. Greedy bastard.

The group shuffle down the gangplank. The Athenian crew can't look at them. Sailors on other ships stand and stare.

A girl greets them. She wears purple silk, and gold shimmers at her ears and throat.

'I'm Ariadne, daughter of Minos, princess of Crete.' She takes a garland from a slave's arms and puts it around the neck of the first Athenian and kisses the boy's cheek. 'We thank you for your great sacrifice.'

Thesea's the final one in line. Ariadne stares as if trying to get the measure of her. The garland tickles Thesea's neck. Then she feels cold metal slipping down the front of her gown.

Ariadne kisses her and whispers, 'Run. Run *into* the labyrinth.' She steps back and smiles, the dimple in her cheek revealed. 'Come, we've prepared a feast for you.'

They're mad. Thesea follows them to the tables. *Every single one of them.*

Thesea's spent her life expecting death at the Minotaur's hands, teeth or trampled underfoot.

The rest of the Athenian's have been sacrificed and there's not a monster in sight. Only Minos and his men. Thesea's witnessed it. Sex and blood, all at once.

'Your turn.'

She's untied. A hand clamps her wrist. She's not agreed to this. This isn't sacrifice for the greater good. It's rape and murder. She pulls the knife from her dress and plants it in the man's neck. He has a soldier's reflexes. His sword bites her arm.

Ariadne's plan doesn't seem so stupid now. Run. Whatever is in the labyrinth can't be worse than this.

'Get her.'

'No,' Minos calls from the heart of the carnage, 'leave her. She'll starve in there. Or he'll find her. Let him have a live one. Poor sod deserves a bit of fun.'

There's laughter. She runs faster in case they change their minds. When she looks back over her shoulder the soldiers are dragging the bodies towards the maze's mouth.

Let him have a live one.

The novelty of a warm, writhing body instead of a cold, already ill used carcass. She pictures the bull headed giant sitting on a throne of bleached bones, tearing the flesh from a human leg with his teeth.

Thesea feels like a bucket of hot water has been poured down her arm. It's slick down to her wrist. There's a relentless drip from her fingertips. Her heart thumps to compensate. A contrary feeling, making her weak and energised all at once. She tears the hem from her gown and binds her arm.

The labyrinth's endless corridors of white marble. Blind endings. Steps and turns. Arches and pillars. It's baffling. Thesea turns a corner to find a fountain, the water making music. In a courtyard there's an altar laid with roses. Elsewhere a lyre nailed to a wall. Smells without source – jasmine, fire and cooking fish. These anomalies don't help her to orienteer.

Thesea remembers being lost in the forest as a child. The trees' pretence of familiarity. The maze is the same. Alive. When she leans against a wall it moves beneath her skin as if breathing her in.

I'm going mad.

I'm going to die.

She lays down, head on the ground. Stone shifts beneath her cheek, like something exhaling. Her skull trembles. Vibrations announce the Minotaur's approach.

There's a roar that could shatter rock.

She pulls herself up to a sitting position.

Let him come. I was bred for death.

The Minotaur's an abomination. Union of earthly woman and divine bull. His outline fills the corridor. His horns throw long javelin shadows on the floor. He lowers his head and breaks into a run.

The Minotaur halts beside her. Thesea tries to be calm as he picks her up. She's cradled in his arms. He smells, she thinks, like the summer rain on warm earth.

She's being carried along a corridor. Its proportions are less grand than the rest of the labyrinth. The Minotaur's bellowing is no longer just sound, it's becoming speech.

'Daedalus! I've found one. She's alive!'

The workshop's around the next corner. Daedalus looks up from his bench. Thesea sees a frowning mouth, crooked nose, a pair of goggles and a flash of grey hair. He sheds the goggles to reveal blue eyes.

'Quick, on here.'

Daedalus clears the bench with a single sweep of his arm, his tools shrapnel flying to the floor. Thesea's laid down, a body on a slab. She's heard of this Daedalus, dubbed *the cunning worker*. His constructions are wonders. He's so complicated that his king is his patron *and* enemy and he's ended up imprisoned with a beast in the jail that he was commissioned to make.

Will he convert her into a terrible machine or will the pair of them sit down to feast on her?

'Fetch my medicine chest.'

The Minotaur looks about in panic. The workshop's a mess of prototypes and parts. It smells of grease and metal. Boxes spill maps, sketches, cogs and wires. Others are sealed with triple padlocks.

'The leather one, there.'

Thesea feels a cold ring of metal on her chest. It's connected to tubes that Daedalus puts in his ears. He tells her the name later. Stethoscope. Daedalus checks the integrity of her bones. Lays a flat hand on her abdomen. Then he unwraps the binding on her arm.

'It's just a flesh wound. She's lost some blood though. Get me the Glenrothes.'

The Minotaur holds out a bottle of amber liquid but Daedalus is too busy with needle, syringe and vial. He nods to the Minotaur, 'Pour me a glass.'

'It's not to clean her wound?'

'Single malt? Are you joking? That's for me. We'll use the cheap stuff on her arm.'

The Minotaur fusses over her so much that Daedalus sends him away.

'Can you feel this?' He prods at the edges of the wound with a needle. 'No? Then we'll begin. Look away.'

Thesea refuses. She watches the needle pierce numb skin.

'What's your name?'

'Thesea.'

'Greek?'

'Yes.' Of course Greek. Where else? 'Minos. I didn't know . . .' Her sentence collapses.

'He's as crazy as a sack of snakes.'

They lapse into silence. Behind Daedalus there's a lit candle in a niche. It illuminates a painting of a young man lying on a rock, his complexion ashen. The sky behind him is red, the horizon a dark line. White nymphs reach for him with pale hands.

A pair of enormous wings are strapped to his arms.

'What's that?' she asks.

'A gift from the Minotaur.'

'He's an artist?'

'No. He just thought I should see it. It's called 'The Fall of Icarus'.'

'I don't understand.'

Daedalus finishes his embroidery. Flesh is reunited.

'We'll talk later.' He drops the needle into the bowl. 'You should get some rest.'

∼

Thesea's mouth is dry when she wakes. Daedalus dozes in a chair. She looks at his sketches but can't fathom their purpose. She helps herself to water from the jug. Slices cheese onto bread.

She looks into an alcove, then realises it's a balcony. The Minotaur's below her, in a vast field. He waves.

'Feeling better?'

'Much.'

She recognises now that the stretched mouth is a smile.

There are bodies laid out in a row. Ariadne's flowers are tangled with torn clothes. She recognises a wave of black hair. A scarf. A necklace. They remind her that mauled flesh was someone she once knew.

The Minotaur's stripped to the waist, shovel in hand, knee deep in a hole. Behind him markers stretch down the hill and out of sight.

He's burying them, she thinks. *Each in their own grave.*

'I'm going for a walk.' Thesea stretches, trying to lengthen her muscles.

'Sure,' Daedalus rummages in a box, 'you're not a prisoner. Take this string and use it to find your way back.'

'Call if you get lost. I'll come.' Then the Minotaur adds, 'If you feel faint put your head between your knees.'

'How will you find me?'

'I will.'

Daedalus follows her down the corridor and whispers in her ear. 'Be careful. He's different, depending where he is in the maze.'

'He can't always speak, can he?'

'Not just that. He's not always so affable.'

'How will I know?'

'You'll know.'

∼

Her walk exhausts her. The Minotaur lays a blanket over her knee when she returns and fetches extra cushions. She watches him work the bellows for Daedalus and together they shape metal. Flames and fatigue bring sleep but not for long. Thesea sits upright, wet faced, choking on a scream.

'You're safe.' The Minotaur kneels before her, clutching her hand.

'You've no idea.'

'I do.'

'I'm sorry, of course you do.' He dignifies the dead with burial.

The Minotaur reaches into his pocket and brings out a brass ring. 'Minos gave me this when I was a boy. His captain held me down while he put it through my nose. Daedalus was kind enough to remove it.'

Daedalus tells her everything later. How Minos sniggered as he threatened to castrate the Minotaur when he reached manhood. How they branded the delicate flesh of his inner thigh.

'I'm not an animal,' the Minotaur tells her.

'No, I know you're not.'

Thesea is holding *his* hand now.

Thesea cries less in her sleep. She walks further each day using her string as a guide. Daedalus won't let her chalk arrows on the floor. *Just in case we get unwanted visitors.*

The Minotaur accompanies her when he can.

'What's your favourite place?'

'The beach near where I grew up. Not far from Athens.'

'Why?'

'Because I've never been anywhere else.'

'I want to show you something.'

She follows him deep into the maze on a bewildering journey from which she'd never return without him.

'Here.' He puts his palms against a wall in a tentative gesture. 'Yes, here will be perfect.'

The Minotaur prises at the stone with his fingertips, pulls out a few blocks and lays them carefully on the floor. He peeks through and once satisfied, he enlarges the hole. The blocks become a stack. Thesea tries to put her hand through but she can't. It's as if there's a hidden barrier. The Minotaur reaches in with ease.

'Why can't I?'

'I don't know,' he shrugs. 'Daedalus can't either. It frustrates him too, knowing I can wander around out there. Now, take a look.'

There's a room on the other side. What stuns her is the view from the window on the far wall. She knows by instinct the slow turning jewel out there is home, even though she's ignorant of astronomy. That the blue is ocean after ocean. Brown is the ground that should be beneath her feet. She can't reconcile this paradox. That the labyrinth is *down there* and *up here*.

'Daedalus says that's the moon,' the Minotaur points to a silvery ball, part in shadow.

The moon. She can't see Diana, goddess, huntress and lunar mistress. It's just a ball of rock.

'Is Daedalus a god?'

'No. He says this is a place where men are gods.'

'The gods don't exist?'

'Not always. I don't know if this is before or after.'

'Is that natural?'

The Minotaur continues to stare out of the window. 'I'm not the person to ask about what's natural and what isn't.'

Thesea's giddy. A place where the fates and gods have no sway. They're insignificant, or will be, or were. So is she.

It's terrifying. It's liberating.

∽

'It's that time.' Daedalus looks at the calendar and shakes his head.

The Minotaur's digging again. Thesea takes him a jug of water. The bodies laid out on the ground are black skinned. The flower of Ethiopian youth.

Thesea makes an approximate count of the markers. The Athenian tribute would only occupy a corner of the graveyard.

'So many?'

'From all over the world. And more than you think. There are mass graves in the corner. It's the work of more than one man. The slaughter of innocents is a family tradition.' A dynasty of psychopaths. 'Luckily Ariadne's not like that, although Minos doesn't know it.'

'Ariadne?' Thesea's forgotten her. The sudden warmth in his voice makes her feel jealous.

My sister. Half sister, really.'

'Were you close?'

'We still are. I talk to her through the wall, although it's hard to catch her alone. Minos watches her all the time. He went even crazier after his wife fell in love with my father.'

'What happened to your father?'

'Minos ate him.'

'Oh, I'm sorry.' There's not much she can say to that.

The Minotaur nods, his eyes lowered.

'Why doesn't Ariadne hide in here with you?'

'Is that what I'm doing? Hiding?' He digs as they talk. A consummate sexton.

'I'm saying all the wrongs things. I'm sorry.'

'No. You're right. Minos would rip this place up looking for her. And she stays to make sure Minos treats his prisoner well.'

'Who?'

'Icarus. Daedalus' son. She's in love with him.'

'Icarus.' The outstretched wings.

Thesea happens upon the wrong part of the maze. The Minotaur sits and seethes, his eyes embers in the gloom. Steam rises from his nostrils. He could erupt at any moment.

She backs away, afraid.

'Daedalus, which is the real Minotaur?'

'We're all made of different parts. One's not less real than the rest.' He shrugs, seemingly less concerned with the semantics of the soul than she is.

'You're lying.'

'I'm not.' He doesn't look up from the machine that whirs in his hands.

'An omission's as bad as a lie.'

'I've missed this,' he smiles.

'What?'

'You remind me of my wife. She saw through me like I was water, too.'

'Don't change the subject.'

'That's exactly what I mean.'

'Tell me or you won't get a moment of peace.'

He sighs.

'She did that as well. If there's anywhere that all his parts are united it's the heart of the labyrinth.'

The heart of the labyrinth is the heart of the Minotaur. Daedalus shakes a finger at her when she demands a blueprint.

'I burnt it. What do you think would happen if Minos got hold of it?'

Yet here she is, due to string and intuition. Here is the Minotaur laid bare.

Thesea's disappointed when he snorts at her but from his embarrassed look she can tell he's speechless, not dumb. There's no doubt that he's more man than animal. His body's beautiful. A giant construct of muscle slabs laid on bone. His tail, a curl of a thing, sits above his buttocks.

Thesea holds out her arms to him. His black eyes are liquid in this light. He buries his face in her palm. His nose is wet, his tongue large and rasping.

He can't kiss me, not like a man kisses a woman.

He lays his immense head in her lap. His physiognomy defies her fingers. She touches the curve of his horns.

'Your neck must hurt.'

He snorts again, tilts his head one way, then the other as she rubs his neck and shoulders. She massages the knots until they soften. His bones click under her hands. He grunts, grateful.

When he pulls her down beside him, she stiffens. Brutality is all she's seen of sex. The Minotaur undoes the memory with a torrent of tenderness.

There are only these moments, Thesea thinks, *I must make them last*. But he draws her on to the next moment and then the one after.

Thesea's dream's a riot. She can see each bead of blood, each gash, each contortion. It's a churning sea of screams. A man's voice carries above it. Sweat pricks her forehead. She opens her eyes. Daedalus is shaking her awake. She can still hear the man, shouting. He's close.

'It's Minos. Hide.'

'What about the Minotaur?'

'He'll know already.' Daedalus shoves her in a cupboard.

Thesea kneels and peeps through the keyhole. Minos comes in, followed by a line of men. A line of human string.

'Daedalus,' Minos folds his arms, 'make it obey me.'

'It's *him*, not *it*. And what do you want him to do?'

'His duty.'

'As what?'

'A weapon. I want him to march at the head of my army. I'm going to remind my dissenters who I am.'

'The Minotaur's no killer.'

'Then he's no use to me. Persuade him. We march at the next full moon. If he's not with me then the first place I'll come is here. There'll be nowhere to hide. I'll pull this place down brick by brick. Oh, and I'll execute your precious Icarus.'

'Someone should put a knife in him.'

'I've tried to persuade the Minotaur to do it while he's visiting his sister but he won't. He says it would be murder.'

'Then we have to leave.'

'Not without Icarus and Ariadne.' Daedalus fiddles with a set of cogs. 'And I don't know if the Minotaur can.'

She snatches them from him.

'Explain.'

'This isn't a prison. I just wanted somewhere to keep him safe.'

'What have you done?'

Thesea's already guessed. It's why the Minotaur knows who's where. Why the walls breathe and the floor sighs.

'He's like his father. The stuff of gods. He can punch holes in time and space. He *is* the labyrinth. It's made from him. Don't look at me like that. This way he'd never be lost or trapped.'

'And being able to travel outside?'

'An unforeseen consequence, but he can't stay away for long. I don't know what it would mean if he tried to leave for good. Part of him is in here. In the fabric of this place.'

The Minotaur's out of breath from running. 'I got here as fast as I could.' He stands so close to Thesea that she can feel his relief and body heat. He looks from her face to Daedalus'. 'What did Minos want?'

Thesea puts her head next to his.

'I'm not trying to fight with you but we have to stop Minos.'
'We can stay in here. Forever if we have to. He won't find us.'
'What about Icarus and Ariadne? What about all those people?' She remembers diving beneath the surf and breaking through on the other side. From then on each moment catalogued, her life finite. She's defied fate. She's seen a future where even divinity is expendable. 'We can stop him.'
'How?'
'We'll need Ariadne's help.'

Daedalus has kept them out of the workshop until it's ready. Thesea glances at the Minotaur. His mouth hangs open.

A copy of the Minotaur's head is on Daedalus' workbench. It's perfect, down to its eyelashes and moist nose.

'Did you find it?' Daedalus asks.

Thesea nudges the Minotaur who's still staring.

'Right, yes.' The Minotaur hands him a tube. 'The shopkeeper said this will glue anything together.'

They all turn back to the head that's watching them.

'There are a couple of things missing.'

Thesea knows right away what Daedalus means.

'Your horns.' The old man nods at him. 'I'll get the hacksaw.'

'I'll need them in a fight.' The Minotaur backs away.

'You're not going to fight.'

It's only when Thesea puts a hand on his arm that the Minotaur relents. She stays but has to turn away. There's the rasping see saw sound of metal on horn.

Afterwards she uses his forelocks to cover the stumps.

'How does it feel?' Thesea asks later.
'Strange. My head's lighter.'
'Will this work?'
'It has to.' He curls a strand of her hair around his finger. 'I feel like I was asleep before I met you.'

'And before you I thought my life was forfeit and I didn't care because I had nothing to fight for.'

'Thesea, if it doesn't work . . .'

'Don't say it.'

'If it doesn't work, don't wait for me.'

'It'll work.'

'It would be all right. I don't want you to be alone.'

'Shut up and kiss me.'

'You should know my name. It's *Astaurius*.'

Sword, shield and helmet have transformed Thesea into Theseus. Girl into boy. She carries the fake head in a bag. It's heavy.

As she and Daedalus leave, the labyrinth walls dull as if a light's going out. She pauses and presses her lips to the stone but it's devoid of life. It's as they planned. The Minotaur's reversing Daedalus' design. Taking the god given power of Olympus back within himself. If he's got it right, he'll use it to make one final door and come out somewhere else, nothing remaining of him in the stone to tether him there.

The ground shakes beneath their feet, a subtle tremor spreading out from deep within the maze.

Astaurius.

Daedalus is as encumbered as Thesea. He looks hunchbacked because he's wearing a folded set of wings beneath his cloak. He hefts the second pair in a sack.

There's another rumble. Behind them there's the distant sound of collapsing masonry. The maze is a construct that can't withstand the world without the Minotaur.

'Hurry.' Thesea takes the spare wings from Daedalus.

Ariadne's waiting for them. The watchman lies at her feet. Blood stains his tunic. Ariadne is Minos' daughter after all. Thesea tries to hide her shock with a question.

'Is that what you're wearing?'

'It would look a bit odd if I was dressed to travel rather than for a party, wouldn't it?' She looks at Thesea like she's a simpleton. She's planned revels to distract the court. 'At least this way I'll be able to take some things of value for us to live on.'

Ariadne wears silks, too many layers considering the mildness of the day. Her yellow hair's bound up in an elaborate coil, studded with gems. Gold bangles tinkle on her arms.

'Clever girl,' Daedalus laughs. 'Where's Icarus?'

'Here's a map. He's at the top of this tower. Father has the only key. I couldn't get it.'

'Leave that to me.' Daedalus, lover of locks, will tease out its secrets. 'What about the guard?'

'I took him a cup of wine.' Her smile makes Thesea shudder. 'Icarus knows where we're meeting. Tell anyone who asks about the wings that you're part of the entertainment. Are you sure those things will work?'

'Certain.'

A shockwave escapes the labyrinth.

'What's that?' Ariadne asks.

'Your brother. We best go. He's going to attract a lot of attention.' Daedalus squeezes Thesea's hand. 'Goodbye dear.'

'We'll go this way.' Ariadne pulls Thesea away. She takes one last look at the maze. Another quake nearly floors them but Ariadne just laughs like it's an adventure. 'There's an Athenian ship in dock. I can play the distressed captive but can you be a convincing kidnapper?'

Crete gets smaller. Thesea's still holding up the Minotaur's head. The ships in port bear witness to the feat. The Minotaur's dead. The gods are no longer on Minos' side. The news will carry around the world on the tide.

Minos is a speck on the dock. Thesea can feel his eyes burning into her, even at this distance but he won't risk his darling girl. Ariadne's played her role so well that Thesea wonders at the upbringing necessitating that kind of skill.

Once they're safe on open sea, Thesea goes to the prow to be alone, cradling the Minotaur's head in her arms.

The sun's a red ball shrouded by fog. Thesea waits for Astaurius on the beach.

He'll come. Any day now.

She listens to news of Daedalus' escape and the nations refusing Minos' demands. He's forced into unwinnable wars on too many fronts.

Gulls' cries carry over the water. There's the lonely lap of waves. A figure walks up the shore towards her. He looks familiar.

'It's you,' he says.

Thesea takes up a fighting stance, sword in hand.

'Don't you know me?'

It's the fisherman's son, the one who used to plague her. She lowers the sword a fraction.

'I live up there, with my family. Remember?' He points to a house high on the cliff. 'These are for you.'

A generous gift of line and net. A loaf of bread. 'If you want to fish, come and ask. I needn't be the one to teach you. My mother or sisters can show you.'

When Thesea eventually knocks at the door it's his mother that answers. The promise holds true. The women cluck about her, teaching her to fish and forage, to cook delicacies in the embers of a fire.

She sits with his mother one evening, learning how to repair nets. She admires the older woman's dexterity.

'I was pregnant before I wed. By another man.'

Thesea looks up but her teacher's intent on her task.

'My husband knew. He was good to me. I came to love him

very much. There's many who'd judge me, not knowing my story.' She sniffs. 'It's no one else's business. It's a hard thing bring up a child alone. How far gone are you?'

Thesea's startled. Her stomach only show's a slight fullness. She blushes.

'My boy didn't eat for weeks after you were taken away. He's loved you since he was a child. He loves you, no matter what.'

Thesea doesn't want to listen. She feels like her reclaimed life is over without the Minotaur.

Astaurius, why don't you come?

'So that's what happened. Come and kiss me goodnight.'

Helena comes first, still posturing and playing out the tale. Next, Astaurius, unusually tall and strong for his age. When they laid him on her belly she didn't know if she was disappointed or relieved that he didn't have horns and a tail.

'Are you coming?' her husband asks.

'One minute. You go ahead.' She tidies the platters away, folds up a pile of clothes.

When she's sure she'll be left alone she takes out a key. It unlocks the chest in the corner, which is hers alone. The Minotaur's head looks up at her. She raises the lamp and light animates the liquid eyes. Daedalus' work was a marvel built to last.

Her husband's dozing. She blows out the lamp and lies down beside him. Her throat thickens and she tries to swallow the tears. He rolls over and a gentle hand wipes her face. She takes it and kisses it.

Her husband says, 'I wonder what happened to Daedalus.'

Daedalus and Icarus. Flight is so much more certain with polyurethane resin than with wax.

The sun is dazzling. They soar.

JESS HYSLOP

TRIOLET

I

An elderly lady lives at the end of our street. She has hair puffed out like a small white cloud and an air of dwindled grace. She wears bangles round her skinny wrists, floral skirts that reach to her ankles, shoes with Velcro fastenings. Her name is Mrs Entwistle. She grows poems.

Mrs Entwistle's poems sprout from flowerpots and vases, ice cream tubs and pencil pots, watering cans and china teacups. They spill from window boxes and climb crooked trellises, spreading over red brick and plastic drainpipe. Their leaves can be large or small, rubbery or velvety, dark or light. Some bloom in violent bursts of magenta and azure, some in delicate constellations of white stars, and some have drooping, elongated heads that toll their verses like bells.

Lisa and I walk past Mrs Entwistle's house every weekday morning on our way to work. It sits at the corner where we part, I heading left to the train station, Lisa turning right to the bus stop. Each morning we admire the poems blossoming in the front garden, and sometimes Lisa puts out a hand to touch the daisy-like flower that bobs, inviting, over the low brick wall. At her touch the plant perks up on its stalk, as though clearing its throat. Then it recites, in the tones of a jaunty schoolboy:

Welcome, footsore traveller,
Welcome to my door.
Come sit and have a cuppa
Before you have to leave once more.
But if you have to rush along,
I wish you a good day.
Perhaps when you're less busy
You'll find time to come my way.

The ditty always makes Lisa laugh, and it puts a smile on my face too. We go to work with lighter steps, and promise each other that we really will pay a visit to Mrs Entwistle soon.

II

Sometimes – rarely – Mrs Entwistle gives away her poems. Sarah Ealing, who we know through Bob and Carol, has one – an elegant perennial with curling leaves and a single violet bloom. Sarah claims to have had the poem for seven years now, and that it needs nothing but a bit of watering every other day and it's as healthy and happy as ever. I ask to hear it, one time when we're over there, but she stays my hand before I can touch the leaves.

'It's private,' she tells me, and blushes.

Lisa exclaims about it as we walk home. 'That blush!' she says. 'What do you think it's about, her poem?'

'I don't know,' I say.

'Well, it's got to be sex, hasn't it?' says Lisa. 'I bet it is. Gosh. And she always seems so, you know, staid.'

'Staid?'

Lisa looks up at me. 'You know what I mean. Sarah's never been married, Carol said. And she's as old as we are.'

I shrug. 'She's always seemed nice to me. Maybe she's just had bad luck. And anyway, who're you calling old?

Lisa hooks her arm through mine. 'I'm jealous,' she admits. 'I want a secret poem.'

'Maybe we should call on Mrs Entwistle then.'

'This weekend,' says Lisa, firmly.

But that Friday my father has a fall and breaks his hip, and we have to go out of town to visit him and look after mum, and we forget all about our visit to the old lady at the end of the street.

III

It's two months later, in mid May, when Mrs Entwistle hails us from her living room window. Lisa and I have just said our morning goodbyes and are about to part ways when the old woman's voice drifts out across her front garden.

'Good morning, Mr and Mrs Lewis!' she says, and her face goes all over wrinkles as she smiles. 'Would you care for a quick cup of tea? I have something for you.'

We pause, I with my briefcase in hand, Lisa with her folder tucked under her arm.

'Morning, Mrs Entwistle,' I say, then hesitate. 'I'm afraid we'll be late for work.'

Lisa gives me a don't-spoil-this look. 'Perhaps we can step in for a minute,' she says.

I give her a no-we-can't look, and she shoots back a well-I'm-going-to look.

'Yes, in fact, that would be lovely,' Lisa says, loudly for my benefit. And she unlatches Mrs Entwistle's front gate and goes up the path, dodging the enthusiastic flora that burgeons on either side.

'Wonderful!' says Mrs Entwistle, and disappears from the window.

I dither on the pavement. Lisa looks back at me from among the flowers. 'Oh, come on, Jim.'

'But the office – ' I say.

'A poem, Jim!' says Lisa. 'A poem, maybe. Just for us.'

I remember that visit to Sarah Ealing, picturing the flush that rose in her cheeks, the secret blooming behind her eyes.

I sigh. 'All right, then. One cup of tea.'

Lisa holds out her hand, and I take it as I join her outside Mrs Entwistle's door. But I brush against something as I do so, and when I look behind I see a plant springing back into place. It's an unruly bush with dark, serrated leaves, amongst which heavy scarlet flowers lurk and peep. The contact with my skin wakes the poem, and the bush begins to speak.

The Jackdaw Prince, old as the hills,
Though newer than the moon, some say;
His realm of air, hung above the world,
In a cradle of storms. All black feathers he,
And pinprick eyes. The Cat King will not catch him.

Mrs Entwistle opens the door. She smiles at us, then purses her lips at the bush as it continues with its poem. Its voice is low and scratchy.

The Prince swoops over earth; his wings
Bring fright, but they delight the Turtle's daughter,
Who swims beneath the void. The Cat King yawns . . .

'No discipline, that one,' says Mrs Entwistle. 'I keep cutting it back, and cutting it back, but no! It creeps right out again.'

The plant is giving me the creeps too. Its poem is odd, the rhythm jarring, the imagery scatterbrain and strange.

Mrs Entwistle notices me eyeing it. 'Oh, don't bother about it, dear,' she says, patting me on the arm with a jangle of bracelets. 'It'll drone on all morning. Do come inside.'

We leave the bush whispering tales of the Jackdaw Prince, and follow Mrs Entwistle into the house. Inside, the place is tidier than I expected. I had pictured plants proliferating in the hallways, jostling for space on every surface, bursting from drawers and trailing down the walls – but in reality the house is neat and clean. There are many poems, yes, but they are lined up evenly on tables and windowsills. Diminutive plants are placed strategically on side tables, whilst the larger ones are pushed into corners out of the way. The wallpaper is pink and yellow and the whole place is very cheery.

Lisa follows Mrs Entwistle into the living room, where there is a faded three-piece suite that looks as though years of use have moulded it into the form of perfect comfort.

'Do have a seat. I'll get the tea.'

'Can I give you a hand?' I ask, but the old woman waves me away.

I put my briefcase on the floor and Lisa lays her folder on the glass-topped coffee table. We settle together onto the couch.

'Only a few minutes,' I tell Lisa.

'I know, I know,' she says reluctantly, and in truth I understand how she feels. The house seems to welcome visitors with the enthusiasm of a favourite aunt, and now that I'm inside I'm loath to leave its hospitable embrace. I feel very cosy sitting there with my wife, waiting for tea.

There's a poem on the coffee table, a cascade of blue florets on narrow stalks. I consider touching it, but then I remember the bush in the front garden and I think better of it.

Mrs Entwistle comes in with the tea things on a plastic tray. 'It's so nice you could come in,' she says as she pours and stirs. 'I haven't spoken to you two in such a long time. But I see you in the mornings, sometimes. You seem very happy. I trust everything's well?'

We tell her that yes, we are very happy and that yes, everything is well. I ask after Mrs Entwistle in return, and she says that she is very dull, but tells us instead about her grandson who is just starting university. Then she mentions that she has heard about a man in Japan who also grows poems, and whom she'd very much like to meet one day.

Lisa seizes her chance. She has been holding in the question the entire time; I can tell by the way she's turning her teacup in her hands. Now it pops out: 'You said you had something for us?'

'Ah yes. So I did.' Mrs Entwistle pushes herself out of the armchair and goes over to the windowsill. Her bangles clack against one another as she chooses a ceramic flowerpot from among the many receptacles that line the sill. When she turns back to us, we see that climbing from the soil inside the pot is a delicate, twisting stem. It curls upwards in a miniature helix, and bluish leaves sprout from it at intervals like tiny steps on a spiral staircase. At the summit of the stem are two flowers. They have small, rounded petals and are a merry yellow.

Lisa flashes me an excited grin. 'A poem!' she exclaims. 'For us?'

'Exactly, my dear. It sprouted last week, and I knew immediately who it was for.'

Mrs Entwistle hands the pot to Lisa, who takes it reverently. 'Look, Jim.'

'Yes,' I say. 'Very pretty.'

'Can we listen?' asks Lisa.

'Of course.' Mrs Entwistle sits down again in her armchair and smiles at us. 'It's yours.'

'Go on, Jim. Touch it,' Lisa orders.

I reach out a finger. It looks very big and unwieldy next to the graceful little plant. Carefully, I touch one of the petals.

The spiral stem flexes. The leaves twitch. The flowers dance, ever so slightly.

Two lovers lie together sleeping,
In their dreams their lives they share.
Entangled in their secrets' keeping,
Two lovers lie together. Sleeping
Is the world without, none peeping
On the inner world, the bedroom where
Two lovers lie, together, sleeping.
In their dreams, their lives, they share.

'A triolet,' says Mrs Entwistle. 'How exquisite.'

'Oh, Jim!' Lisa breathes. Her eyes are wet.

'It's beautiful,' I say, and I mean it. The plant's voice was like water lapping gently on a far-off shore, and its words conjured alluring memories of Lisa and me, together, on our honeymoon in Saint Lucia eight years before.

I've the urge to kiss Lisa right then and there, but she's still holding the pot and the last thing I want to do is make her drop the poem.

We don't go to work that day after all. Once we've said our goodbyes and our thank-yous to Mrs Entwistle, we go straight home and take the poem to our bedroom, where we place it safely on top of the chest of drawers. Lisa touches it again and we listen, enraptured by the seductive verse. Then we make love right there in the mid-morning sunlight, and it's like we're newlyweds again.

IV

Lisa and I listen to the poem almost daily after that. We shiver with delight at the leaping rhymes, and we marvel at the movement of the words, the shifts and pauses that bring new meaning to the repeated lines. Lisa looks up 'triolet' on Wikipedia and we agree that it is indeed an exquisite form.

We show off the poem when Bob and Carol come over for dinner, but when they ask to hear it we shake our heads.

'It's private,' we say as one, and Lisa giggles.

Bob and Carol look a little sour. I make up for it by pouring them both another glass of Merlot.

'I think that was a bit mean of us,' I say later, when our guests have gone home.

'Hmm. Maybe.' Lisa is washing up, and her hands pause under the suds. 'It's true though, isn't it? It *is* private.'

I slide my arms around her waist. She gives a little start, then laughs. I brush my lips across her hair. It smells of Fructis shampoo, of Bob's cigarette smoke, of the Bolognese sauce we just had.

'It's private, all right,' I murmur. 'It's extremely private.'

She turns and kisses me, and I don't care that she still has the wet rubber gloves on; I pick her up and carry her upstairs.

A few months after Mrs Entwistle gives us the poem, I get a promotion at work. Lisa's thrilled at first. She books a table at The Vine and we toast my success over a shared platter of *hors d'oeuvres*. But the glow of achievement wears off after a couple of weeks and the downsides start to reveal themselves. The promotion comes with a transfer to another office much further afield, so I'm out early and late home. I don't catch the train anymore either, so Lisa's left to walk alone in the mornings past Mrs Entwistle's house. She tells me that the old lady often leans out of the window and asks after us.

'She says to tell you congratulations,' says Lisa, as she watches me eat a late supper of cold chicken and salad.

'That's nice. Tell her I say thank you.' I should go round and say it myself, of course, but I have even less time now than ever and somehow it always slips my mind.

I never forget to water the poem though. It sits in our

bedroom, under the window, and the flowers are merry and yellow as ever. I am beginning to believe what Sarah Ealing said, about hers having lasted for seven years straight. I hope ours is as hardy.

V

I am beginning to suspect that Lisa's in a mood with me. Work is demanding at present, so I often don't get home until eight or even nine in the evening. Lisa says hi when I come in the door, asks me about my day, and sympathises about the lateness of my return – but all the while she's got this look in her eye that says we-really-need-to-have-a-talk.

I don't have the energy to start that conversation, but I do apologise. 'I'm sorry about this, hon. I really am,' I say. There isn't really anything I can do, however. Work is work. And as my dad always says, 'You gotta do your time.'

'It's OK,' Lisa says, but I can tell that it isn't. She doesn't laugh like she used to when we watch *Mock the Week*, and she doesn't touch me at all when we go to bed.

Then, one evening when I come in, Lisa is sitting watching a wildlife programme. Onscreen, some tanned presenter is washing a baby elephant, which is lying on its side and swishing its tail in contentment. I take off my coat, then come up behind the couch and lean down to kiss Lisa on the top of the head. She whirls, startled, and almost elbows me in the face.

'Jim! I didn't hear you. Miles away.'

With the elephants? I want to joke, to bring a smile to her face, but I can't make the words come out. When I walk into the kitchen my feet feel heavy. I go to the fridge and take out the leftovers Lisa has put by for me. I place the Tupperware on the counter and then I pause, and just lean there for a minute. My head is reeling.

When I bent to kiss Lisa, her hair smelt of cigarettes.

Logically, I know there could have been any number of people smoking around Lisa during the day: people at work, in the street, at the bus stop. But the smell had been too familiar. Too familiar by far.

That night, even though I have to be up at six the next morning, I go to touch the poem sitting on the chest of drawers.

Lisa stops me. 'Not tonight, Jim. I'm tired. Okay?'

'Okay,' I murmur. 'Okay.' Then I glare at the yellow flowers as if this is all their fault.

VI

Coming home one evening the following week, I find a cigarette butt on our front lawn, lying in the grass under the living room window. It's small and wet and squished, but I pick it up and hold it between my fingers and look at it for a long time.

I don't say anything to Lisa. She doesn't say much to me either. It's becoming the way of things. But that night, I creep out of bed and, very slowly, pick up the poem in its ceramic pot. Then I carry it downstairs and put it on the dining table at the rear of the living room. I pull out a chair and sit in front of the plant. In the darkness, the yellow of the petals palls to grey.

I touch the curlicue stem, gently, and a voice like a Saint Lucian beach recites:

Two lovers lie together sleeping,
In their dreams their lives they share.
Entangled in their secrets' keeping,
Two lovers lie together. Sleeping
Is the world without, none peeping
On the inner world, the bedroom where
Two lovers lie. Together, sleeping.
In their dreams, their lives they share.

Maybe it's just because it's late, and I'm tired and agitated and heartsore, but the final two lines sound different to how I remember them. I touch the plant again, and again it delivers the poem. I listen hard to the last part.

Two lovers lie. Together, sleeping.
In their dreams, their lives they share.

Where once it prompted an intense wave of satisfaction, the couplet now makes me uneasy, as though there's some sinister meaning lurking beneath the innocuous words.

I sit there in the dark and listen to the poem over and over, trying to uncover the secret of those lines.

Eventually, brain throbbing and eyes aching, I give in. I take the poem back upstairs, then slide back into bed and stare at the ceiling. I think about Lisa and the cigarette butt. Then I think about lying, and sleeping, and dreaming, and sharing.

VII

My head is pounding from lack of sleep, but I get up at my normal time of 6am. I dress in my usual work clothes: suit (grey) and tie (navy blue); clean shirt; smart shoes. Lisa stirs under the duvet but does not wake. I do not kiss her goodbye.

I take my briefcase and coat from the hall and go outside. It's November, and the morning is clear and cold. The car starts on the third try, and I reverse out of the driveway. I drive round the corner and park the car where it won't be spotted by Lisa when she heads out for the bus. Then I walk back round to Mrs Entwistle's house.

It's early, so the old woman doesn't open the door when I first ring the bell. It's only after several minutes of waiting and ringing and waiting and ringing again that I hear the slow shuffle of her feet descending the stairs. When she opens the door, it's only by a crack, and she keeps the chain on.

'Who is it?'

I feel a moment of shame when I see the fear and suspicion on her elderly face, but then I think of Lisa and the cigarette and I thrust the feeling away.

'It's me,' I say. 'It's James Lewis.'

'Oh! Mr Lewis.' Mrs Entwistle sounds relieved. 'I didn't know who it was, this time in the morning. I didn't know who it could be.'

'Can I come in please?'

She blinks at me, still bleary from sleep. 'Is something wrong?'

'Yes,' I say. 'Yes, I think it is.'

'It's not Lisa?' she asks, concerned.

'Look, can I come in?'

'Yes, yes, of course.' Mrs Entwistle backs away and fiddles with the chain. It takes her a minute, but then she has it unhooked and it falls away. She opens the door wider. She is wearing a mauve dressing gown and no slippers. Her feet are small and blotchy, roped with swollen blue veins. 'Come in, come in,' she tells me.

I step over the threshold and close the door behind me. Mrs Entwistle beckons me into the living room. There, she gestures to the couch, but I shake my head, so she remains standing too. She studies my face.

'What is it, James?' Her anxiety appears genuine, but I don't trust it. Like the poem, it seems to be hiding something.

'The poem,' I say. 'The poem you gave to Lisa and me.'

'Yes, I remember. A triolet, wasn't it? Most lovely.'

'Lovely!' I snort. 'I don't think so. Oh, I don't think so.' I'm shaking my head over and over; I don't seem to be able to stop.

'What's this?' She frowns. 'I thought you liked it.'

'It's changed!' I say, and suddenly my frustration all rushes out at once. 'It's changed, you old hag! It's all gone wrong!'

I half expect Mrs Entwistle to cringe away from me, but instead the old woman's face goes hard. 'It hasn't changed, Mr Lewis,' she says primly. 'None of my poems change. It's not in their nature.'

'I'm telling you, it's different,' I insist. 'I was listening to it last night, and it – '

'It won't have changed,' Mrs Entwistle repeats. 'The poem is still the same poem. But, I suppose, it may have grown.'

'Grown? Grown? What the hell does that mean? It doesn't look any different. It's the poem that's different.'

She shrugs. 'If you insist,' she says, in the tone of a teacher humouring a wrong-headed pupil.

My anger builds. 'You're some kind of witch,' I accuse. 'These poems, you give them away like they're presents, like they're blessings. But they're not. They're not. That thing – it's some sort of spell, isn't it? And now Lisa . . . Lisa . . . '

My knees feel suddenly weak. I drop onto the couch. 'It's ruined everything,' I moan.

Mrs Entwistle stands over me. 'I'm no witch,' she says, 'and my gift to you and your wife was no spell. It's just a poem.'

'But what does it *mean?*' I cry. '"Two lovers lie' – what does it mean by 'lie'? What kind of lying? And which lovers? Which two? 'In their dreams', it says. In whose dreams? In mine? Who's sleeping? Am I sleeping? Is Lisa? With whom? Jesus, *what does it mean?*'

Mrs Entwistle looks down at me with sad eyes. 'It's a poem,' she says again. 'It means what you make it mean. It means what you think it means.'

I put my face in my hands. 'Great,' I groan. 'That's just great.'

On my way out, I brush again against the bush with the red flowers.

The Jackdaw Prince, it says, old as the hills . . .

'Shut up!' I growl at it. 'Goddamn it, can't you just shut up!'
The Cat King will not catch him, it replies, gravely.

VIII

I don't go to work that day. I don't go home either. I just get in the car and drive. I take the A-road out of town, and then I take every back road I come across until I'm way out in the countryside. There are no clouds in sight, and the air is a pale winter blue.

I follow a winding road and find myself at the top of a ridge, overlooking a steep-edged valley. I can see for miles. There's a viewing area by the side of the road, with a faded sign and a small car park. I pull over, tyres crunching on the gravel, and then I just sit in the driver's seat looking out at the fields and the woods, the verges and the hedgerows, the hills and the villages spread out below. I gaze at the vista of greens and browns, and think about how, if I were to touch any of those plants, they would remain silent. They would not spout pernicious, ambiguous verse. They only mean one thing: themselves.

The thought is comforting, and after a while I drift into sleep.

It's dark when I awake. I check my phone and find I have four messages: three from the office and one from Lisa. I turn the phone off. Then I start the car and drive carefully back into town. I feel much calmer.

The November night has come early, and the lights are on in the windows of all the houses in my neighbourhood. I head home, but when I get to the house I find myself driving right past it. I drive past Mrs Entwistle's place too. But when I get to Bob and Carol's I ease on the brakes and let the car dawdle outside. They haven't drawn their curtains yet, and I can see right into their front room.

Peeping on the inner world, whispers a voice at the back of my mind.

I cannot see Bob, though their car is in the driveway. Carol, however, is sitting in an armchair with her back to the window. Her left hand is lying on the armrest, palm up, fingers curled slightly inwards. The top of her head peeks out above the chair, and it lists slightly to the right. She is asleep.

I wonder where Bob is. I wonder if I would find Lisa at home, if I went back there.

Together, sleeping.

Bob and Lisa, I think bitterly. *And in another sense, Carol and me. Except I've woken up. Poor Carol.*

I drive on before my lingering gets too suspicious, and I surprise myself again when I stop outside Sarah Ealing's house. Only once I'm there do I realise why I've come.

Her poem; yes. I can picture it now, with its lone violet flower, the petals curving upwards to cradle the stigma waiting at its heart. And Sarah's blush, I can see that too. We had thought it mere embarrassment at the time, but now another detail of the incident springs to mind: how Sarah's eyes flickered to Lisa as she put a denying hand upon my own.

Seven years, Sarah had told us; her poem had flourished for seven years. Now, sitting outside her home, I ache to know whether the plant remains as hale as it was that day. Had it 'grown' like mine and Lisa's, so perversely? Or did it endure still, as elegant as it ever was?

I summon my courage. Leaving my briefcase on the passenger seat and my phone, switched off, in the glove compartment, I get out of the car and go ring the bell.

Sarah does a double-take when she opens the door. She's wearing pyjama bottoms and a knitted, oversized jumper. There is a pair of reading glasses perched on her nose, and her hair is pulled up into a scruffy ponytail.

'James,' she says. 'Did you – Did I forget – Did we arrange . . . ?' She peers behind me, presumably looking for Lisa.

'No,' I say. 'No, don't worry.'

'Then why . . . Sorry, but why are you here?' Her gaze moves over me, and suddenly I'm aware of my hair, dishevelled from my nap in the car, and my crumpled work clothes. 'Are you all right?' she asks.

I open my mouth and shut it again. I honestly don't know if I'm all right, but I suspect that I'm not.

Sarah looks at my car, parked in the street, then back at me. 'Do you . . . Do you want to come in?'

'All right,' I say.

I wipe my shoes on the mat, though they're pretty much spotless as all I've been doing is driving around all day.

We stand awkwardly in the hallway.

'Would you like a – ' Sarah starts, but I interrupt her.

'Your poem,' I blurt out.

Alarm flits across her face. 'My poem?' Her tone is wary, but also – I think – ever-so-slightly wistful. 'What about it?'

I pause, biting my lip. 'Can I . . . Can I hear it?'

'It's – '

'It's private, I know.' I smile at her wearily, trying to show her that I understand; I understand now what she meant by that blush, by those words. 'I know.'

She looks at me, her expression guarded.

'Please,' I say. 'I'd really like to hear it. Please.'

Her eyes soften. Slowly, she reaches out and takes my hand.

GEORGINA BRUCE

CAT WORLD

My sister Oh and I go to the corner shop and buy a packet of Doctor Rain's Travel Gum. Oh wants Cinnamon Sour, and I want Spearmint Buzz, but Oh wins because she's older and it's her money. We run out to the back of the yard. Oh runs with her hands in her pockets, one hand curled around the Gum. I am never allowed to carry it because she says I might drop it, but I definitely wouldn't. We go to the railway line, where the trains used to come down. There's an overturned crate to sit on and a bit of plastic tarpaulin to haul over our heads. I say, let's do it at the same time, don't start without me. And Oh laughs and says everything with you is like that, you never want to do anything by yourself. But some people are just like that, so what are you going to do?

So we sit together and unwrap the gum at the same time, and we put it in our mouths at the same time, me watching her to see if she is going to do it right, and she waits for me, and I smile and say chew! So we do it together. And then we are gone, and I see her body falling through space, turning and turning like a brown stick in the milky galaxy. That bit is not real, Oh always tells me, but sometimes it's my favourite bit of all.

Then we are there in Cat World. Oh is all clean and her hair is in braids. I guess mine is too. We are sitting in the kitchen at a large wood table, like a slab of wood cut out of a tree just to make the table, and I say, let's do the thing. She says, I don't want to do the thing, we always do the thing. I think about sulking but I decide not to waste the time and so instead I get up and look out at the garden where all the cats are stalking through the long grass. Let's play in the garden, I say. We could ride on the horses. Oh says, those aren't horses you idiot. They're swings. You're no fun, I say, but secretly I'm a bit relieved, because I don't want to walk in the garden with the cats. We raid the fridge and eat all the sugary yoghurts, and afterwards we press our faces against the window and point at the cats, then the gum loses its flavour and we are back on our crate in the rain.

I want some more, but Oh shakes her head and presses her lips firmly together. She needs it, she says. She needs it more than I do. She stuffs it right at the bottom of her bag, and tells me I'm not to touch it. I'm cold and it's starting to rain. Big fat plops of rain splash onto my head. Don't cry, Little One, says Oh. Come on, we'll do the thing. She drags the tarp over our heads again and I clamber into her lap. Her arms wrap right around me, holding me like a baby, and she rocks me gently back and forth. I suck on my thumb and say wah wah goo goo gah, and Oh says, hush now my little baby. She's a lovely little baby isn't she? Look at her, little diddums, yes she is.

Oh has to go to work. A big ship has landed, and the tourists have real money in their pockets. We want real money, paper money, not the stupid plastic money because it's no good for us. We can't buy anything with it. I'm too young to work, according to Oh, but I'm eight, actually. Oh is twelve, and she's been working for years, ever since the men came for our Mummy. They took our everything. I don't want to go to work, but I don't want Oh to go to work either. I want her to stay with me and do the thing, and play and go to Cat World, but then we wouldn't have any food and we would die. Oh says we are going to run away to the real Cat World. When she has saved enough money, we are going to find a boat. There are some women, Oh says, who are like mothers. They are kind. They can help us get away.

We do our exercises. Oh makes me remember all the things she's taught me. Hit them in the balls, she says, and put your fingers in their eyes, and bite their ears. All right, I say, jeez louise, I know all this. Oh laughs and musses up my hair and says, just looking out for my little sis.

We drag the tarpaulin over to the side of the tracks where there are some big bins, and put the tarpaulin over the bins, so it's like a tent. Oh is pleased. She says she didn't notice the bins until now. Oh gives me the sleeping bag and my teddy, and our little bag, and makes me put the picture of Mummy in my pocket. I make Oh give me a lot of kisses, and I tell her I want a story, but she says no story tonight, just close your eyes and go to sleep and when you open them again, I'll be back.

I like the sound of rain falling on the tarpaulin. It's a good sound. Nobody walks around the railway tracks at night in the rain. I could light a match if I had one. It would be safe, probably. I'll tell Oh in the morning: we can have a light when it rains, maybe a fire. It's very dark, but with my eyes closed I imagine I'm going to sleep in Cat World, in a real bed, with Mummy and Oh sitting either side of me, just quietly sitting, and a light on in the hallway outside the room.

Then I open my eyes and it's morning. Light is coming through the blue tarpaulin, and it's sort of milky and nice, even though it's still raining. I'm dry and warm, so I just lie there for a bit, thinking how nice it would be to wake up in Cat World for real. And I think what shall I say to Oh first of all, will I tell her about my dream or will I go and get her a cup of tea from the tea boy in Edward Road. She's quiet when she's been working, but she'll give me some money to buy tea and maybe some fruit. So I decide to get the tea first, and that's when I realise she's not there.

She's not curled up in the sleeping bag with me, or crouching under the tarpaulin, watching the rain. I lift up a corner of the plastic and look outside to see if she's there, but she's nowhere.

She hasn't come back.

I'm not going to cry, I'm not. I'm a big girl. I'm going to get back into the sleeping bag and curl up and close my eyes and dream about Cat World. And next time I open my eyes, she'll be back.

Rain makes the neon shine and hurt my eyes. I hide in a narrow alley, behind a giant blue bin. My stomach growls at me, and I think about climbing into the bin and looking for food, but I don't, because what if someone catches me? What would they do to me? Oh says they can do anything they like to us – there are no laws about what happens to little girls who live on the street. I am watching the door on the corner, where men are stepping in and out. They laugh loudly and slap each other on the back. Their eyes are bright and cold.

Smells from a nearby café drift up my nose. Bacon and eggs, hot greasy sausages bursting open in the pan. My pockets are empty. I check them, anyway, for the thousandth time. Finally, the door swings open and a girl steps out. I recognise her: it is Book.

'Book! Book! Hello!' I wave at her and she looks back at me, not smiling.

We know Book from the old days. Her mummy was my mummy's friend. They used to talk for hours, over the fence between our back gardens. Book and Oh used to play together, and I was not allowed to join in because I was too young and stupid to understand their games. Instead I used to lean against my mummy's leg and listen to her talk about the government. She did not like the government. No one did.

'Little One? What are you doing here?' Book says. 'Where is Oh? You're soaked! Come in out of the rain.' She takes me by the hand, and her pointy fingernails dig into my skin. She leads me to her sweaty, perfumed cubicle at the back of the hotel. It is the size of a single bed and it's not possible to stand up in there.

'I've lost my sister,' I say. I want to wail. I'm so hungry, too. But Book is very calm. She sits with her legs crossed on the bed, so I do the same. My hair is dripping onto the blankets.

'She didn't come back yesterday, or the day before,' I say. My voice sounds strange to me, having not spoken to anyone for two days. 'I've been waiting and waiting. Can you help me find her?'

Book looks startled. 'I don't think that's possible,' she says. She rubs her hands over her face, pushes her black hair back, sighs. 'Girls disappear, honey. They don't come back.'

'No,' I say, making Book raise her eyebrows at me. 'She has to come back.'

And then I think, what if she's gone without me? Maybe she found the women who help, and she went on a boat, and she forgot me.

'Poor little thing. Hey. You could work here,' says Book. 'I'm sure if I spoke with Mr Cow—'

I shake my head, stricken with fear. I cannot.

'You always were a big baby.' Book laughs. 'But if you won't work, I can't help you. And if Mr Cow finds you here, he'll make you work. Trust me.'

'Did she come here? Did she go anywhere else? Did she have any other friends?' I am trying not to cry, but the tears are bubbling out of me.

Book shakes her head. 'Don't be sad,' she says.

'I can't help it.' I wipe my nose and eyes. 'Aren't you sad?'

Book makes a funny expression, turning the corners of her mouth down. 'I don't know,' she says.

For some reason, this makes me cry even harder than before.

Book shushes me. 'Don't want Mr Cow coming in here.' She yanks up a corner of the thin mattress, and digs around in there, eventually coming up with a little plastic bag.

'Here,' she says. 'This is all I can do.'

She hands me a crumpled bit of paper, which turns out to be a five-pound note. So old and used, it feels soft, like it might dissolve in the rain. Then she gives me three sticks of Travel Gum – Spearmint Buzz flavour.

'That's it, honey,' says Book, closing my fingers around the gum and money. 'You'd better go now.'

Three sticks of gum means three visits to Cat World. And that's when it hits me: I bet Oh's gone to Cat World! She's probably there, waiting for me, right now.

I run to the railway yard and get under the tarpaulin. Everything is wet now and I can't get warm, but I have money and I could buy a match and make a fire. When Oh gets back, she might want that money for something, though. And she probably has a match already. So I just try to find a dry bit of blanket to sit on and unwrap my first stick of gum. It tastes minty and sweet, and reminds me I'm hungry.

Then I am falling through space and I can see Oh's brown-stick body turning and turning, but it can't be her, so maybe it's me, or maybe it's just like the titles or something. This bit isn't real anyway.

When I get to Cat World it's raining there too.

I'm in the kitchen and Oh isn't there, but I feel like she must be around somewhere, so I don't panic. I make myself some cereal and eat it, shovelling it in, with my Travel Gum wedged in the side of my cheek. Fruity Loops. My favourite. It doesn't matter what I eat here, no one ever tells me off and the refrigerator is always full of stuff. In the garden the grass has grown extra-long, probably because of all the rain, and I can't see any cats around, but the horses are swinging back and forth.

I look all over the house, even under the beds and in the wardrobes. Oh is very good at hiding; we used to play it all the time when I was little. Just in case she's hiding somewhere, I call out her name: Oh! OH! Where are you? But there is no answer.

After I don't find her, I sit back down at the kitchen table and look out at the rain. I've got this horrible feeling Oh's out there, outside, with the cats. That means I've got to go out there, too. Outside. With the cats.

But the gum is losing its flavour so I chew as slowly as possible and stand in front of the refrigerator, looking at the photographs held on with fridge magnets. There is Oh when she was little, holding Mummy's hand. Mummy's hair is all different colours. I'm inside Mummy but you can't see me yet. They are sitting on the horses and Oh is laughing really hard, like something is just too funny. I wonder who lives in our house now.

And then I am back under the tarpaulin, and my bum is cold, and I curl up as small as I can and try to think about what to do next.

Book brings me a cup of soup with bits of pasta floating in it. The soup is cold. She brings me some bread too, and I eat it all because the food in Cat World is comforting but it doesn't fill you up. Then she helps me hang out the blanket to dry.

She rolls her trouser legs up over her knees and pulls her hair back into a ponytail. 'I love the sun, Little One, don't you?'

I shrug, because it's not exactly warm, really, and go back to beating the blanket with my hands to scare the bugs away.

'How's it going, sweetie? All on your lonely only, eh.'

'I need some matches,' I say, holding my palm out to Book. 'Gonna make a fire.'

'Ai! You can't make a fire here, Little One!'

'Why not?' I close my fist and shove it in my pocket. There are the two sticks of gum and the soft silky note brushing against my knuckles. 'Oh always makes a fire if we get too wet, or she makes us run around until our clothes get dry again.'

'That's why Oh always smelled like a dying dog, I guess,' says Book.

'She does not!' I put my hands on my hips, and Book laughs.

'Chill out, Little One. I'm just kidding.'

I remember that Book was the one who never let me join in her and Oh's games. She said I was too stupid to understand and then when Oh got mad she said, 'only kidding!' So, nothing's changed.

Before she goes, she gives me her jumper and two matches. 'Don't freeze to death,' she says. 'But be careful about that fire. You don't want anyone to see it.'

In the end I wait until it's very dark and raining again, and I build the smallest fire in the world under the tarpaulin. When I light it the space fills up with smoke and I can hardly breathe, but I get warm and I decide to go back to Cat World.

This time something is different. At first I'm not sure what it is, because everything looks the same, but the feeling is different. So I take a look around and see what I can find. It's just that the back door is open.

The door has never been open before.

The cats can get into the house.

I can go outside.

With the cats.

I stand behind the door, ready to slam it shut if a cat tries to get past me. The horses are swaying back and forth. I can feel the sun on my face, and when I close my eyes, bright white blobs fall down the inside of my eyelids.

I can hear voices that sound like they're coming from far away. Laughter, some crazy kids laughing. I smile. It must be Oh. I just know it is.

And I want to get to her, find her, bring her back.

But she's outside.

I could run through the long grass to the tree. I could shout all the way, so the cats can hear me and get out of my way. I'm a brave girl. I'm a big and brave, clever girl.

So I pull the back door open wide, and take a deep breath.

But there is one, right on the doorstep! A black cat, licking its paw. It looks up at me with green eyes and opens its mouth wide like a yawn, and its huge teeth sparkle in the sun.

So instead I go upstairs and I climb into my bed and all my toys are in there. I have a memory of my Mummy sitting on the edge of my bed. I think I can feel the weight of her, near me. She reads me a book, and then she says, time to sleep! And I say, no Mummy, just five more minutes, but she says, come on Little One. She gives me my teddy, the soft black-and-white cow, to squeeze, and I close my eyes and put my head back on the cool white pillow.

The little fire has gone out, and everything in the tarpaulin stinks of smoke. Everything is dirty and wet. Everything is cold.

I think if Oh came back now I would punch her in the face. I would claw her eyes out. I would kick her head in. I hate her! She went without me. She is probably on a boat right now, sailing to some other country where she can be safe and live in a house and grow up, and she has already forgotten all about me.

Book comes and brings me half a sandwich and a cup of tea. She is wearing new jeans that are bright blue, and trainers with orange and red flashes all over.

'Mr Cow took me shopping,' she says. She does a little twirl under her umbrella. 'Not bad, eh?'

I sniff. I pull my knees up to my chest and try to wrap myself around the warm plastic cup of tea.

Book shrugs.

'Hey, Little One,' says Book. She takes off her jacket and puts it around my shoulders. 'Poor thing. Look at you! You can't carry on like this. You'll freeze to death.'

I try to shrug, but all that comes is a shiver.

'Come back with me,' says Book. 'We'll get you cleaned up. Get you a lovely warm bed.'

'Can't,' I say. 'What if Oh comes back?'

'Silly,' says Book, rubbing my arms through the jacket. 'She'll find you at Mr Cow's, won't she? It'll be the first place she looks.'

That's right, I think. Book is right. So I allow her to pick me up and put me on my feet, and we walk holding hands towards the town.

Mr Cow looks inside my mouth and in my ears.

'What are you looking for?' I ask, but Book shushes me.

'She's scrawny,' says Mr Cow.

'She's young,' says Book. 'She's fresh.'

They are talking about me like I'm not even there.

I have a blanket on the floor. The floor is made of straw, so it's warm at least. There are about ten of us in the tiny, square room, all clutching our blankets. I thought I would have a cubicle, a real bed, like Book does – but she says you have to work really hard to get one of those.

No one in the room says anything to me, and I am too shy to speak to any of the other girls.

I wind myself up in my blanket, and try to make myself small. Sometimes the door opens and Mr Cow or Book comes in and wakes up a couple of girls. They leave the room together. Sometimes the girls cry, and Book puts her arms around them, mothering them. She shushes them and pushes them gently along. If it's Mr Cow, he doesn't say anything. Just grabs their arms and shoves them out of the door.

What happens in the other rooms? I want to ask Book, but she doesn't look my way. Besides, I'm not sure I really want to know the details. I know the facts – Oh told me all of that ages ago. It's bad, but you can survive it. It's work, that's all. It's the same work Oh did, before she left.

Some of the other girls cry, but I don't feel like crying. There's just this big dry stone inside me now.

Mr Cow says there are rules. He does not let us chew gum. He says it is unladylike, and the customers don't like it. The customers want us to be *there* the whole time. So Book goes around the room and picks up every girl's blanket and shakes it so all their private things fall out: matches and beads and photos, and white pieces of Travel Gum. Book collects all the gum in a plastic bag. When she gets to my blanket, she shakes it out just the same, but I have already hidden my last stick of gum under my foot, and I stand on it the whole time she is looking.

'Good girl,' says Book. She hands me the photo of my Mummy. 'Don't worry, hon,' she says, whispering into my ear. 'I'll give you some later, don't tell the others.'

When she is gone, I fold my blanket up and put the photo and my last stick of gum at the bottom, careful not to let any of the other girls see me do it. Is this what Oh had to do, I wonder. Did she use up all the flavour and have to go into the room and be *there*, the whole time? I look around at the sea of wide, frightened eyes, and one by one, the girls look away. We are not little girls, I think. We are something much more terrible.

It's not real, I think. It can't be real. Somewhere there is another me, a me who is asleep in bed with her mummy sitting next to her, her mummy's weight on the bed next to her. Maybe she is dreaming this. But when I wake up, it's because Book is shaking my shoulder, and her face is close to mine. I can see the make-up smeared over her skin, the little holes where it has sunk down into her pores.

'Little One,' she says. 'Come on, get up.'

She smooths down my dress with her hands and quickly brushes my hair, then runs a smear of lipstick over my mouth. It's greasy and tastes bad.

'Don't be scared, Little One,' she says. 'There's nothing to be scared of.'

'I've changed my mind,' I say. 'I want to leave.'

'You can't leave now. Mr Cow's looking after you now.' Book fiddles with my hair, pushing it behind my ears. 'You don't want to be ungrateful.'

She presses two pieces of Travel Gum into my hand. 'See? I'm helping you.'

I throw the Travel Gum away, behind me, hoping it lands on some other girl's blanket.

'Don't help me,' I say. 'You've helped me too much already.'

Book grabs my shoulders and puts her face right up to mine. She whispers, hissing through her teeth. 'You want me to call Mr Cow? I'll go and get him, shall I, and tell him what a bad, ungrateful little bitch he's bought?'

I shake my head. I let Book lead me out of the room.

She leads me along a narrow corridor and down two flights of stairs. I notice that the stairs carry on going down, probably going out to the back entrance. Book pushes me along the corridor, and into a room with a bed in it. She gives me a mean look and slams the door shut. I hear the lock being turned.

The room is pink, the colour of bubblegum and dolls' dresses. I climb up on the bed. The bed covers are pink, too, and lacy and frilly. My legs don't touch the floor, they dangle down. I swing them back and forth. I have my last piece of Travel Gum in the pocket of my dress. That, and the five-pound note. That's all I've got.

A key turns in the lock.

I jump up from the bed, and run to behind the door.

The man has long hair and a beard, and he is wearing jeans and trainers. He looks kind of nice.

He says, 'Where are you, honey?'

Then he unbuckles his belt.

The black cat licks its paw and rubs behind its ear. It keeps looking at me with its green eyes.

From far away, I can hear Oh's laughter. Sunlight sparkles over the whole of Cat World.

The black cat stops washing, and pads towards me. It slinks around my legs, around and around, mewing and purring. It's hungry.

Oh says, you've got to hit them really hard in the balls, because that's where it hurts the most. You've got to use all your power.

What's power? I want to know.

She taps me in the middle of my forehead, then my chest, then my stomach.

I'm too little, I say.

Oh waggles her eyebrows up and down to make me laugh. Little is good, she says. You've got the element of surprise.

His face goes bright red and he doubles over. I might have killed him, but I don't want to stay to find out. I bolt out of the door and race down the corridor. I'm aware of Book somewhere behind me, screeching, but all I can think about is getting down the stairs and out of the hotel. I feel like I could take off at any time, just fly up into the air as I round the corner of the stairs, leap down the next flight, jump into the stairwell and land on my feet.

There's a fire door at the bottom of the stairs, but there's no one there. No guards, just the door. I take it in fast. No guards. No padlock. I hurl myself at the door, and as it swings open, an alarm blares out. It's too late, though. I'm too fast. I am off and running, running on my bare feet on the wet roads, and I don't stop until I get to a long street with houses, and then I duck down an alley and let myself into a back garden, and then out through the thorny bushes into the long grass beyond.

I follow her voice, Oh's voice, through the long grass. The cats wind about my legs. The cats follow me and run ahead. Oh is laughing, laughing in that hard, silly way of hers.

I think she is spinning around and around in the grass. Around and around, with her arms out, spinning until she falls over, and the world keeps spinning her around.

It's all right, Oh, I call out. I'm coming, I'm nearly there.

Through the tall trees I catch a glimpse of her dancing in the meadow. The sunlight bounces off the grass and the flowers. She is laughing.

The cats run towards her, their tails flickering in the long grass, and I run towards her, too, fast as I can. But my foot strikes something, and I stumble and fall, hurting my hands.

I'm not supposed to see it but I do.

She is lying with her face pressed into the grass. Her hair is all different colours. The men have been here. Her clothes are torn and bloody, her skirt bunched up and twisted round her waist. There are big red gouges down her legs, red and blue inside and squirming with white worms.

And the cats sit a little way away, licking their paws and rubbing them round and round their bloody mouths.

Then we're in the kitchen and the back door is shut.

You're a silly, says Oh. You didn't see anything, really. She picks me up and sits me on her lap. There we go little baby, who is a little diddums, is it you? Is it my little baby? Don't cry, Little One, don't cry, don't cry.

And by the way, she says, don't stop running.

The sun is bouncing off the flowers in the meadow. Despite everything, the sun feels good. I hold my arms out and spin around and around, until I'm so dizzy I can't stand up, and I fall into the soft grass and laugh so hard it's like I'm crying.

Maybe she is somewhere in the tall grass, somewhere, hidden away. Like my mummy was hidden, after the men came, and we looked for days and days, but the cats found her first. Wherever she is now, I know Oh is not coming back. And I want to be sad, but I can't, because I haven't got the time. I want to chew Travel Gum and live in Cat World, and lie down here until my body turns into grass. But I can't. I have to get to a place where there is a boat. I have to find the women who help. I have to keep running, because it's what Oh told me to do. Because I'm the only one left in our family, and I have to remember everything.

So I stand up, and brush the grass seeds from my dress, and carry on.

TIM MAUGHAN

ZERO HOURS

0714, WANSTEAD

NICKI IS AWAKE even before her mum calls her from the other side of the door. She's sat up in bed, crackly FM radio ebbing from tiny supermarket grade speakers, her fingers flicking across her charity shop grade tablet's touchscreen. She's close to shutting down two auctions when a third pushes itself across her screen with its familiar white and green branded arrogance. Starbucks. Oxford Circus. 4 hour shift from 1415.

She sighs, dismisses it. She's not even sure why she still keeps that notification running. Starbucks, the holy fucking grail. But she can't go there, can't even try, without that elusive Barista badge.

Which is why she's been betting like mad on this Pret a Manger auction, dropping her hourly down to near pointless levels. It says it's in back of house food prep, but she's seen the forum stories, the other z-contractors who always say take any job where they serve coffee, just in case. That's how I did it, they say, forced my way in, all bright faces and make up and flirting and 'this coffee machine looks AMAZING how does it work?' and then pow, Barista badge.

But Nicki doesn't work like that. She's not one of those girls, she doesn't feel comfortable playing it that way. She just likes to keep her head down and get the work done, get out, get home.

Her tablet pings once, flashes a notif, pings again and flashes a second. Two auctions won. Both lower than she'd like, both lower than the national minimum, but it's a start. It's a reason to get out of bed. Her mum shouts her again, she hollers back. Before she gets up though she's got the CopWatch wiki open in front of her, checking her route. London Transport Police drone spotted at Mile End, actual cops doing spot checks at Bank. Fuck it. She's gonna have to change her route – she's not put credit on her legit Oyster card for time, and she's only reasonably sure the three hacked ones in her wallet will get her through to Zone 1 from right out here in the forgotten sprawl of Zone 4. Even if they do, re-routing round these checks are going to put an extra half hour on her trip.

She's out of bed, pulling on clothes, before her mum calls her for a third time.

0920, Oxford Circus tube station

As she reaches the exit barrier at Oxford Circus there's some kerfuffle on the other side, cursing and shouting, and as the crowd gets out of the way she can see what's going on; security theatre breaking it's own fourth wall as two cops wrestle with a guy and get him to the floor, gloved hands pulling back his hood to reveal the shock of his warped face, mutated beyond machine recognition into a disturbed alien mask. Nicki has seen it before, but it still surprises her that people would go to those ends, pumping their face full of QVC home Botox injections just to fool the cameras.

Misuse can lead to dangerous long term side effects, the EULAs warn. Plus they just look fucking painful. Apparently the swelling goes down after a while, but the stretch marks remain – plus if that's the only way you can do business inside Zones 1 & 2 then you need to start jacking your cheeks and forehead up with that shit all over again.

Nicki's in the barrier gate now, people crowding behind her, eager to get out or crane a look at the guy that's pinned to the floor. She glances back. No retreat. She steps forward and pops her wallet on the reader, hoping the right card is out of the RFID blocking envelope. She holds her breath. The gate bleeps dully, the barriers swing open, and she's stepping out, head down, pink hoody up, past the sprawled, screaming guy with the face made of balloons.

1235, Pret A Manger, Oxford Street

Two hour shift down and she's not even seen a coffee machine, let alone some hipster barista she can flutter eyelashes at. She's been stuck in a cold backroom sticking vacuum packed, pre-sliced organic cheddar into authentic French artisan baguettes she pulls out of a box from a bakery in Croydon.

Her phone chimes in her pocket, vibrates against her hip. Shift over. She peels and drops plastic gloves into the bin and heads out to the main counter, is surprised by the sudden mass of bodies – it had been dead when she got here, but the early lunch crowd is in now. There's the fucking coffee machine, steamy and hot and out of touch. She contemplates hanging around to see if she can grab the barista's attention, but it's getting too busy in here for that sort of shit, plus she needs to clock off and go, get to the next job.

She finds the manager, he'd been all gruff and short with her when she turned up, but he seems more chilled now, friendlier – despite the fact the shop is getting busier. Maybe that's why. He smiles and winks at Nicki, and she pulls out her aging Blackberry and scans the QRcode he shows her on his tablet.

Another chime, cash register sounds kerching, kerching, kerching

Shift completed!
£12.64 received.
Achievement unlocked!
Sandwich Stuffer Pro badge!

1330, OUTSIDE STARBUCKS, OXFORD STREET

Nicki sits soaking up skyscraper-focussed rays, eating self made ham sandwiches out of tin foil wrappings, leeching wifi from Starbucks. Somewhere overhead rotors buzz, and she catches a glimpse of one of those Dabbawallah.net tiffin drones straining against it's own payload as it vanishes behind cliffs of steel and glass, delivering Indian food to penthoused analysts in those tall, metallic tins that swing like bombs from its underside.

She glances back down at her Blackberry, checks CopWatch again. More random stops on the Central line. Safer to walk. Lunchtime over.

1415, BOOTS THE CHEMISTS, HOLBORN

Boots is busy, a steady flow of post lunch shoppers. Occasionally one of them stops and asks her or one of the two other zed-contractors she's stacking shelves with for directions to some product they don't even recognize the name of. She smiles politely, tries to explain she's zero hours, and offers to find someone to help them. Invariably the customers just tut and twirl on their heels, walking away from her mid sentence. The two other girls she's working with keep their heads down, don't even bother to look up. Maybe it's the best strategy.

The work is fiddly, annoyingly so. Usually shelf stacking is pretty straightforward – but this time they're all on lipsticks and each one needs to be slotted into the correct little plastic hole on the display depending on colour and shade. Get it wrong and the shelf knows, and buzzes the app on her phone. She guesses it's probably telling someone else too, building stats on her, trails of data ranking her for efficiency.

She watches the other girls, both about her age. Similar clothes, with the oversized Boots t-shirts they were given over the top. She wonders how much they are getting paid – all the auctions are secret. Did they undercut her or the other way around?

As she gazes at them the one nearest her, the one with the tight, straight black bob of hair, slips two of the lipsticks into a silver envelope and then into her jeans pocket. She recognizes the envelope, it's made of the same material she keeps her Oyster cards in when she doesn't want them to be scanned. RFID blocking. She pretends she hasn't seen anything, turns back to the shelf and the lipsticks and the endless stupid holes.

1845, Boots the Chemists, Holborn

Nicki and the other two zed-contractors are in the manager's office, waiting for her to get off a call. It's nice in here, Nicki thinks. Warm and quiet. There's chairs and one of those old desktop computers with the big displays. Nicki wonders what it's like to have a job where you get to sit down all day.

The manager gets off the phone, and near silently walks over to them, showing them each her tablet so they can scan the QRcode. Nicki is last, before her the girl with the bobbed hair and light fingers. Chimes and kerchings. Nicki glances a look at the surface of the girl's two-seasons-ago iPhone, catches perfectly rendered text on its OLED screen.

Shift completed!

£19.84 received.

Nicki feels a rush of jealousy, anger. The girl is getting paid more than her. It's pence, but.

The manager reaches Nicki, presents her with the QRcode. She scans it. Chimes and kerchings.

Shift completed!
£19.24 received.
Achievement unlocked!
Shelf Stacker Pro Level 2 badge!

The manager thanks them all, and the three girls shuffle out of her office, Nicki at the back. Something stops her before she makes it through the doorframe though, a cold grip of rage and injustice. She turns back to face the manager, who looks at her over the rims of her Samsung branded spex.

– Yes?

Nicki looks at her, at the floor. Rage tinged with shame.

– That girl, with the black hair. She took some lipsticks. Put them in an RFID bag.

– I see.

The manager touches the side of her spex, talks to an unseen security guard. She thanks Nicki and taps her clipboard-tablet, gives her another QRcode to scan.

Chimes and kerchings.
Achievement unlocked!
Shop-cop Pro badge!
£5.20 bonus received!

2127, WANSTEAD

Nicki lies on her bed, surrounded by books from what's left

of Wanstead's library. Dali, Gaudi, Picasso, Bosch, Warhol, Giraud. Her sketchbooks sprawl open around her, pencil scribbled designs sprawling across multiple pages; figures and textures, architectures and crowds, trees and towers.

Nicki is on her tablet, transferring credit from the Retail-Warriors app to her PayPal account. She checks the total. £3,467. Still not enough to cover the first term of graphic design at the Wanstead Community Academy.

Maybe next year.

She slides the books off her bed onto the floor, sets the alarm for 0645, and slips under the sheets. She'll have to wake up early again, before even her mum calls her.

DAVID TURNBULL

ASPECTS OF ARIES

Spring 2039

ON HIS APPROACH to the checkpoint at the border Rik noted with some satisfaction that the baby in the back seat crib was fast asleep. Although he had heard that this happened sometimes Rik had never been lucky enough to transport a child that slept all the way through. Mostly he ended up with payloads that bawled their little heads off from beginning to end – puking and stinking up the interior of the car into the bargain.

Smiling to himself he drove slowly past one of the border guards. When she saw that the words *Infant Courier* were stencilled in large letters on the side of Rik's vehicle she waved him into the priority lane, holding up the queue of traffic to let him through.

Rik pulled up in front of the security booth, applied his handbrake, and then checked that the armband with its *Aries* symbol was visible on the left sleeve of his bomber jacket. The clock on his dashboard read four thirty-four. He was making good time for his evening delivery. The baby was still sleeping, seemingly unaffected by the fact that the car was no longer in motion.

Another guard stepped out of the booth. The symbol on

his armband showed that he was a *Sagittarius*. Rik would have expected nothing less. He was still on his home ground in the *Fire Zone* after all. He rolled down the window as the guard scribbled down the car's make and registration number.

'Destination?' he asked once Rik had shown him his ID card.

'*Earth* Zone,' replied Rik.

The guard made a note of this.

'Purpose?' he asked.

Rik nodded at the crib. 'Have to deliver a baby born under the wrong star sign to its newly assigned parents.'

The guard peered through the back passenger window.

'D.O.B.?' he asked.

Rik told him his own date of birth and checked his paperwork for that of the baby. These were duly entered onto the guard's sheet. 'Just going to run all of this through the astrology software on my desk,' he said. 'Check if there's anything untoward in the stars that might impinge on the rest of your journey.'

Rik watched as the guard returned to the booth and sat down at his PC. The engineering department had given his car a full service the previous weekend, so Rik thought it highly unlikely that there was any real risk of a mechanical fault. But if the software identified a high probability of a road traffic incident it would be unlawful for the guard to allow Rik to proceed.

A few months back the motorway portents had prophesied a blow out of his front tyre. As a consequence he'd been forbidden from travelling and had ended up stuck with an ill-tempered *Pisces* baby in a grotty B&B for four nights. Since that day he'd always taken the precaution of ensuring he'd fully replenished the supply of nappies, milk formula and gripe water stored in the car's cargo space.

Rik stepped out of the car to exercise his legs. After a moment the guard who had waved him into the priority lane came sidling up beside him. 'I couldn't do your job,' she said. Like his her armband bore the symbol for *Aries*.

'It's essential work,' he told her. 'See that poor mite in the crib there? She's a Taurus. Her paperwork says she was born on April 22nd. Can you believe that? Her parents didn't even have the common decency to conceive her at a time that would ensure she was born under a compatible Fire sign. If the authorities left it to them to raise her who knows what kind of problems social services would end up having to deal with? That's the kind of the thing the Grand Council of Astrologers has worked so hard to stamp out . . .'

The guard held up her hand, halting him in full flow.

'Actually it wasn't that aspect of your job I was referring to.'

She pointed to the twelve-foot tall, electrified fence that separated the *Zones*.

'I'm a big supporter of segregation, believe me. That's why I could never do a job that involved crossing over into the *Earth Zone*. It makes my flesh crawl just looking through the fence at all those creepy *Virgos* and *Capricorns*.'

She gave a little shudder, emphasising her point.

'I keep myself to myself,' said Rik. 'Get my job done. In and out – sweet as a nut.'

'You go into *Air* and *Water* as well?' she asked, nose pinching slightly as if there was a bad smell in the air.

Rik nodded.

'I do pick ups as well as deliveries. There are irresponsible parents across all the *Zones*. Never seems to be a shortage of displaced kids who need to be reassigned to a compatible family.'

'Turns my stomach to think of a *Taurus* kid being born over here in *Fire*,' she said and leaned in to the passenger window. 'She got a name?'

'Not yet,' replied Rik. 'They don't like to give them names till they're with their reassigned parents. It affects their equilibrium in later life.'

'She's definitely a *Taurus*?'

Rik nodded again.

'Poor thing. I wouldn't wish that on my worst enemy.'

Her colleague poked his head around the door of the booth and waved his clipboard. 'All in order. No negative portents predicted.'

As Rik started the car's engine once more the baby finally stirred a little. Through the mirror he saw a little pink hand clawing playfully at the air. 'Soon be settled in with your selected parents,' he said, releasing the handbrake and pushing gently down on the accelerator. The barrier went up. He pulled onto the M6 and passed from *Fire* into *Earth*.

Summer 2043

The room in which Rik was incarcerated was damp and dark.

He could smell the mildew that speckled the walls. Somewhere water was dripping onto the concrete floor with a pronounced and regular smack. The room shuddered as the aerial assault above toppled yet another building up at street level. Dust and clumps of plaster fell onto his head and shoulders.

He knew that if the entire ceiling came down he wouldn't be able to dive out of the way. His wrists were bound to the arms of the chair. His ankles were bound to the legs of the chair. The chair itself was bolted to the floor of the room. He tried to blink away the dust that was getting into his eyes. The effort was painful. His eyelids were swollen and bruised from the beating he had taken.

The light went on – suddenly illuminating his dank surroundings. Rik tensed. He knew what this meant. The light switch was just outside the door. *He* was out there; hand poised around the door handle, ready to enter – his torturer – his tormentor.

The door opened with a slow groan.

Rik felt his heart quicken.

'Have you had sufficient time to consider whether there is anything you wish to tell me?' asked the torturer. He was pushing a small trolley before him. An object covered in a white cloth sat on the trolley. Rik eyed it with growing consternation.

The torturer smelled strongly of coal-tar soap. He was dressed immaculately in a starched white shirt and a plain blue necktie. His black shoes were polished to a fine shine. A *Leo* symbol was tattooed onto his left cheek.

'Well?' he asked, leaning toward Rik.

His breath smelled of peppermint mouthwash.

Rik was so parched that he felt as if his tongue was stuck to the roof of his mouth.

'There's nothing I can tell you,' he managed. 'I don't know anything.'

The room shuddered again as another bomb hit home.

'You hear that?' asked the torturer. 'Your friends in the *Earth* Zone are striking at our homeland. Murdering innocent *Leos*, *Sagittarians* and *Arians*.'

'I have no friends in the *Earth* Zone,' said Rik. 'The hostilities have more to do with the dissolution of the *Grand Council* than anything you think I might have done.'

'But the *Earth* forces appear to have accurate intelligence,' said the torturer and slowly circled him like some predatory insect. 'They must have obtained their information from somewhere. Suspicion naturally falls upon people such as yourself.'

He was behind the chair now and Rik found this all the more unsettling. Beads of sweat tumbled over his swollen eyes. 'I've told you a dozen times,' he said. 'I didn't give anyone any information. I didn't have any information to give.'

The torturer's hands pressed down on his shoulders and gripped them as if he was about to offer Rik a massage. 'It's a fact, though, that you travelled regularly back and forth between *Earth* and *Fire*,' he said, squeezing ever so slightly.

'It was my job,' said Rik. 'I was an *infant courier*. I made deliveries and did pick-ups. I went into *Air* and *Water* as well.'

The torturer went on squeezing his shoulders.

'We are not at all concerned with what you may have done when you were travelling in the *Air* Zone,' he said. 'We are in an alliance with *Air*. But *Water* is an entirely different prospect. The turncoats in *Water* have thrown their lot in with *Earth*. You occasionally slept overnight in one or other of the Zones, did you not?'

'If I had a long journey,' agreed Rik. The torturer's thumbs carried on rubbing and rubbing against his shoulder blades. 'But I only stayed in authorised non-segregated transit motels – in line with the provisions of my travel permits.'

'Perhaps,' suggested the torturer, 'you had other reasons for spending the night? Perhaps you were having secret liaisons with some *Scorpio* whore? Perhaps she was fucking information out of you?'

'Never!' cried Rik. 'I was good at my job. I took pride in my work. I would never have jeopardised my career for the sake of an unlawful relationship. And, as I keep repeating, I didn't have any information worth passing on to anyone.'

'Are you sure about that?' asked the torturer. 'Are you sure your loyalty to your own kind was not infected and compromised in some way by your constant contact with those of inferior star signs?'

Now his thumbs and fingers squeezed hard around the cartilage of Rik's shoulders. Rik cried out in agony. He would have writhed and kicked had he been able to move his arms and legs. Instead he shook his head violently left to right. This just made the torturer laugh and squeeze all the harder. So hard that Rik thought the cartilage was bound to snap.

'Are you sure?' he kept asking. 'Are you sure?'

'I'm sure,' Rik kept screaming. 'I'm sure.'

The torturer relented.

He walked slowly in front of Rik's chair, laboriously cleaning his hands with a strongly perfumed wet-wipe. As the pain in Rik's shoulders began to recede he was almost overcome by a wave of dizziness that could so easily have robbed him of consciousness had not the torturer pulled the trolley closer and caused fear to punch him wide awake.

'You do know that your silence will eventually be in vain?' asked the torturer. He neatly folded the wet-wipe and placed in the breast pocket of his shirt. 'Our military astrologers predict a resounding victory for the forces of *Fire* and our glorious allies in *Air*.'

'Then you have no need to do this to me,' said Rik, bruised eyes transfixed by the ominous object beneath the sheet on the trolley.

The torturer carefully removed the sheet, folding it into a perfect square. What sat beneath this was a small black box with a handle protruding from one side and two electrical wires running from the other. On the end of the wires were metal-toothed bull-clips.

'Quaint, don't you think?' the torturer asked him. 'I collect devices like this. It's my hobby. This particular model is known as the *Tucker Telephone*. It's based on the design for an old fashioned hand cranked telephone and was developed by the resident physician at Tucker State Prison in America way back in the 1960's. It runs on two dry cell batteries and its sole purpose is to deliver a rather unpleasant electrical shock.'

'I have nothing I can tell you,' insisted Rik.

'I will give you ten more minutes to consider whether there is anything at all you wish to confess to,' said the torturer. 'If you decide at that point to maintain your stubborn silence I will attach these clips to your scrotum. The pain when the teeth dig into your flesh will be excruciating. But it will be nothing compared to the pain you will experience when I crank up the current.'

Autumn 2047

Rik ducked as a stray bullet ricocheted from the window ledge and sank itself into the wall with a dull thud. He ran his hand across the embroidered Aries symbol on the arm of his flack jacket. The words above the symbol read – Fire Forces and the words below it – Aries Division.

There were no civilians any more. Everyone was conscripted to the war effort – either as an active combatant or a support auxiliary. Although nothing had ever been proven, Rik's record as a suspected spy made it inevitable that he would be considered expendable and therefore sent on active service to the front line.

Now, after months of bloody and brutal fighting, the war was almost over.

The capital city of the *Air* Zone had all but fallen. The ruins of bombed out buildings were being systematically combed for survivors and the last remnants of organised resistance were centred on the two hundred or so pupils who had barricaded themselves into their High School. The offensive unit that Rik was attached to had been dispatched to finish them off.

The military astrologers had been correct in their predictions of a *Fire* and *Air* victory over *Water* and *Earth*. And the victory was total. Over a period of eighteen months following their surrender the country had been thoroughly cleansed of everyone born under a *Water* or *Earth* star sign and a failsafe system of compulsory terminations or induced births put in place to ensure that children were only ever born under *Fire* or *Air*.

However, the military junta that had assumed command in *Air* became greedy and ambitious, seizing territory that had clearly been designated as the rightful province of *Fire*. It had not taken long for such disputes and infractions to descend into all out war. Of course astrologers on both sides were keen to insist that the portents of the stars were on their side. Nevertheless *Fire* had the superior weaponry at its command and the traits associated with the star signs of its citizens turned out to be far more resolute and determined.

Now it had all boiled down to this – a poorly armed band of defiant teenagers facing off a crack unit of battle hardened troops from *Aries* division. From the shattered window of the burned out warehouse they were occupying opposite the hastily fortified gates of their school Rik could see some of the kids moving hurriedly back and forth along the corridors. They seemed impossibly young.

This wasn't something he had any stomach for.

However, his encounter with the torturer had turned him into an avowed coward and he knew with an absolute certainty that he would not risk any potential retribution by questioning the validity of an order issued by his superiors. In the current climate the slightest thing could be interpreted as flying in the face of the stars and immediate execution was the most likely punishment.

Their sergeant was calling them into a huddle to begin her briefing.

She was a veteran of the Zone war and had the wounds to prove it. The last two fingers on her right hand were missing and her face was cratered with the deep pockmarks of penetrating shrapnel. Amongst these pits and lesions her holographic *Aries* tattoo was still visible on her left cheek. These were mandatory now and Rik sported one himself. It was apparently just as important to differentiate between those born under *Leo* and *Sagittarius*, as it was to differentiate between those born *Gemini*, *Libra* or *Aquarius*.

Because of the sergeant's facial disfigurement it had taken Rik a good while to figure out where he knew her from and why her voice had such a familiar ring to it. It had been her throw away comment after they had massacred an entire brigade of *Libran* commandoes that had finally brought clarity to the matter.

'Bury their stinking corpses as soon as you can,' she'd ordered. 'It makes my flesh creep just looking at them.'

Rik had known in that instant that she had been the guard who had chatted to him that day so long ago when he'd been held up at the border. As he recalled they had taken up a nodding acquaintance from that point, acknowledging each other with a wave each time he passed in or out of the *Fire* Zone on his delivery routes.

He was sure that she must be aware of his previous profession from his military records but if she had any inkling of their fleeting acquaintance she never let on. Desperate to avoid any sort of discussion that might eventually lead to speculation on the accusations once made against him Rik had taken great care not to mention it either. It didn't stop his thoughts turning to that mild mannered *Taurus* baby he'd been delivering that day. And it didn't stop the cold shiver that ran through him whenever he considered what might have become of her.

'This will be a full frontal assault,' the sergeant was saying. 'There's a contingent of snipers from the 5th *Sagittarian Rifles* stationed on the football pitch behind the school – just in case any of them try to make a break for it.'

She turned to face an eager faced woman standing to the right of Rik.

'Templeton,' said the sergeant. 'You and McNeil take the rocket launcher to the fourth floor and fire on the gate. Once the fortifications are breached we go in all fucking guns blazing.'

Around him Rik heard the sound of high-fives and shoulders being slapped. He forced a smile onto his face and feigned being as gung-ho as his comrades.

'Remember,' said the sergeant, 'These are kids. Not all of them are armed. So you only shoot the ones who return fire.'

'That's outrageous,' complained one of the grunts. 'You're saying because of their age we should spare them? We can't be expected to do that. They'll only grow up to be thorns in our sides. We can't go against the astrologers and the astrologers' reading of the portents is that for the sake of our own futures we must eliminate everyone born under an *Air* sign. Every last filthy one of them!'

The sergeant held up her three-fingered hand, in the manner she had done the first time she and Rik had met at the border station, in the manner he had seen her do a dozen times or more since joining the unit. 'I wasn't suggesting they are *spared*, dick-head,' she spat. 'I was suggesting you *spare* ammunition. There may be other struggles ahead of us. If we take as many of them prisoner as possible the *Extermination Camps* can finish the job.'

Rik shuddered at the mention of the *camps*. Ever since their existence and purpose had become public knowledge they had been the dark material that fed the dreadful nightmare that seemed to constantly re-occur whenever he closed his eyes to sleep.

In these terrible dreams he would see all of the children he'd once delivered to re-assigned parents. They would be lined up one behind the other – all of them now eight or nine years old – the boys and the girls – Gemini, Libra and Aquarius, ahead of them Cancer, Scorpio, Pisces, Taurus, Virgo and Capricorn. Each one of them trembling in terror as their turn to endure the penetrating needle of the fatal injection drew ever nearer. All of them looking at him with accusing eyes – You did this to us. You did this . . .

Rik blinked and shook his head as images from the dream tried to replay in his head. Templeton and McNeil were already departing with the rocket launcher. The other troopers began loading magazines into their assault rifles. Trembling slightly Rik did likewise.

'We go on my word,' said the sergeant.

Rik shouldered his rifle and decided in that instant that his one act of defiant mercy would be to shoot to kill – regardless of any immediate threat posed to him.

WINTER 2051

Rik knew from the smell of disinfectant and the starchiness of the sheets that he lay upon that he was in a hospital bed. His eyelids felt heavy. When he tried to force them open the light stung so badly that he had to close them immediately.

I'm lucky to be alive, he thought.

It had not been long after the triumph of *Fire* over *Earth* that the *Leos* began to air their grievances. They convinced themselves that the military hierarchy, who were mainly *Sagittarius* and *Aries* by birth, were conspiring to exclude them from the spoils of victory. Their astrologers confirmed this to be the case and pointed out that *Leos* were being discriminated against in the job market and afforded only the worst slum housing.

They set up autonomous *Leo* enclaves – called them *'prides'* – started posturing about how *'lionhearted'* they intended to be in the defence of their cause. Splinter groups began to engage in kidnap and hostage taking in order to press for concessions to their unjustified and increasing unrealistic demands. When this strategy failed they resorted to acts of terror – suicide bombs and hi-jacking.

The *Sagittarian* and *Arian* astrologers consulted the stars and proclaimed that it was written that the world must also be cleansed of *Leos*. Horoscopes, based on date and time of birth, were compiled to select which serving soldiers should be seconded to the elite genocide brigades.

Rik was amongst those given carte blanche to search and destroy.

Rik's torturer had been a *Leo* and it was his face that Rik saw when he was carrying out his orders. The sadistic animal had never given Rik his name, but it didn't matter – not any more. He was a *Leo* and there were enough of them to around.

It was his neatly trimmed hair, his clean-shaven jaw and his manicured fingernails that Rik saw whenever he executed a *Leo* at close range. It was the sickly smell of his soaps and lotions and the lightening jolt of the electrical current jarring though his genitals that he remembered when he shot a *Leo* in the head and tasted the splatter of their blood on his lips.

The memory of what he'd endured in that damp underground room made it easy to hate and despise his cowering victims. A cold logic took hold of him. In times past sections of humanity had used nationality, race or religion to justify intolerance against another. Why not birth date and star sign? Accepting that premise became easy too when it was so obvious that the *Leos* felt the same way about *Sagittarians* and *Arians*.

It was while on a mission to cleanse an inner city *Leo 'pride'* that Rik's unit had been the target of a booby-trapped car parked by the roadside. He remembered the white, searing light of the explosion and moments later lying on his back, the wind knocked out of his lungs, looking up at the dirty, smoke filled sky, his ears ringing so badly he thought that he must have burst both eardrums. He couldn't feel his legs or his arms and he had wondered if any of the severed limbs scattered about him were his. He had wondered how long it would take his *Arian* comrades to avenge this cowardly attack.

He had no recollection of how he had arrived at the hospital, or how long he had been bed ridden. But he hoped there was an end to it now. Surely he was so badly wounded that they could no longer expect him to carry out front line duties?

His head felt oddly heavy when he tried to turn on the pillow. When he reached up there was some kind of hard structure encompassing the area just above each ear. Perhaps a brace holding together repairs made to injuries to his skull? He patted his chest and his arms and his legs. He seemed to be covered in some type of rough, fleecy material that he assumed must be a newly developed type of dressing and concluded, therefore, that he had been severely burned by the explosion.

'You're awake,' said a voice from somewhere near the side of the bed. 'Excellent.'

Rik opened his eyes. The light stung, but not as badly as it had done a moment ago. Blinking rapidly he was gradually able to make out the image of a doctor standing over him. He was bald headed and bespectacled, his white tunic had been fashioned on the design of a military uniform, there was an *Aries* symbol, encompassed by the words *Aries Forces – Medical Division*, embroidered on his left sleeve. He sported a holographic *Aries* tattoo on his cheek.

'How do you feel?' he asked.

'Groggy,' replied Rik. 'Confused.'

'Perfectly understandable in the circumstances,' said the doctor.

He turned and motioned to someone who was hovering in the doorway.

'I have a visitor for you,' he said.

A girl of around twelve or thirteen years old entered the room and stood shyly beside the doctor, watching Rik from the corner of her eyes. She was dressed in a school blazer, also fashioned on the design of a military uniform. There was a badge with an embroidered *Aries* symbol on her left sleeve. It read *Aries Forces – Youth Division*. She too sported an *Aries* tattoo on her cheek.

'This is my daughter,' said the doctor. 'You won't remember me. But when you were brought here I was sure that I recognised your face. I checked your records. You were an *Infant Courier*, were you not?'

Not sure where this was going Rik nodded his head. Again he felt the unusual awkward weight of it on his neck.

'I am in your debt,' said the doctor. 'My wife and I were unable to have children. But the stars sent you to us and you brought us our daughter.' He put his arm around the girl and hugged her close to him. She blushed and smiled at Rik.

'She was born in the *Water* Zone,' said the doctor. 'To a *Cancer* mother and a *Scorpio* father. But she was blessed, like her mother and I, to be born under *Aries*. And it was by your hand that we were united.'

All Rik could think about was the other babies that he had delivered into *Earth*, *Air* and *Water*. Given what had transpired none of them were in any way blessed.

'I simply had to bring her to see you,' the doctor was saying. 'To show her what a glorious thing you have become. To show her that you are again set to become her saviour and protector.'

'What are you talking about,' asked Rik.

'You have been unconscious for some considerable time,' replied the doctor. 'Partly as a consequence of your injuries and partly due to the coma it was necessary for us to induce.

In that time the problem of the *Leos* has been resolved. But it is the *Sagittarians* who have now risen against us.'

Rik felt his heart sink at the depressing predictability of it all.

'The years of struggle have taken their toll on military resources,' continued the doctor. 'Neither side any longer has sufficient munitions to fight a war in the modern sense. The treacherous *Sagittarians* have taken several cities and slaughtered innocent *Arians* who previously fought alongside them. They defend these cities like mediaeval fortresses. *Sagittarian* archers raining deadly arrows down on our brave soldiers each time they attempt an assault.'

'So I assume that the astrologers have consulted the stars?' said Rik, not even attempting to disguise the sarcasm in his voice.

'They have,' agreed the doctor. 'And the stars decreed that we must create a new type of soldier – one hewn from the damaged material of our wounded. Our innovative scientists have developed a material known as *silverwool*, part synthetic and part organic, impervious to arrowheads. We have found ways to enhance body mass and muscle tissue. We have created resilient headgear implants in order to enable our storm troopers, our *rams*, to lock horns with the enemy in close mortal combat.'

Rik patted the coarse fabric that covered his body, panicking when he could find no discernable trace of a joint or a clip that held it in place. He reached up and touched the curvature of the hard material that encompassed the sides of his head.

'What have you done?' he screamed. 'What have you done?'

'Nurse,' said the doctor, 'bring in the mirror.'

A young woman in a militarised version of a nurse's uniform wheeled in a full sized mirror. She sported an *Aries* badge on her sleeve and a tattoo on her cheek. The doctor and his daughter stepped to one side to give her space.

'Get out of bed,' said the doctor. 'See what we have created. You and thousands like you, my friend.'

Rik stumbled out of the bed and stood before the mirror. He was appalled by what he saw. His thighs pumped up and bulked out – his shoulders even bulkier and impossibly broad. Every inch of him covered in wiry curls of coarse *silverwool* armour. Lacquered brown horns, curved into ferocious spirals on the sides of his head. His feet split and reformed into cloven hooves. They had made him into a killing machine – a dreadful *Arian* warrior.

This was far worse that anything the torturer had been able to come up with. It was the *dehumanisation* that had started with segregation taken far beyond the persistence of psychological indoctrination and given actual physical form. A tear welled in his eye and was lost amongst the frizzy curls of *silverwool* on his cheek.

He looked at the three of them – the doctor, his adopted daughter, the nurse peeping out from behind the mirror. They gazed back at him with awe and he sensed how thoroughly they had already pinned their warped and polluted hopes on him. Their soft flesh and puny stature was nothing compared to what they had made of him and he was ashamed at the disdain he suddenly felt for them.

Then it hit him – like some stark prophecy written in the stars. With an almost painful crystal clarity he understood that when the last *Sagittarian* was finally hunted down and destroyed, the seeds of yet another war would be sewn – a war between those who had been *adapted* and those who had not. And with it the dark dawning of the age of the true *Arian* would usher in its final solution.

HELEN JACKSON

BUILD GUIDE

THE NEW APPRENTICE was a slight, childish figure, maybe 150cm tall and massing about 50 kilos. She clung to a grabrail and glared at us. She looked nauseated. She wasn't what I'd hoped for.

The Gaffer said what we were all thinking: 'Great. They've sent us a little girl. She's no good to us. Did you know about this, Peggy?'

I shook my head and sighed. I was too old to wrangle teenagers. The Earthside contractor we worked for had embraced the New Modern Apprentice scheme. They got government subsidies, tax breaks, and good PR. We got a stream of unemployed – possibly unemployable – youngsters. This was the youngest yet.

The Gaffer spoke to the kid. 'What's your name, girlie?'

'Grace Benjamin Murray, *gramps*,' the kid said, pointedly. She spoke with spirit, despite still being doped up from the shuttle journey, in a pronounced South London accent. Eltham, maybe, or Kidbrooke. One of the rougher estates. The Gaffer didn't rise to the challenge.

'How old are you, Grace Benjamin Murray? Fifteen?'

Murray kept her head up. 'I'm nearly nineteen and I've been through full training.'

Diego snorted. 'What, six weeks groundside? Think that'll help you up here, nearly-nineteen?'

Murray looked fit to explode. She reminded me of myself at that age: scrappy and determined. I stepped in before she could say something she'd regret.

'Peggy Varus, foreman's assistant,' I introduced myself. 'You'll be bunking in with me. The Gaffer's Rasmus Larsson, Mr Larsson to you.' I nodded at the Gaffer and hoisted a thumb Diego's way. 'He's Diego.'

'Mr Fernandez to you.'

'In your dreams,' she said, letting go of her grabrail and attempting to step forward. As she floated, her face went distinctly green. I barely got the sick bag to her in time.

The Gaffer looked disgusted. Diego burst out laughing. I hustled the kid away before she could get herself in more trouble.

'Can we keep her inside?' asked the Gaffer. 'I haven't got time to babysit.'

We were running through the week's build guide for the *nth* time. Although we'd each be fed our step-by-steps on the Head Up Displays, it helped to know the full operation by heart.

'I don't see how,' I said, pausing the build guide at step five and pointing at the holo. 'It's a four person job from here onwards.'

We'd received a steelwork delivery along with our problem child and were ready to move onto the main truss extension. We'd also received a new boatload of tourists. The hotel accommodated fifty sightseers, keen to view the Earth from space. It'd take twice that many once we completed the new wing.

'Could we adjust to use the three of us plus an arm?' asked the Gaffer.

'Not a chance. Roboarm-1 will be doing the heavy lifting,

Diego'll be attached to R-2 in order to come in from the offside, and R-3's giving rides to the visitors.' The Gaffer looked thoughtful. I headed him off: 'We'll never get permission to requisition R-3.'

He nodded acknowledgement. We'd asked before, without success. 'Can we re-programme the build to use a maximum of three people?'

'I already looked at it. Today's on the critical path: we'd lose a lot of time.'

This wasn't quite true. I could see a way of reprogramming, but it would affect the delivery schedules for several suppliers I wanted to keep happy. I knew the Gaffer wouldn't question me.

He frowned. 'Okay, we'll take her out. But I don't want her causing trouble. Watch her, Peggy.'

I contemplated Murray as we suited up. She was over her space-sickness and handled her suit fasteners with confidence. It looked as if she'd stayed awake during training.

'Hey, nearly-nineteen,' said Diego. 'D'you know one end of a podger wrench from the other?'

Murray pulled the wrench out of her tool belt. 'Sure do. Used to have these in the gang.' She paused and lifted it in a raised fist, spike end forward. 'Pointy end for stabbing, blunt end for hitting, right?' Diego blanched. The Gaffer pushed forward and grabbed it from her.

'No way were you in a gang, girlie. Stow this and stop menacing Diego.'

Murray took the podger back, but didn't replace it on her belt immediately. She floated it near her hand. 'Was too. Steel erector gang. Started straight from school. I'd done eight months when the recession hit and we got laid off. I know what I'm doing with a podger.'

'Oh yeah?' said Diego. 'Fifty quid says every nut you put on today needs tightening by a real erector.'

'Give over, Diego,' I said. 'That's not a fair bet.' It takes several shifts to figure out how to apply the right torque in microgravity, and fifty pounds was more than an apprentice's daily wage. I expected the Gaffer to intervene. He stayed quiet.

'Too right it isn't fair,' said Murray. 'It'll be the easiest fifty I've ever earned. Wanna make it a hundred?' She held out her gloved hand to shake on the bet, an awkward Earth gesture that made Diego sneer.

'Helmets on,' said the Gaffer.

I got a glimpse of Murray's resolute expression before the gold visor hid it. I admired her commitment to making a fast buck. She'd go far, if she could master her over-confidence. Maybe I should take an interest in her?

'Clip in, Murray,' I said, passing her a line. 'Attach the other end to the red rail as soon as you get outside. Understand?' She nodded, hooked in, and looked back at me. Her body language said she expected something else. I waited.

'Where's my secondary line?' she asked. She really had been awake during training.

'We can't use secondary lines today. With the four of us, and the build order we've got, we'd get tangled with two lines each.'

'Safety handbook says no-one's to go out without primary and secondary lines.' Murray spoke quietly. She moved back, away from the airlock. She sounded even younger without her attitude.

The Gaffer entered the code to open the airlock inner door. As the release alert beeped, I did my best to sound reassuring.

'Construction Manager Caldwell set the build order. If she says it's safe, it's safe. We work without a secondary line all the time.'

'But what if it breaks, or comes loose? Safety handbook says – '

'Safety handbook? Not so tough now, are you, nearly-nineteen?' said Diego.

Murray shut up, and pulled herself into the airlock with the rest of us. We exited on the off side of the space station. Diego and the Gaffer headed to their positions. I kept Murray near the airlock door. If she panicked I wanted to be able to stuff her back inside straight away.

'This is freaky,' she said, floating a step away from the door. She didn't sound scared any more, she sounded awed. I could remember my first time well enough to know what she was experiencing. Space is different from the neutral buoyancy lab. Sure, the suit floats in the pool, but in space...

'I'm floating inside my suit!'

'How're you feeling? Any nausea? Headaches? Dizziness? Anything strange happening to your vision?'

She brought her legs up and pushed off, drifting until her line pulled taut. Over the radio, I could hear her laughter: bubbling glee rather than hysteria. Looked like she wasn't going to pass out on me. Next step, dealing with the view.

'Murray, pull yourself back in now.' She didn't obey immediately, still caught up in the sensation of floating. I raised my voice a notch. 'Murray!'

'Yeah, yeah, yeah. I'm coming.' She remembered enough of her training to grab hold of the line rather than using her legs to manoeuvre; I've seen plenty of apprentices floundering as they kicked off against nothing at all. Murray's return wasn't elegant or fast, but it wasn't bad. She had promise.

'We're going round to the Earth side. Use the green grabrails, hand over hand like this,' I demonstrated, 'don't try to float. Stay behind me.'

She kept up, until the Earth rose in her vision. I heard her indrawn breath. She stopped dead. I'd been expecting it – the view from Earth-Moon L5 is something special – and carried on moving steadily.

The planet was the only colour in the sky. There wasn't much cloud that day; big banks of white over the Americas, but vivid blue elsewhere, with the landmass of Europe clearly visible. I always liked being able to see England. I missed home.

'Beautiful, isn't it?' I said. 'It's a real challenge to ignore those visuals. This is where you have to remember your training and focus on the job you're here to do. Can you do that, Murray?'

She reached for the next grabrail and hauled herself forward. She'd almost caught up when she spoke. I swear I could hear the shrug in her voice.

'Where's the big deal? Seen it a million times.'

She seemed to mean it. I stopped.

'Seeing it on a screen's hardly the same as being here.'

She took her right hand off the rail and brought it up to her helmet. 'Nah,' she said, cheeky. 'The view was better in the movies, without all this Head Up Display crap getting in my face. Are we starting work or aren't we?'

I got moving. I'd noticed a similar attitude in the last apprentice. The way these kids took space for granted made me feel ancient. It was time I moved Earthside, if only I could find the right successor. If the company had had a decent pension plan, or I'd managed to skim enough, I'd have taken retirement years ago.

Diego was plugged on to Roboarm-2 when we reached our work point. The Gaffer got us started, steadily talking us through the build, step by step, reinforcing our HUD visuals, keeping everyone together.

The three of us worked well as a team. The Gaffer and I had been on the same crew for eleven years. I knew he'd make sure we got the job done, and he knew I'd deal with the paperwork without bothering him. Diego was into his third year with us and the Gaffer was training him well. Still, a fourth pair of hands – even clumsy hands – came in useful.

Construction Manager Caldwell had done a nice job of allocating tasks. For the first hour or so, Murray's role was restricted to nudging the position of steelwork lifted in by R-1. She'd had enough time in the neutral buoyancy pool to understand near-zero weight doesn't mean near-zero inertia. She did okay.

Her troubles started when she had to use tools. It took her nearly a quarter of an hour to get her first nut onto a bolt. She struggled with the gloves. It was painful to watch. When she'd finally got it tightened, I moved over to check it. It needed a finishing twist. So did the next one, and the next, much to Diego's delight.

'Looks like my drinks'll be on you tonight, nearly-nineteen.'

Murray swore viciously and promptly got worse. She dropped her podger, grabbed for it with reflexes conditioned to Earth gravity and missed. It headed in the direction of the main hotel viewport. The Gaffer pushed out and snagged it.

'Take a breather and calm down,' he said, before passing it back. 'And, Diego, concentrate on your own work.' Diego was working well. He and the arm operator had a smooth rhythm going; they made a difficult job look easy.

'Hey,' I said to Murray, 'come over here for a while and watch how I do it.' She did. I explained what I was doing and got her to repeat it. She dropped her wrench again. It was a long day.

Towards the end of the shift, Murray had mastered catching a dropped wrench. She'd done it often enough for her reflexes to adjust to microgravity. She was still struggling to do fine work with her gloves on: I made a mental note to give her a nut and bolt when we went in so she could practice overnight.

She was getting better at applying torque, and she was really working at it.

'Nearly,' I said, tightening off one of her connections.

'I'm gonna get this right, Peggy. Here, try that.'

'Nearly, again.'

'That?'

'Another nearly.'

I thought she'd lose patience, but she kept at it. As we moved onto our last step of the day she'd all but got the knack. Her last-but-one joint was almost good enough to let through. The rest of us had finished work. Diego and the Gaffer were watching. There was certainly enough torque for it to hold. I paused ... considered letting her have it ...

'I'll check it myself if you don't hurry up,' said Diego.

I had to call it.

'Almost, but not quite,' I said. Murray was already putting on the last nut, handling her podger neatly.

'Here,' said the Gaffer, 'let me check that one.' It took a while for him to pull over. 'Hey, nice work, girlie.'

'Yeah?' said Murray. She hung nearby, a little too close.

'This is good for your first day out.'

'Good enough?'

The Gaffer gave the nut one last adjustment.

'Nearly. You'll get the hang of it tomorrow. Should I take that hundred out of your first week's pay?'

Murray turned up early for the next workshift, carrying her gloves and practice bolt. Construction Manager Angela Caldwell was talking to the Gaffer while I checked the lines. Caldwell had her long grey hair tied back and wore a singlet that showed the scars on her arms.

I greeted Murray as she came in. 'Keen to get outside again, are you?' I asked. I was pleased. Enthusiasm was natural in a kid her age.

'Nah, not specially. Wanted to talk to the Gaffer about today's build.'

The Gaffer heard and turned, one eyebrow raised, breaking off his conversation with Caldwell. Although he and I went through the build guide every day, we didn't expect input from the rest of the team. Not that it was banned; it just wasn't traditional.

'Angela, this is our latest apprentice, Grace Murray,' he said. 'Murray, Construction Manager Caldwell. What did you want to talk about?'

Angela Caldwell gave Murray a level, assessing look. They were about the same height. Murray didn't speak. I hadn't seen her intimidated before. Diego arrived during the silence, realised something was going on, and kept his mouth shut. The Gaffer prompted Murray.

'Come on girlie, speak up. You've got something to say about the build order?'

Murray could speak nicely when she wanted to; she'd learnt to smooth out her accent.

'It'd work better if we did steps eighteen and nineteen first, then went back to step one,' she said. 'We'd get the biggest section bolted into place early, meaning we could separate into two teams after that. We could get five steps ahead of the day's programme.' She looked away. 'Plus we'd be able to use two lines for the full shift.'

Diego rolled his eyes.

'Is that what this is about?' asked the Gaffer. 'You're going to have to get used to working with one line. It's perfectly safe.'

'It wasn't safe for Batukhtina.'

They'd shown the same training video back when I apprenticed. Batukhtina was an early casualty; she'd been doing a solo repair on ISS-2 when her line snapped.

The video is silent. For the first few minutes Batukhtina's visor reflects the space station. Look closely and there's a face at the viewport: her colleague . . . watching . . . helpless. Then, Batukhtina stops reaching towards him, turns away, and relaxes, facing the Earth, arms and legs spread-eagled.

She had floated gently away with sixty-nine minutes of oxygen and no way of getting back. It gives all of us the shivers. Just thinking about it reminded me how much I wanted to go home. If I found someone I could trust to take over my work I'd be on the next shuttle back to Earth. Sure, I'd miss the view, but I could live with that.

'We have stronger lines now,' I said, 'checked and replaced regularly. Two lines is fine for tourists, but it slows us down.'

'My way'd be quicker though, even with secondary lines.'

Caldwell took over. She didn't appreciate the implication her site was dangerous.

'Interesting idea, Murray, but you're thinking like an Earthworm. There's not enough manoeuvrability in your spacesuits to be able to work with the main steelwork in the way. Plus, I designed this order to keep you near the others. Your inexperience is much more dangerous than working without a secondary line. You'll do everything as a full team until I say otherwise.' Caldwell turned to the Gaffer. 'That clear, Rasmus?'

'Perfectly, Construction Manager.'

'Way to go, nearly-nineteen,' said Diego once the door hissed closed behind Caldwell.

Two weeks on, we finally split the team. The Gaffer and Diego went off to fit struts at the hotel end of the truss, while Murray and I checked and tightened nuts along its bottom chord. It was real monkey work.

I took a brief break to admire the Earth. Vivid patches of blue showed through heavy cloud cover. Murray didn't stop. She was working steadily, using her podger like a pro, movements well adapted to the lack of gravity. Even Diego no longer doubted she'd done construction work before. I was beginning to think she was made of the right stuff.

'Must have been hard for you, getting made redundant,' I said, on a suit-to-suit channel for privacy.

'Yeah,' she said, not breaking her rhythm. 'Mum'd lost her job too. Granddad looked after us, but he died last year . . .' She faded out. I turned to look at her, giving her the chance to continue if she wanted. She didn't.

'Something's bugging me,' she said, full-volume again. 'These are Boltefast nuts and bolts. The construction models spec SureEng.'

'"SureEng *OEA*'. That's Or Equal and Approved. These are approved.'

'Who picked Boltefast? Would it be the Gaffer?'

I didn't hesitate. I'd faced tougher questioners than this kid. Plus, I was interested to see if she'd follow up.

'Probably. He's answerable for costs once a project's on site. Or it could have been Head Office.'

'And who approved it?'

'Angela Caldwell, most likely.'

She nodded and dropped the subject, only to come back to it the next day.

'I still don't get the equal and approved thing,' she said. I was pleased she was bright enough to keep asking the right questions, although I was glad we were talking suit-to-suit again. I hoped I was the only one whose ear she was bending.

'Those brands,' she said. 'I looked them up. The Boltefast are lower grade. They're not equal to SureEng. Their shear strength is lower.'

'Lower but high enough.'

'Who says?'

'If Caldwell approved them, Caldwell says.'

'It's your initials on the change request.'

'Then I made the suggestion and Caldwell approved it. It's pretty routine.'

She stayed quiet for a moment, pulling out a bolt and looking at it. She was getting pretty good at fine manipulation wearing gloves.

'They're cheaper,' she said. 'Who makes the saving?'

She's nearly there, I thought, willing her to work it out. I didn't answer. When she spoke again, she seemed to have changed the subject.

'There was this guy I worked with before,' she said. 'His wages went further than everyone else's. He had the latest tech, ate out a lot, nice clothes. I liked him. Always got the first round in at the pub.'

'Uh-huh?' I said.

'His sister-in-law, see, she ran a galvanising firm. Hot dip and powder coating. We used her on almost all our contracts. Must have been good.'

I knew then she was the one – my ideal successor. She confirmed it with her next question:

'Do you think Boltefast is good in the same way?'

'Yes,' I said, looking straight at her, 'I'd say it's good in exactly that way.'

She nodded. Time to put my exit strategy into action.

'I'm thinking of requesting retirement,' I said. 'I'm too old to be wielding a podger. But, I need someone up here to take over the paperwork.'

'Doesn't the Gaffer deal with it?'

'He's never been interested. I'd prefer to pass it on to someone else. Someone who'd keep me in the loop, as it were.'

'That person would be taking a risk, wouldn't they? Perhaps half the risk?'

'I wouldn't say half. Eighty:twenty, perhaps?'

'Sixty:forty,' she countered.

'It takes time to build up contacts,' I pointed out. 'Eighty:

twenty for the first three years, seventy:thirty when you finish your apprenticeship.'

'Hey!' called the Gaffer, on the open channel. I looked up and he was coming our way. 'You two are getting behind. Problems, Peggy?'

'No, nothing,' I said.

'Girlie?'

'Nah.'

'Get a move on, then.'

We finished the shift in silence. I was happy to let her mull it over.

'Is it true Caldwell got those scars working on the London Olympic stadium?' asked Murray.

We'd just come in from a shift, a couple of days after I made my offer to the kid. I was waiting for her reply, confident it'd be yes. Who doesn't want to earn a little extra on the side?

Construction was a day ahead of schedule, the Gaffer was whistling happily, and Diego had gone easy on Murray for a few hours.

'That's the rumour,' I said. 'Must be forty years ago. How'd you hear? She doesn't talk about it.'

'One of the tourists.' The Gaffer stopped whistling and turned to look. We weren't supposed to fraternise.

Murray continued. 'Old guy. Used to be a labourer.'

'What were you doing in the hotel?' asked the Gaffer.

'He came over here,' said Murray. 'Wanted to see how we did things.'

'More to the point, what's a labourer doing in the hotel?' asked Diego. 'Won the lottery?'

The Gaffer and I laughed. Murray shook her head.

'Nah, he's been saving all his life. Always dreamed of going into space, he said.'

'What'd he know about Angela Caldwell?' I asked.

'He worked on the stadium too. He was off sick when one end of the lower tier collapsed. She was apprenticing with the steelwork gang. Eight people were killed. They pulled Caldwell out of the rubble two days later.'

Diego whistled. 'No wonder she likes space.'

Diego and the Gaffer had finished changing. Murray was going slowly; I guessed she wanted to talk.

'I need a volunteer to check the oxygen tanks,' I said.

'That'll be you, nearly-nineteen,' said Diego, suddenly out the door, the Gaffer right behind him. I sat down and waited to hear what was on Murray's mind.

'He was nice, that old guy,' she said. 'I hadn't thought about the tourists. What if there's an accident?'

'There won't be.'

'But what if something fails?'

'It won't. Everything's checked. I wouldn't let anything past if I wasn't completely confident.' I was lying, but not much. There's always the possibility of component failure. My specification changes only increased the chances a little.

'He's probably someone's granddad.'

'He's perfectly safe,' I snapped. 'Talking to tourists is likely to get you in trouble. So is gossiping about Caldwell.'

She looked guilty at that. I took pity on her.

'You can head off,' I said. 'I'll do the tanks.'

I should have known better than to be soft on an apprentice. She knew I'd be occupied for at least half an hour. She used the time to grass me up to Caldwell.

Of course, Caldwell came straight to me afterwards.

'Whistle-blowing!' I said, disappointed. I hardly believed it; Murray had seemed so promising.

'How much does she know?' asked Caldwell. I shrugged.

'She obviously hasn't worked out your role.'

'Let's keep it that way. Arrange a safety infraction tomorrow and I'll fire her on the spot. Once she's been shipped home in disgrace no-one will believe her.'

Easy for Caldwell to say; she wasn't at risk of exposure. I was sure I could come up with a better solution.

'Here, clip in, Murray,' I said, holding out a prepared line.

Diego sailed through the door. 'I'll take that one. Nearly-nineteen's not ready yet.'

He was right; Murray hadn't fully sealed her suit.

'You're not suited up,' I said, pulling my hand back, 'and she'll only be a moment.'

'So get another line ready quickly,' said Diego, taking the line and clipping his suit in before I could think of a reason to stop him. He was finished and waiting to go well before Murray.

'Taking your time, nearly-nineteen?' he taunted.

'Get lost.'

'Enough!' said the Gaffer. 'You two are working together today. I need Peggy with me on the central connector point. Diego, no messing around, understand? Peggy, I want a second line for girlie here.'

The Gaffer's order was a relief. I'd drawn a blank trying to come up with a reason for Diego and Murray to swap lines. I broke out two extra lines and checked them.

'No need for me,' said Diego.

'Safety handbook applies to you too,' I said, throwing one his way.

'First I've heard of it,' he said.

'Just clip in.'

'Nah, remember what Caldwell said? I'm in no danger so long as nearly-nineteen's fully restrained.'

Murray ignored him and clipped in, doubly safe, to my frustration.

'Leave it,' said the Gaffer, punching the airlock code. Diego laughed, and lobbed his secondary back to me. I considered calling him back. I could say I'd spotted something wrong with his line. I nearly did it . . . but I needed to act before Murray was sent Earthside.

I decided. A warning would do the job. It was a shame; I'd always liked Diego. But, Murray needed to be taught a lesson about telling tales.

I watched them as best I could from the opposite end of the truss, but I was still looking the other way when the trouble came. The first I knew was Murray shouting for help over the open channel. The Gaffer looked round, swore once, and headed towards them.

Diego was without a line, moving steadily away from the station. As I watched, Murray flung herself after him. She got her trajectory wrong, would have missed him by a mile even if her line had been long enough.

'Murray,' I said. 'There's nothing you can do. Come away now.'

She didn't reply. She'd pulled herself back in and was fiddling with her line. She launched towards Diego again, this time with her secondary line attached to the end of her primary to give herself more length. She'd got the reach, but her angle was still wrong. She tried to correct mid-jump. It didn't work.

She pulled in, sighted more carefully, and pushed off. It was an elegant dive, with the heading exactly right. Diego held out his arms. She got to within two meters, the line snapped tight, and she stopped.

'Nearly,' said Diego, softly.

She held position, looking at him as he drifted off. She said nothing. He relaxed his arms, but didn't turn away. I could see Murray reflected in his visor.

It seemed a long while before the Gaffer's voice interrupted.

'Grace, you did good, but pull in now. We're going to try and grab him using R-3. I need you out of the way. Diego?'

'You really think an arm pick-up might work, Gaffer?'

'I've gone through it with the operator on duty and she's confident. Fifty pounds says it'll work.'

Murray was shaken and wary as I helped her back inside. I watched the footage of the rescue later – as did most of the Earth's population. It looked like a slow-motion ballet. Murray's dive turned her into a hero.

Angela Caldwell avoided me that evening and the next day. I engineered an encounter outside her bunkroom, but all she said was 'I'm not going to be sent Earthside over this, Peggy,' and pushed past. A highly visible accident wasn't what she'd had in mind, especially as we couldn't pin it on Murray. Murray the hero.

We were kept in for a shift while Caldwell inspected every piece of kit we used, as per post-incident guidelines. The following morning everything was back to normal – a new sort of normal.

'Psych has given you a sick note for the week,' said the Gaffer to Diego. 'Why not use it?' They were both suiting up.

'And let you lot mess up the build? No chance.'

'Think you're irreplaceable do you, Diego?' said Murray.

'Too right,' said Diego. 'You're barely competent with that podger, Grace.'

Murray grinned. 'At least I don't wander off half-way through a shift.'

They both laughed.

The Gaffer put his visor down. 'Let's go, then. Diego, you're with me to finish the central connector. Peggy and Grace, you're together. Secondary lines for everyone.'

There were no complaints.

'Diego and I are doing another interview tonight,' said Murray as we worked.

'You're quite the media stars.'

'Yeah, everyone loves a heroic failure, especially when there's a happy ending.' She was quiet for a while. Then: 'They love an honest whistle-blower too.'

She hand-tightened a nut, as comfortable with delicate movements in her gloves as she would be bare-handed. I thought hard. I'd missed my chance to get rid of her; negotiation was my best option. If she talked I'd be in serious trouble.

'The media might like whistle-blowers, but bosses don't,' I said. 'You've made a good start here. Why spoil it?' She stopped working. I pushed on. 'What about Diego? If you go public tonight, he'll be associated with you. It'll end his career too.' I paused to let it sink in. 'How about we increase your cut to thirty percent from the start and say no more about it?'

'You tried to kill me!'

'Thirty-five.'

'I want you out of here.'

'That's the plan. Thirty-five, and I move groundside as soon as I can.'

'No.'

I turned away and tightened a couple of nuts, giving time for her confidence to falter. 'I won't go any higher than thirty-five,' I said, my back to her.

'No,' she repeated. 'You meant that line for me and the others saw it. What will Caldwell do when I tell her it wasn't an accident?'

It was a good question. Caldwell had plenty to hide, but this was outside her comfort zone. I didn't know what she'd do. Still...

'You're missing something,' I said

That shut her up. I wish I could have seen her face as the penny dropped.

'Caldwell's in on it,' she said, a statement rather than a question.

She moved away from me, turning to look at the point where her lines clipped onto the rail. I was close enough to reach out and unhook them. I hoped she was scared. If I was lucky she'd quit before the end of the day and my problems would be solved.

I wasn't lucky.

I retreated to my bunk to watch Murray and Diego's interview. I couldn't bear to be in the common area while they were broadcasting.

It was sick-making stuff: Diego joking about how he'd misjudged Murray at first and Murray all forgiveness.

I wished I dared switch off.

It seemed every Earthworm with a connection had a question to ask, and Murray wanted to talk to them all. She even got in a tribute to her dead granddad, who taught her right from wrong.

The longer it went on, the more tense I got. I held my breath each time Murray spoke. She chatted and laughed.

Finally, the flow of questions stopped. The pair said their goodbyes and signed off to the world. I breathed a premature sigh of relief.

The broadcast continued on the staff network. Diego moved away from the camera. Angela Caldwell came into shot.

'We have a special announcement,' Caldwell said. I didn't like the complicit look that passed between her and Murray. 'Grace, would you?'

Murray smiled.

'We all know how much Peggy Varus deserves to be rewarded for her work.' I swear the hairs on the back of my neck stood on end when I heard my name. 'I'm delighted to announce she's been promoted to a management role at Head Office. Congratulations, Peggy!'

My orders came through seconds later. I'd been allocated a groundside desk job without any opportunities for creativity. Congratulations were hardly appropriate, although everyone chimed in with good wishes over the open channel.

A second message pinged in almost immediately. Caldwell would be taking on my construction duties until a replacement arrived, with all paperwork being handled groundside in the meantime.

My head was spinning. Caldwell hadn't used a podger in a decade. And, how did she and Murray plan to keep their scam – *my* scam – secret with Head Office nosing into everything?

I turned up for the start of the next shift as usual and offered my services to the Gaffer. I needed to find out what the situation was.

I still hoped Murray and Caldwell would buy my silence with a cut. I'd salted away some money, but not enough for comfort. I needed that on-going income, or I'd never retire.

'I've re-jigged the programme from today onwards,' announced Caldwell. It was news to me. I looked at the Gaffer. He knew about it.

'What's going on?' I asked, as casually as I could. Diego and Murray had yet to arrive.

'We've got a delivery the day after tomorrow,' said the Gaffer.

'Nothing's scheduled,' I said.

'SureEng nuts and bolts,' said Caldwell. My jaw dropped. 'I ran some spot checks and I'm not comfortable with the shear strength of the Boltefast ones. We're going to replace the lot.'

I closed my mouth and took a deep breath.

'I don't see how ... we'll never finish on time.'

Caldwell pulled up the full build guide.

'We've changed a few other material specifications,' she said. I looked at the changes in despair. Caldwell had been talked into dismantling our entire scheme. Murray's negotiation skills were better than I'd realised.

Caldwell continued: 'It turns out the new suppliers can deliver sooner, which gives us a bit of leeway.'

'We need more than a bit!' I said, looking at the Gaffer for support. 'Especially when we're already behind because of the accident.'

The Gaffer looked pained at mention of the accident. He glanced at Caldwell. *He knows*, I realised.

Murray and Diego swung in.

'Ah,' said the Gaffer, pleased with the distraction, 'right on time. How did you get on?'

'What have you been doing?' I asked.

'Fraternising,' said Diego. I frowned. Nothing was making sense.

'The hotel operator has agreed we can have R-3 for two hours every morning,' said Murray. I looked at the revised build guide again. The extra arm would get them back on schedule within weeks. Everything I'd achieved had been reversed; no-one but the shareholders would make money out of this job.

'Thanks for coming down, Peggy,' said the Gaffer, 'but we've got things under control. Take a couple of days off.'

'I asked a favour while I was talking to the hotel manager,' said Murray. 'She's given you permission to spend as long as you like in the skylounge. Enjoy the view.'

I was shipped groundside on the shuttle that made the SureEng delivery, fittingly enough. It didn't have passenger facilities, so I suited up for the journey. The gang waved me off.

Angela Caldwell looked more relaxed than she had in years. She confided she was enjoying working with a podger and having a holiday from management. I might have known she'd be the type to go straight.

The Gaffer wouldn't look me in the eye. Eleven years we'd worked together and he barely said goodbye.

Diego shook my hand.

Murray hung back until the others had left. I could still see myself in her; she'd got exactly what she wanted: acceptance, a place on the gang, and an honest living. Her dear old granddad would have been proud. Would she regret giving up the money, I wondered, when she reached my age?

'Better start saving for your retirement now,' I said. 'Or you'll be working until you drop.'

She recoiled. 'That's better than being like you,' she said.

'Oh, but you could have been, if you'd had the courage. You nearly made it.'

I put down my visor. I hoped Murray would see herself, reflected in gold, as I turned away. But, deep down, I knew she saw a tired old woman whose schemes had failed; I was a build guide Murray would never follow.

E. J. SWIFT

SAGA'S CHILDREN

You will have heard of our mother, the astronaut Saga Wärmedal. She is famous, and she is infamous. Her face, instantly recognizable, appears against lists of extraordinary feats, firsts and lasts and onlys. There are the pronounced cheekbones, the long jaw, that pale hair cropped close to the head. In formal portraits she looks enigmatic, but in images caught unaware – perhaps at some function, talking to the Administrator of the CSSA or the Moon Colony Premier; in situations, in fact, where we might imagine she would feel out of place – she is animated, smiling. In those pictures, it is possible to glimpse the feted adventurer who traversed the asteroid belt without navigational aid.

We knew her only once, on Ceres.

You will have heard of what happened on Ceres.

Ours is one of many versions of Saga's story. Widely distributed are a number of official biographies, and you can easily find another few dozen from less reputable sources. She is the subject of documentaries and immersion, avatars and educational curricula. We were not consulted in their production. But then, we did not know her; we only knew her contradictions, of which there were many. One small but significant example: she renounced her European passport in order to gain Chinese citizenship, yet she gave each of us a traditionally Scandinavian name.

We can say for certain that Saga was born in Umeå, Sweden, where in winter the darkness lies low and thick and heavy and the snow crunches underfoot with that particular sound heard only on Earth. Ulla, the oldest of us, remembers Umeå snow. She remembers the flakes falling on her head and the cold tingling sensation as they melted through her hair into her scalp. At least, this is what she says, and so we agree that this is how it was.

We know that Saga grew up in Umeå with a single mother. The biographies depict her as an exceptionally clever child, excelling in the fields of science and mathematics. A solitary creature. Decisive. Sure. In some editions, Saga herself is quoted:

It was when I saw the lights for the first time, the Aurora Borealis. The most beautiful thing on Earth. But it wasn't on Earth. That's when I knew what I wanted to be.

So she did what every child who wishes to be an astronaut must do. Saga taught herself Mandarin.

By age sixteen she was fluent. She applied to the most prestigious university in Beijing to study astro-engineering, and graduated with the top marks in her year. She was promptly accepted as a trainee astronaut in the Chinese Solar System Administration, a move almost unheard of for Europeans, and especially at such a young age. From there her career took off in meteoric fashion. News of her escapades was celebrated across worlds. She mapped the Martian planet. She led the first missions to Jupiter's moons.

The biographies are less interested in Saga's domestic life, if we can refer to it as such, and even between us we are not entirely settled on the details. We were raised by our fathers and grandmother. We knew Saga only through occasional communications from the outer planets, and nothing of one another's existence. She sent us the debris of space. In our bedrooms we stored asteroid crystals and jars of red dust from Mars. We dreamed of Saga sailing through the stars, tailed by comets.

In her transmissions, she would tell each of us the same thing.

She loved us.

We must work hard.

Seek wisely.

Dream deeply.

Her hologram, flickering gently the way we imagined ghosts might, would flood us with bewilderment. We wanted to touch her, but when we put our fingertips to hers, there was nothing but air.

Since we found one another, we have spent many hours puzzling over the mystery of our existence. We do not mean this in an existential manner, although of course we ask those questions as much as the next human being. The mystery we share is something more personal. We would like to know why Saga chose to create us at all.

Ulla's conception must have been an accident – still early in her career, it was not a good time for Saga to have a child, and an abortion would have been more practical. Ulla was born in Umeå (or says she was, as she says she remembers snow. But her father brought her up in Beijing, where, we imagine, he lived out his life awaiting Saga's return. He waited a long time) but the greater question is why she was born at all. Could Saga have been unaware of her predicament until it was too late? How had she failed to take precautions?

Five years later, Per appeared on the Moon colony. He may have been intended, although a relationship with his father was not. (Nonetheless Per's father did his best until Per reached sixteen, upon which date his father moved to Mars, we imagine, to search for Saga. He searched a long time.) Per grew up among space farers. Pilgrims, adventurers, criminals on the run, ambassadors, colonists and writers: all passed through Moon and recounted their tales whilst Per, in his first paid job, served them cups of mulled moonshine.

None of us are astronauts, but we have travelled. It is true that much of our journeying was done before we were born. Ulla went to the Moon and back, the size of a fingernail. Per went as far as Mars, and felt its heavy gravity pulling him down against the lining of Saga's womb. Signy, we believe, was conceived on a ship orbiting Europa under Jupiter's yellow gaze, and later returned to Earth and entrusted to the care of Saga's mother in Sweden. Signy is the only one of us to have known our grandmother.

It was in the year preceding Ceres that we learned the truth. Saga had recorded a transmission on Mars where she was readying for her latest expedition to the dwarf planet, which at that time was being prepared as a mining centre for the asteroid belt. Ceres would cement China's wealth and fund the Republic's empire for a long time to come. We had a hazy awareness of these events, but if we are honest, we did not tend to pay much attention to the expansion. You have to understand that it was a painful thing, to consider the world our mother had chosen over us. Most of the time we preferred not to think of other worlds at all. We were trying to live our lives as unobtrusively as we could, and avoid people discovering the identity of our mother.

Of course, we couldn't help our dreams.

We were to discover that we have very different lives. Per is a shuttle engineer – we assume he inherited most of Saga's genes. Ulla teaches the old Earth art of yoga and works primarily with pregnant women. Signy is employed by the Earth Restoration Commission and travels to blighted patches of ocean or forestry. We thought it interesting that we had each taken a restorative, vocational pathway. We were feeling for one another's personalities, on that first night.

Saga had contrived for the transmission to reach us at the same moment across our locations of Moon Colony, Tianjin and the Indian Ocean. It arrived with Per over breakfast: spinach and eggs; he always has them poached. Ulla received it when she returned home from an intensive Bikram class: she had been working on her own practice that day, and her mind was still revolving through salutations. Signy was the last to view it, from the cabin of a ship, which despite Signy's best efforts smelled of stale sweat and salt, as did her clothes.

The transmission was short. Saga was in uniform, with the rén arrow and crane wings of the CSSA logo visible at her collarbone. There was nothing to suggest where in the solar system she might be, but we were shortly to find out.

Quite calmly, Saga delivered her revelation. *It is time for you to find one another*, she said. She knew where we were, which surprised us. She also knew what we did, which surprised us more. She invited us to join her next year on the space station orbiting Ceres, from where she would be leading an anniversary expedition down to the surface. (She did not clarify the nature of the anniversary, but later we learned that the first space probe to Ceres had been sent by NASA, several centuries ago in 2015, when NASA was still a guiding force.)

What did we feel, watching Saga's transmission?

We were bewildered by her. What did she mean by telling us we were multiple? She had thrown our lives into turmoil – how could we not hate her a little for it?

Were we angry? Yes, we suppose we were angry too, although we did not admit to anger when we united, not at first.

We were in awe. Saga inspired awe. She inspired admiration. Listening to her low hypnotic voice throwing our lives into turmoil, we could only gaze upon the famous eyes the colour of an ocean on a stormy day (as the biographies describe them), and feel ourselves slowly losing oxygen, or perhaps we were injected with oxygen, high on it, at once starved and sated, propelled into a delirious state that made us not ourselves, or more purely ourselves than ever before. Our heartbeats quickened. We sweated minerals. Our mouths were dry but we wanted to break down and sob. We wanted carpets and cushions to soak up our tears.

Saga wanted us there. She did say this; our memories are united on this point. Saga wanted us to witness the expedition to Ceres. She was excited to have us there, together.

(Later, when we reflected upon the transmission, we realised that she did not say the word *together*. But she was excited to see us there. Have us or see us? Does it make a difference? We think it does.)

There was no question of not going. We had some concerns – the political climate being somewhat unstable, since the revolution on Mars, and rumours of possible war – but this was not enough to deter us.

We quit our jobs or took extended leave. We met our new siblings on the Moon. Per was there and it made sense to travel together, even if we would be in suspended sleep. At first we assumed we would want to ride out the long journey, using the time to get to know one another, but Per explained that would not be possible: ships were not equipped to entertain passengers, and hibernation was cheaper and actually far more comfortable. We understood, but we felt a little strange when he used that word, passengers. Perhaps we had been thinking of ourselves as being like Saga, as though we had absorbed something of her spirit after all, but we were not astronauts. We would be civilians, not even emigrants, largely a nuisance, and only undertaking the journey because Saga Wärmedal had ordered it and footed the bill.

It was when we saw the cost of our trip that we realized the extent of Saga's influence.

In the week before the flight we talked about ourselves and about Saga. We compared our fathers and our bone structures and the colours of our irises. Signy had Saga's nose. Ulla did not, but she might have done, before she changed it. Per and Ulla had inherited her broad shoulders, we decided, plucking up images. We knew when we finally saw her in person we would be studying every detail, comparing her physique with our own, adjusting the swing of our step a little, to match hers.

We agreed that there were things that must be said to Saga. We would be calm: we would not air our grievances like a committee, but we would ensure that Saga understood what we wanted to tell her. It was difficult to find a common language to describe our loneliness. Signy favoured metaphors. She was poisoned, she said. She was a bird whose migrational compass had been distorted and who no longer knew where to fly, and so flew everywhere, unable to find home. She was a penguin in the Antarctic gone mad, one of those ones that wandered inexplicably out into the ice sheets, where nothing awaited them but starvation.

We considered Signy's metaphors and felt that the penguin was not quite right. Penguins were too close to comedy, and this was a sad, unfortunate matter. We agreed that Signy should not mention the penguin. The bird, we said, was a better analogy.

Per talked pragmatically about the events of his life. His partner had left him. She said he did not know how to love her, or even what love was. It was she who pointed towards his peculiar childhood. Brought up amongst adults, she said he had never been innocent. It was his mother's fault, she said.

His mother had plucked out his heart and hurled it among the stars, and the stars were cold things, whatever people said. Love to his mother meant a word travelled through a vacuum, uttered by a hologram. How could that be love?

Now there was another woman in Per's life, a slender girl from Mars, but Per feared it would go the same way.

Ulla explained that she was obsessed with pregnancy, but would never be able to have children. It was not that she was infertile – this was a thing in her head. Ulla had seen a therapist, once a week, for the past three years. She told the therapist about our mother, the astronaut, who was without doubt the origin of this affliction. She told the therapist that the idea of bearing her own child was at once abhorrent and the only thing she wanted in life. She did not need a partner; she would happily purchase the requisite DNA. But something was holding her back. She taught yoga for pregnant women, gazing at their swollen bellies. She dandled the babies of friends, and without exception the babies fell in love with her, laughing and squealing with delight, but after handing them back to their parents Ulla would run out of the house or the playgroup or the coffee shop, and breathe in and out of a panic bag, paralysed for hours in the grip of terrible attacks.

Despite our disparate lives, we had found something in common: a series of disastrous relationships. We agreed that Saga had cost us love in our adult lives. We were dysfunctional. We would tell her this.

We were welcomed to the orbiting station above Ceres by a CSSA official. He did not mention Saga, which we thought strange, but invited us to a viewing platform from where we could see the dwarf planet drifting softly below. He brought refreshments, and there he left us. We surveyed Ceres with dubious eyes, knowing this sphere of rock and water was the latest thing to have a hold over our mother. Down there was her version of love. We saw a white planet, a cream planet, a planet with pale lemon sorbet swirls. We saw veined marble; we saw old polished bone. We pointed out to one another the dark spots where smaller asteroids had crashed into the planet's surface. We pontificated aloud that Saga's mission would be dangerous, whatever it was. We theorised on likely locations for the mining base. We knew nothing, but believed that we must say something. We had to reassure ourselves of our right to be aboard. We were passengers. We were nervous.

She entered the viewing platform alone. Our mother, the astronaut, in our sights for the first time since our births. There was the tall, lean figure, there were the eyes the colour of an ocean on a stormy day, flecked with recklessness, just like the documentaries said.

As soon as she appeared we knew we had been right to be nervous.

It was clear that Saga was not expecting us. She recognized us in the way that we might recognize a celebrity from a photograph – disorientation, followed by slow comprehension. She looked shocked. Yes, we agreed afterwards that she looked shocked. She said:

What are you doing here?

It was a horrible moment. Taken aback, we rushed to explain. The invitation – the transmission! We had replied. Had she not received our replies? We did not like to say, had she not paid for our flights, arranged for our stay, organized all of this?

Gradually the shock faded from her face. *Of course, of course.* She smiled. But we were thrown, obviously, by this peculiar greeting.

Struck by a terrible shyness, we felt our tongues grow huge and clumsy. How should we introduce ourselves, how should we greet her? We had agreed before that we would address her as Saga, but now alternate possibilities ran through our heads: mamma, mŭqīn, mom. We were stunned by the lean, stark beauty of her face. Her youthfulness shocked us, although we knew, we had read, that she had had no restorative work or even enhancements, as many of the astronauts did, to make them faster, sharper, better. We wondered if she were real; we wondered if she might live forever.

We wondered why she had born us and what we were doing there, but all the things we had planned to say evaporated.

Saga spoke in Mandarin, although Signy swears there was a moment when we all digressed into Scandi.

She said our names.

Ulla, Per, Signy. Look at you! I'm so happy you could come.

(But that moment of shock?)

She asked us questions. She wanted to know about our little, insignificant lives, and all we wanted to know was her, her inner life, her private thoughts. Alone in her ship in the outback of space, did Saga ask the questions we all asked? Did Saga wonder where she came from, if there was a god? We wanted to know, but did not dare to ask.

We did our best to make ourselves interesting; gave her the answers we thought she wanted to hear. The evening passed too quickly. Over dinner, Saga told us about the mission. She told us Ceres would become the most important mining station in the solar system, a source of water and fuel for travellers back to Earth and out to Jupiter and Saturn. We watched the way she held her chopsticks, scooping up noodles with easy elegance. We mirrored her gestures. We were offered wine, but Saga took only water. Her storm-at-sea eyes surveyed us, smiling. We thought she was pleased, and this gave us a feeling of warm satisfaction.

The next day we watched her descend to Ceres. She had her own ship, and it was built, she had told us, to her exact specifications. She gave us some technical details that we did not understand.

We watched Saga's ship land, and the others of the mission followed. Saga appeared first on the surface link. We watched her suited figure lope across the surface of the planet. In the low gravity she appeared like a mythical being gliding over her territory. The expedition team were to meet with another team stationed on the surface. They had been drilling for samples for some months, and would perform the extractions today. Big results were expected.

Before the astronauts could reach the drilling station, the transmission cut out. There was confusion in the room: what had happened to the link? An engineer came and tried to fix it. She could not get a picture. We watched, silently, hoping everyone would forget we were there, but of course they did not. After a few minutes we were told that there had been a technical mishap (nothing to worry about, only the connection) and were escorted firmly from the room.

We went to the viewing platform and stood about aimlessly. Ceres hung, mute and ghostly against her velvet backdrop. This was how we came to witness Saga's exit.

We saw a pinpoint of fire, small but distinct on the surface of the pale planet. A brief flare, there then vanished.

We saw a ship emerging from near the point of flare. It grew steadily larger, catching flecks of sunlight, like the carapace of a golden insect. Although there were no identifying markers, we knew, we sensed that it was Saga. We turned to one another, pointing.

Isn't that – ?

Was that an explosion?

It must be –

We watched the lone ship orbit the planet several times, gaining velocity. It was then that we realized what was happening. Saga was preparing to leave. Her ship made one final circuit, before it shot away in the direction of the outer solar system.

We stared without comprehension. On Ceres, a cloud bloomed where the fire had been. Saga was gone.

At first there was media attention. People wanted to interview us. Our pictures were broadcast: Saga's children, said the captions. Witnesses to her final farewell. That was what they called it, the media. Saga's final farewell. We thought it wrong: it implied she had said goodbye before, and this was not the case, and she had not said goodbye now, not to us. Saga became a rebel. She had thwarted the CSSA, and some even believed she had caused the explosion, which was the result of unstable gases released by the drilling. There was a warrant for her arrest. Interplanetary outrage was so great that the CSSA backtracked and declared themselves Saga's eternal ally, and wished her safe travels, wherever she was going. Later it was announced that the whole thing had been a set-up: Saga had been dispatched on a secret mission, known only to the Republic of China. Mars made a bold statement: the truth was that Saga had defected. She was working for another planet now. She was an agent, a double-agent, a triple-agent.

The solar system held its breath, anticipating a dramatic return. Months passed. There was no sign of Saga.

Next the experts appeared. Doctors and psychiatrists spoke to Saga's colleagues and analysed her state of mind. Fellow astronauts agreed: yes, she had been distracted, yes, there had been lapses. She had fallen prey to star sickness, said the doctors. It happened sometimes, to astronauts. She had been consumed by a kind of madness.

We thought of Signy's penguins in the Antarctic. Had Saga gone the wrong way?

Our opinions were sought, and discarded (we had little to say). The frenzy passed more quickly than we expected. We are less interesting; not so photogenic as our mother. We lack the thing which makes her magnetic, the reckless spark in the storm-sea eyes. We did not know enough to make a story.

We returned to our old lives on Earth and Moon. Once a year we met. We talked about Saga, speculated as to her whereabouts. We did not believe she was dead. We were not sure if she had gone mad.

Every few years there was a new rumour or sighting. Her ship had been spied upon Dione. The wreckage of her ship had been found in the asteroid belt, and a human spacesuit was drifting through the skies. But no, Saga herself had been witnessed in the embassy on Europa. We examined these theories, shared our musings late into the nights.

The years passed.

Now we are sept-and-octogenarians, unavoidably middle-aged. We have partnered, we have separated, some of us have children, some of us have money. We have weathered break-downs and crises. We have dreamed.

We are wiser, enough to know that what we know is nothing. We can seek but we may not find.

We decided to return to Ceres. The colony is fully established now, an independent civilisation. Its population increases steadily. There is provision for tourists.

This time we take a shuttle down to the planet surface. Still a little wobbly with the after-effects of hibernation, we support one another, steadying elbows, watching our steps. We are amused by the low gravity, find ourselves acting like children. Even Per wishes to see how high he can jump. After a night to acclimatize, we are taken on a tour of the capital, before we suit up and board a surface transport out to the mining station. The constructions loom as we approach. The machinery is colossal. Our guide, a tall young man with thin, bird-like arms, is deferential and eager to please. He knows our mother's name, of course. He shows us the plaque. The letters are glittering minerals which he tells us are from the mines. He says, proudly, that Ceres is the largest supplier of fuel in the solar system.

The plaque says:

This marks the last known flight of Saga Wärmedal.

We ask him for some time alone. He nods respectfully. We stand around the plaque. We suppose this is what we have come to see. We remember her ship, streaking away like a comet. This is the last place that she was seen. We think that she was never really seen.

There is a place on Earth beneath the Siberian permafrost, where those who died in the gulags of the twentieth century are said to be buried. With every winter, a new layer of ice crystals hardens over the tundra, fusing and compacting upon what lies below, sealing the mass graves forever. It is said that their descendants still search for bones. There are women who go out day after day with ice picks and radars, their boots crunching on the new fallen snow with that particular sound, heard only on Earth.

They are looking for something. They are prepared to spend a lifetime looking.

CAROLE JOHNSTONE

AD ASTRA

WE HAVE A lot of sex because it's a way around the things we can't say. The things we can't do. The things we don't want to *think*. We've always been very good at that; even when we hate the very thought of one another, we can still fuck. I used to think that it was because we were that couple: the ones who never forgot how to be horny, the ones who could go to sleep on an argument but never at the expense of a shag. Because we were grown up, emotionally astute. Because we could compartmentalise. Now I realise that none of that was probably ever true. We keep on having sex – as much of it as we possibly can, even when it hurts – because it makes us feel safe, like having a parent stroke our fevered brow through the worst kind of night terror. And because it's a way to fool each other. Maybe even to survive each other. I hope so. Though I don't have a lot of that left.

I get headaches in zero gravity. You'd have thought that I'd have discovered that during all the training and medical assessments inside the Astro labs, or when they sent us suborbital for the TV studios. I didn't though, and now those bastards get worse every day I'm trapped here with Rick and nowhere to go. Maybe the pain feels the same way too: we're both stuck inside a smooth, almost spherical prison and escape is nothing but dark vacuum.

Rick and I have pretty much stopped talking. There's nothing and too much to talk about; sex is just about our only method of communication and it's usually angry. I don't talk to Rick because I don't believe anything he says anymore and perhaps because I'm afraid that I might; Rick doesn't talk to me because he doesn't trust himself either – I can see that in his blue-grey eyes though he tries to hide it. He wants to tell me the truth, I can see that. He wants to and he can't. Won't.

Today we have to talk because I awoke to a beeped reminder that it was time for the quarterly biomedical checks. I don't want to do them – no longer even see a reason to – but the alternative is to do nothing at all; to sit and stare into that dark vacuum, and that way madness would truly lie, I'm certain.

Rick is in the medical module already, not that it takes me long to find him. Aside from a tiny cabin that houses little more than a bed, there are only two living spaces in our octahedral capsule: the medical module and a larger area between, dominated by the table that we're supposed to eat our meals at every day. We have no need of a cockpit because our pilots are at least 3.57 billion miles away. At least. To use Rick's increasingly irritating vernacular, we've spent the last thousand days of our lives living in a space the size of a fucking RV.

He's strapped himself into the cycle ergometer, but he isn't doing much cycling; instead, he's slumped over its bars, forehead resting on his arms. I wonder if his head hurts too and feel an uncommon twinge of sympathy.

'Hi.'

He jumps, flinches as he looks up as if expecting someone else. 'Hey.'

'Bio check day.'

'Already?'

I try to smile. 'Another glorious day in the Corps.'

Rick tries to smile back. 'That's a good one.' He reaches down to release the seat belt across his torso and unstrap his boots from the buckles on the footrests. When he comes towards me, I pretend not to be afraid of him and boot up the computer, busying myself with the equipment.

Every month we both have ECGs and blood pressure checks. I take and then process urinary, blood and respiratory samples; we don't shit very often – and now even less than before – so I've dropped that test entirely. There are complex psychological exams, which is not my domain; we both answer downloaded and detailed questionnaires: always inscrutable, always the same but different. I scoff my way through them, getting angrier and angrier, while Rick chews the inside of his mouth, brow furrowed in concentration.

Every quarter, I carry out more intensive experiments, mostly cardio-respiratory and functional tests with physical, mental and orthostatic loads. That *is* my domain. It's the only real reason for my being here, I guess. Back in the Astro labs, I specialised in immersion theory, more particularly hypokinetic disorders associated with zero gravity: the effects of prolonged weightlessness on the support mechanisms of the body, the central nervous system, motor function, hand-eye co-ordination and so on. There are other things too, a whole plethora of experiments whose potential results were far less alarming when considered only in aseptic theory: the effects of a hypoxic environment on the immune and metabolic systems, due to the fire-resistant argon mixed into our life support systems; the radiobiological effects of solar radiation on the main regulatory body systems; DNA analysis for genome-based prophylaxis and telemedical management. Rick and I take a lot of pills. Neither of us knows what's in them, though I can mostly guess. I don't discuss the test results with Rick, though he never asks. If he did, I wouldn't tell him because he wouldn't want to know.

Rick is chief cook and bottle washer: chief technical officer and chief science officer; I'm chief medical officer and chief communications officer. That's a lot of chiefs for two people, and the latter has become something of a joke: I record my medical findings and download both that and whatever Rick and I confidentially mutter in our psych exams. I've stopped doing jolly video messages home because I don't think anyone cares. I certainly don't. I have no idea if they reach Earth anyway. The last proper communication was more than eight weeks ago.

Rick reaches for me several times, at first just my hand or my arm as I go about my tests, but then my thighs, my arse, my breasts. This time I bat him away in irritation because today I don't want adolescent oblivion – I don't want to answer his desperation with my own. Rick's looks of reproach grow until I have to give them a response. I think he's depressed; in fact I'm sure he is, but he also has manic bursts of almost uncontrollable excitement that I like even less.

I turn back to the computer screen. 'Later,' I mutter, even though it's just about the only exercise he gets these days. It's like he's gone into hibernation.

Later, we sit at the table and have dinner together. We haven't done that in a while, even though that was one of the things we agreed to do every day. We both have chicken burgers masquerading as dehydrated and rectangular bars, with those bloody golden arches emblazoned on their wrappers. Even now I can't get used to the texture like squeaky polystyrene: those desiccated strawberries that I used to pluck out of my breakfast cereal because eating them set my teeth on edge. I lob it into the air, watching it turn and twist too slowly.

'You need to eat,' Rick mutters, head down and chewing disproportionately fast.

'I'd like to fuck now.'

'Okay,' Rick says, pretending he can't hear the tremor in my voice. He picks up his wrapper and chases after mine before pushing both into the disposal system. We go back to the cabin. In the beginning, we'd do it anywhere and everywhere, but shagging in zero gravity is frustratingly crap and the bed has the best restraints. I've barely strapped us both in before Rick pulls down my trousers and is inside me. It hurts, not because I'm not ready but because he's been there too often – and too often like this. We need to stop, I know that. We need to stop because it's becoming a kind of madness. I arch my back and our restraints rattle around us, pulling us back down. Rick swears into my neck, biting. When he comes with a shout that sounds too much like a scream, I do too. It hurts more than it helps. We need to stop. Because if we don't the madness will lose its power to distract. To dissuade.

Just before Rick goes to sleep, his face more relaxed than it's been all day, I lean in close to his ear. 'Where are we?'

Rick sighs, opens those grey-blue eyes that never look at me. 'You know where we are.'

'No, I don't,' I whisper, though there's no one else to hear us. Probably. 'Do you?'

He doesn't answer me.

Everything is a monumental effort. Every little thing that we do requires so much planning and uses so much energy, yet appears smooth and lazy and unhurried as if we exist in slow motion. It always makes me think of that swan on a lake analogy: existing in zero gravity really is like that, except that the frenzied paddling under the surface is only inside your head.

It takes me an age to release myself from the bed without waking Rick, and by the time I'm free of it I'm almost crying. There's a digital display in the corner of a mounted TV screen – the same TV screen upon which we watched video footage of

Rick's daughter's sixth birthday party three months ago; Rick choking, smiling, laughing, rubbing at my crotch even as she blew out her candles – it blinks 03:45. It doesn't much matter whether I believe it or not, I suppose. Here, it's always night. 03:45 is another existence.

I make my way back into the main living area, pulling on the handholds built into the walls until I'm floating close to the only window built into the capsule. I grip at the handles either side, my face pressed hard enough against the aluminium silicate glass to hurt. Rick calls it *aluminum*, which drives me mad. I blow my breath against it; I whisper. *Ad infinitum*.

There's nothing out there. I stare into the black dark just like I do every night, and there's still nothing. I don't see how that's possible. How can I accuse Rick of lying; how can I accuse him of anything *worse* than lying when there's nothing out there? If we're where I suspect we are then there shouldn't be nothing – there should be trojans and centaurs and dwarf planets. There should be asteroids and ices and early warning collision alarms. I'm not an astronaut; I'm not even an astrophysicist. I don't know enough to mount any kind of attack never mind a defence, but this is what I know, this is what I feel down to my wasting bones and muscles: we are not going home. Regardless of where we are now – where I *think* we are now – that is the biggest and most irrefutable lie of them all. Rick telling me that we've turned around and are going home.

I crane left, imagining the vast solar sail behind us, mercilessly pushing us forwards. And it is vast. When I saw 3D simulations of our ship in flight, our octahedral capsule looked like a little blemish – an imperfection – surrounded by brilliant, golden mirrors reflecting the sun. According to the manual, our solar sail has a surface area of 600,000 square metres. Rick must have told me about 600,000 times that this is the size of ten square blocks in New York City. We never got to see it in the flesh because it was unfurled from our cargo bay once we'd left orbit, but in darker moments I imagine its brilliant face turned and tacked by unseen hands, reflecting photons like balls bounced off a wall, propelling us further and further away from their thrower.

I sit down at the table again and strap myself in. I've stopped crying already because crying in zero gravity is a horrible experience – another reminder that my body is not my own anymore. I look at the walls surrounding the dubious relief of the window. They're lined with black bags and I'm sick of seeing them; they are another example of theory being a better beast than practice. In the beginning, those polythene bags were filled with water and food: a nuclei-rich, half metre thick shield against radiation that was more effective than even metal or the vast water tanks between the living modules and the storage bays.

As we used them up, Rick switched them with bags of our collected shit. The capsule's water recycling system dehydrates them by osmosis, leaving hydrocarbon-rich waste behind. All very clever, of course. But now there's no escaping the fact that there is more dried shit lining our living room walls than there is food or water. And there's no escaping the fact that we breathe recycled air and drink recycled water that was once what our bodies expelled – what they no longer wanted. Everything is used up and then used up again. Nothing goes to waste. It makes me want to scream. Ad infinity is not an option here, but sometimes it doesn't feel that way at all.

I ball my hands into little fists and hiss other words under my breath: *ad hoc, ad nauseam*; I have no idea why, which is probably just as well because they make me feel better. If I allow myself to think of the black bags and the water shield tanks behind them and then the three metre wide storage corridor encircling our living space behind *them*, I might scream and never stop. Even though Rick laughs at most of my Alien movies references, that's the one he knows I'll never use.

Because it's true. In space, no one can hear you scream. No one that can help you, at least. No one that wants to.

They isolated us – all twenty-some candidates – for twelve months inside a terrarium called Biosphere 3, just outside Tucson, Arizona. It was before all the TV companies came on board, so it was half-arsed at best. We could come and go as we pleased – although there was nowhere to go, there were plenty deliveries, plenty parties in the desert. Rick got more out of it than me, because he was on the Infinity astronaut program and I was only another lab tech, but I'd be lying if I said I didn't enjoy the experience. It was nothing like this because it was no preparation for this. And because we were so far down the list of potential candidates that we didn't even need to pretend that it might be.

They wanted a couple. A married couple. Ostensibly because of the confinement to such close quarters and the length of time of the expedition: two and a half years to our destination and about the same back again, but also because of the symbolism. Rick and I represent humanity: the Adam and Eve of a new era. Only I'm not the one who tempted him with the apple, I'm pretty certain of that.

I hadn't liked the favourites. Experienced astronauts, as arrogant as they were foregone conclusions; I've forgotten their names. I'd laughed when they were pulled because they'd got stuck on the US-SS and couldn't get back in time to launch. Bill and Stella Flack were their initial replacements: the chief technical officer of the project and his physicist wife. She got pregnant at the eleventh hour, and remembering his blustering swagger aboard Biosphere 3, I imagine that he was pissed to say the least. There were others, of course, lots of them. I stopped laughing around the time I realised that the candidates were dwindling to an alarmingly low number. I cried the night that Rick's bleep went off; I cried harder when

I watched him crouched over the kitchen counter, phone in hand, his too-white teeth getting bigger.

Space exploration is now exclusively the domain of entrepreneurs and private enterprise. Our expedition has been funded by rap stars and millionaires and TV execs and ex-engineers still greedy for what was denied them in their government careers. The rest of it is advertising and television rights. After we were signed up, we spent more time talking to dicks in shiny suits standing in front of cameras and sound booms than we did training in the Astro labs or the space centre itself.

I remember watching one online interview with the deputy director of Astro Infinity a few weeks before the launch date. When asked about the not inconsiderable risk, he'd waxed lyrical about why it was a risk worth taking: that it harkened back to the days when taking risks to further humanity's knowledge was commonplace; that our expedition was Meaningful. Inspirational. The interviewer's next question had been whether or not he expected us to have sex in transit. That answer got far more hits. And that was the last night that I begged Rick to reconsider, to forfeit our contract, sell the house, pay the fine – anything. He didn't even bother to say no.

I am the weakest link, of course. I'm a lab tech, a grunt, a non-entity. And I'm not American. Rick is a mediocre astronaut, rejected by government programmes, and until now a sailor of not even the closest stars, but he's the All American Jock that the TV studios love to love, and back when I was a struggling student, I modelled underwear online. There were posters of us everywhere, dedicated websites and adzines and pop-ups and cookies. I was almost glad when the launch day came around just so I could escape. Stupid.

I wake up still strapped to my chair. Rick knocks his arm against me as he comes around the table's edge, handing me another rectangular bar. I don't say thank you because he doesn't say anything about me not waking up in bed with him; about spending an entire night sat at a table. I chew the bar – it tastes of synthetic apple – and drink my water. Rick avoids my eyes, though I don't try very hard to meet his. My fear is alive now, bubbling under the surface like magma, reminding me of what we've long left behind.

Rick picks up the remains of our rubbish and disposes of it before kissing me on the cheek. He grabs my left tit and flashes his white teeth. 'No offence.'

I try on a far weaker smile that pulls tight my skin. 'Look into my eye.'

'See ya later, honey.' As if he's going to the office via the subway or Route 25, instead of coasting less than three feet to his computer station, next to the clearspan floor deck; as if we didn't have to catch the escape of someone(s)'s blood post-orgasm where it floated in an ugly, perfect sphere towards the capsule ceiling the night before.

'*Carpe diem*,' I mutter, grinding my teeth. I need to pee, but I hate using the toilet – as much for the effort as the inevitable sample results (a constant flux of galactic cosmic rays has caused tracks of radiation damage in our biological tissues, altering our DNA and lowering our blood cell counts; we're already long past the three percentage points expected over an astronaut's entire career) – so I pretend that I don't. Instead, I push past Rick and his studiously faked industry and then into the smaller medical module.

I don't look at the collated data, nor do I attempt to send it, even though I should have already done so days before. I'm no longer afraid of what that data shows because there's little point, but I'll be buggered if I let them see what they've done to us – even if I suspect that they already know.

There's a laminated A4 page tacked above my computer, a joke that Rick thought might make things better 2.7 years ago:

Lena's Shit List:
GCRs
SEPs
Zero Gravity
Rationing
Re-entry
Her Fuck-buddy

I grab hold of the cycle ergometer, spin myself around onto its saddle and strap myself in. It's only once I've started exercising that I remember to be more angry than afraid. Rick used to make a lot of jokes about re-entry. A lot. They were only funny while I believed it was still a possibility. While we both did. Now it's just another thing that we don't talk about.

It was good at first – aren't most things? We've long left the rocky planets and gas giants behind, but I can still remember the moment we bypassed Jupiter, its pull tremendous enough to slow us to a brief crawl. I remember Rick and I clutching hands as we hung onto the handles either side of the viewing window, watching the white upwelling bands and red downwelling bands, laughing at the tiny black shadow of Europa, trying to find the undulating Great Red Spot; the latter a game that never got old: Spot the Spot. We never did.

After Jupiter, our acceleration began increasing, our continuous thrust gaining a momentum far beyond what we'd been led to expect. I'd wondered a little about that – about the laser beams that had been under development in the Astro labs and how they could supplement the sun's dwindling power at increasing distances. There had been no point asking Rick; he knew as much as me and resented it a lot more.

I start to cry again as my wasted legs pump back and forth, their weakness trembling up into my pelvis.

Ipso facto, caveat emptor. Memento mori.

I loved him. I love him. And I'm scared. When I let myself think; when I let myself *know*, those are the only two things left. We reached Pluto over two months ago. Astro wanted to assess the contracture of its atmosphere: it's getting further and further from the sun and yet its atmosphere appears to be getting thicker, bigger. It's one of the few remaining mysteries of our solar system, but neither Rick nor I have grown any wiser in that regard: all data was collected via telescopes and particle spectrometers; we didn't have to do anything at all.

Finally reaching Pluto was an anti-climax, partly because it wasn't Jupiter and mostly because I had a stomach upset that confined me to the cabin for most of the flyby. If you've never puked in zero gravity, if you've never had to wear an adult nappy because you physically can't strap yourself onto a toilet and aim at a point narrower than a bulls-eye, you can't begin to empathise. By the time I could think beyond any of it, our destination had been reached and we were already going back home, our sail turned and tacked towards the sun. Or so I'd thought.

My thighs shake and shake until I finally stop, my fingers curling against my chest, touching my heartbeat. I can feel my fury dissipating like a coastal fog. I need to feel like there's still something I can do; I need something to happen.

And then it does. There's a gentle hum – no more than that – and then the alarms start going off, flashing fast red. Rick shouts, sounding more alive than he has done for weeks, months.

And I think, is this it? Have we got a collision alarm? Will we see an ice, a short-period comet? Will I finally be able to say – *see? I knew we weren't going back, I fucking knew it!* But as I manage to get free, I hear the servomotor start up and realise that the capsule is turning with the sail in a manoeuvre that was practiced again and again in pilot simulations, and that the alarms are those that warn not of collision but of radiation, which can only mean one thing. A solar flare.

My disappointment is so great that it seems to weigh me

down. In the end, Rick is forced to come to the medical module to get me. His face is the colour of ash, his jaw working as if he's grinding his teeth. I'd forgotten that he could look this way; that he was capable of anything beyond a flat and distant stare.

'Lena, come on! They're turning the ship!'

We collide in an ugly embrace, and then he manages to turn us around. We drift through the living area towards our cabin, alarms sounding and flashing all around us, the servo-motor humming, and I start to laugh, I can't help it – an ugly sound pitched far too high. When we reach the cabin, Rick pushes us towards its furthest wall, and there we hunker down where we're best shielded from the outside, using the bed's restraints to keep us there.

'Close your eyes, baby,' Rick says, and I give him a sharp stare, wondering if he's being cruel, wondering if he's turning one of my few remaining defences against me. But he only looks afraid, he only looks concerned. And so I do.

A week after the solar flare, I take more samples from us both and feed the results into the med computer. It'll take a few hours to properly process our readings against the Rhesus macaque prediction model, not that there's anything I can do if the results are bad. We're not dead and we don't have acute radiation sickness, so I guess the worst we can hope for is reduction of our overall immune system resistance. I'm beginning to suspect that our long-term life expectancy is academic. It's ironic, I suppose, that it's our very distance from home that has probably saved us, but I can't bring myself to feel grateful about that.

We knew the risks, Rick keeps telling me, his blank game face having survived intact. And he's right, of course. They told us that we had at least a twenty percent chance of experiencing a fatal SEP event and nearly a fifty percent chance of experiencing the kind of flare that would kill fifty percent of us in fifty days. I remember Rick laughing at that one: 'wonder which one of us will be the fifty percent?' I'm also pretty certain that there's been some damage to the ship; there are still occasional alarms and Rick spends much of his time hunched over his computer, looking at endless streams of data. I don't understand most of it – not that Rick likes me to look at all, though I know the password – but what I do understand I don't like.

'We're not slowing down.'

Rick doesn't look up from the table, doesn't answer, just goes on chewing his bloody dinner like he's enjoying it.

'Rick, we're not slowing down and even I know that we should be. The photons' pressure on the sails should be working against us now, but they're not. If anything, we're going faster.' My voice drops to a whisper that nearly acknowledges how shit scared I am; that nearly lets me imagine our tiny capsule hurtling into black, starless oblivion. When Rick doesn't even stop chewing, I scream high and loud, hard enough to hurt my throat. 'We're going fucking faster!'

Rick swallows, and then silently plucks my uneaten bar from my hands. 'Are you gonna eat that, sweetcheeks?'

I swallow my fear, I swallow my fury, and the effort is so great that I can't answer him. After a mute second, he unwraps it and starts to eat.

'Where are we, Rick?' I'm a biologist and a mathematician. I have two PhDs and my research into hypokinetic and metabolic disorders associated with prolonged zero gravity had Astro Infinity offer me first a five and then six figure salary ten years ago, but all of my work was theoretical, the minutiae of space travel – not sailing ships and solar flares and walls of my own crap. Never once during those ten years spent in the Astro labs was I afraid of them – those men with no faces in boardroom suits. Not once did it occur to me that they would lie. They told Rick that this was his only chance and they told him that I was part of the deal, and I spent so long trying to get out of going, trying to convince Rick that it was a bad idea that I never once stopped to consider the offer itself. Why us. *Non compos mentos.*

'We're in the Kuiper Belt, aren't we?'

Rick chews, chews, chews.

'Please, Rick, just tell me.' My fingers pull into tight, white fists. 'I already know we are, so just fucking tell me. We never turned around at all, did we?'

Rick looks at me with his grey-blue eyes. 'I've sent them a message.'

My heart momentarily stills. 'You have?'

He nods, offering me the kind of smile that used to make everything better, but before I can ask him what was in the message, what he asked them, what he hopefully *demanded* of them, his smile grows teeth and he leans closer across the table. 'But if I were you, baby doll, I'd be more worried about the things in the walls.'

My heart stutters, stalls, stutters again. I think the word *what*, but I don't say it because I'm suddenly more afraid of Rick than I am of men with no faces in boardroom suits or even of where we are.

He winks, unstraps himself from the table and then deposits his empty wrappers inside the disposal system. 'We're in the pipe, five by five.'

I shudder as he drifts past me on the way to our cabin. He chuckles, but I notice him cast a quick glance like a tic towards the storage hatch, his forehead briefly furrowing. When he looks back at me, his smile has teeth again. 'Ready when you are, sweetcheeks. Boy, are you gonna be sore tomorrow.'

The bile rushes into my throat as he disappears from view. I'm shaking, shaking, but as all my attention is focussed on not being sick, I hardly notice. When the worst of it passes, I unstrap myself and get up. I pull my body towards the viewing window because I can't bear the thought of being near this Rick, of letting him touch me and fuck me, of letting him make me pretend along with him.

I grasp hold of the handles and I stare out at that dark nothing. But this time I let myself see. I let myself picture the framed and beautiful artistic impression of what lies beyond the planets on the periphery of our solar system that we had hanging behind our corner sofa: those coloured, speckled spheres. Green dots in the main belt, orange specks for those objects scattered, yellow and pink trojans, white centaurs. I look and I look and all I see is nothing. Not that it matters; I know that they're there.

I wake up in the dead of night – in the dead of what is night more than 3.57 billion miles away – to a realisation that is so obvious I can hardly believe that I'd never even thought of it before. I'm strapped into my seat at the living room table, so only my hands are free to move without hindrance. They creep over my mouth.

At the press conference a few weeks before the launch, those boardroom suits made us out to be pioneers, explorers into the furthest reaches of our own solar system. We posed holding hands, wearing our astronaut suits and clutching our helmets under our arms while flashes went off all around us, and it never once occurred to me that I wasn't what they said I was – not once. I'm not an astronaut. And neither is Rick, no matter what it says in his job description. I don't know how much this expedition cost, how much it is still costing, but I know that it's too much to rely on the few skills of candidates so far down a list that they were close to its bottom.

My fingers pull at my lips, my gums. My fingernails glance against my teeth. We are not the astronauts, the pioneers. We don't pilot; we don't discover; we don't interpret. We exist. We collect and collate physiological and biological and psychological data on our own body systems, we survive the onslaught of GCRs and SEPs and road test new systems of shielding, communication, junk food. We are guinea pigs, Rhesus monkeys. The domestiques for the true stars, the ones who might come after. All going well. And just like the lab macaques, once we've outlived our usefulness we're expendable – but never without one last great hurrah. Nothing is used up; nothing goes to waste. I think of those astronauts in Biosphere 3. I think of Bill Flack's arrogant swagger. Rick and I were always the ones who were going. I think of those parties in the desert, the faked camaraderie, the cocktails and backslaps. I look at the black beyond that aluminium silicate window. And now we'll just keep going. On and on and on. Until we don't.

Rick barely speaks to me at all now. He eats and he drinks and he pees and he occasionally shits, and the rest of the time he sits at his computer next to the clearspan deck and he looks. More occasionally still, he types.

I've stopped asking him where we are because I suspect that he no longer knows. I've stopped allowing myself to be afraid because it's too much to bear every second of every day. I've stopped looking out of that aluminium silicate window, I've stopped making references to the Alien movies, I've stopped thinking or muttering Latin phrases in common usage. I've completely stopped sending back data via the med computer. It feels like the only weapon I have left. Instead, I type an endless stream of profanities and curses, and if the weight of their efficacy is measured in fury – in desire – then they should worry the suits with no faces far more than any lapse in proper communication.

We still have dinner together; that seems to be the only habit that neither of us can break. I don't know how much food is left. I don't dwell too long upon which might be the worst death: starvation or suffocation, because I guess it hardly matters. We no longer fuck – we no longer fuck often – and Rick's distant blank gaze no longer frightens me as much as it once did. I think he's mad, but that's okay. I'm nearly jealous, though I'm not so certain that I'm not far behind him.

'I've been thinking about when we first met,' I say to him one mealtime, as he's bent over and furiously chewing. 'Do you remember?'

He shakes his head and keeps on chewing. The dark hair at his crown has started to thin. His hair was one of the first things that I noticed about him, that and his thick forearms, his sexy grin, his ludicrously Goodfellas accent. We met at an Astro Infinity Christmas dance, and when he bought me a caipirinha and told me that he was in the astronaut programme, I decided that if he asked me back to his I'd go. He did.

'Why did you buy me a drink?' I whisper. 'Why did you ask me to dance?' I know why. He'd said it was because I'd glowed under the white disco lights like no one else; he'd said it was because I'd turned away from another man and smiled at him across the clichéd crowded room and he'd known. In a smiled, glowing breath, he'd known.

He looks up from his labours and flashes a grin that shows more teeth than it used to. His receding gums are red, pumped full of blood. 'Because ya made my dick sing, baby doll.'

There's no longer any emotion in his words, no smiled intent. I shiver. I shiver again when his head snaps left, looking up at the crap-lined walls as though he's heard something. He does that a lot now – like a cat who's sensed something that you haven't; that you can't – but it never loses its power to freak me out. It's just about the only thing left that does.

He shakes his head as if convincing himself that he's mistaken, that all is well. He unstraps himself from the table and plucks my half-eaten bar from my hand. I think: 'we're in the pipe, five by five,' as he deposits the wrappers inside the disposal system.

I'm suddenly seized with that need to do something again; that need to reassert a control that has all but vanished. 'Rick – '

He turns back around to me slowly, rubbing at his flat crotch. 'Just thinking about you gets me hard, baby.'

This time, I don't feel sick. This time, I don't feel anything at all. Once, I might have believed him, but not now. Thinking about what might happen to us gets him hard. Thinking about going further than anyone has ever gone before gets him hard. Discovering the undiscovered. The fear, the power, the powerlessness. Starvation, suffocation, oblivion. That's what gets him hard.

And that's when I know for sure. We won't survive each other. We won't.

'Don't speak to me anymore.' I whisper it.

He laughs as he heads for his cabin, but I don't look at his eyes because I'm too afraid of what I might not see. This is Astro Infinity's symbol of humanity; the Adam and Eve of a new era. This is what we've been reduced to.

I flinch from Rick's sudden scream – languid terror versus something far more immediate. And requiring a response. When I look left, towards him, his head is cocked again towards the storage hatch, the one that leads behind the water walls.

'Can't you hear it?' he screeches, but I don't think that he's asking me. When he pulls himself towards the ladder, I don't unstrap myself; I don't try to stop him with either words or deed. A cringing, hunkered down part of me flinches as he climbs the ladder, as he opens the hatch. When his torso and then legs disappear upwards into new space, I do unanchor myself, grabbing hold of the table's edge as I try to get closer.

I hear him curse, I hear him bang his body against the three metre wide storage space that surrounds our own. And then suddenly I'm grabbing onto any and all handholds, desperate to reach the ladder. I climb it with shaking limbs; I bash my left temple against the opened hatch as I crane inside.

Rick is on all fours, already close to the turn towards the medical module. He spins slowly around, the skin on his face thin enough to expose the grey veins beneath its surface, his smile a frozen rictus. 'Can't you hear it? Can't you hear *them*?' His eyes widen in almost ecstatic terror. 'They're in here!'

I step down one rung and grab hold of the hatch. He sees me doing it, and then sees what it means. His scream is too late. His weightless scuttle back towards me is too late. I pull down the hatch and turn its wheel. I've already almost reached the bottom again when he begins pounding at it. When he begins screaming. But it's too late for that too. I've already decided not to hear him.

I can sleep in my own bed again. The novelty wears off within days, but while it prevails, it is wonderful. I sleep. I don't dream. I'm not sore. I'm not desperate. I'm nothing at all.

My days are spent listlessly drifting between cabin, living space and medical module. For the first few of these, I can still hear Rick banging against the storage corridor walls and hatch. I start feeling the insidious scratch of doubt behind my eyes, until I sit myself at his computer station and type in his password. I might not be able to understand most of the data, but I know that I'll understand some of it – and despite everything, I still need to know. I need to know what – if anything – they're going to do.

It doesn't work. Rick was never supposed to tell me his password, just as he never knew mine, but after an early blow job less than two weeks into our journey, he told me that it was the date of our wedding. It isn't anymore. And that's when I know what the me that locked the storage hatch already knew. Rick was part of it. Rick was always part of it. Rick and his stubborn, never satisfied hard-on. His endless *need* to be something other than what he was.

I release myself from his station and drift towards the table. I look up at the white curved ceiling and the dimpled dents of the surrounding water walls. I scream. I finally scream.

'Sweetcheeks, Baby doll, Rout, Erb, Aloo-minum, Moss-cow, Dick Wad!' I stop, pulling myself up short against the viewing window, and my eyes follow the frantic scuttle that I'd been ignoring for days. 'Eye-fucking-Rack!'

The words are a better balm than Latin phrases or Alien movie references; they make my heart temporarily sing. Afterwards, I sleep without strapping myself down. I float.

All the days and moments and thoughts – such as they are – morph into one another, until I can hardly tell what time has passed. I've turned off the monitors that blink time, the computers that tell me how much life support is left. I no longer eat.

Instead, I stare out of the viewing window into black nothing. Sometimes I forget to blink. And now there really is an Alien – a thing – inside the walls. Using the capsule as a hamster wheel, I hear it. Banging. Scuttling. Shrieking. It doesn't lose strength as I'd expected; it doesn't grow quieter or any more resigned to its fate.

And then finally – one day/one night – it happens. What I've been waiting so long for. I see something. Finally, through that blank vast window, I see something.

My jaw slackens and my heart remembers what it's for. I feel colours wash over me – not the greens and oranges and yellows and pinks of that framed picture behind our corner sofa – but real colours, real light. Real breath, real life, real horror, real joy. I understand Rick's ecstatic terror a little better. I'm crying, but I can't feel it. I'm shaking, but it doesn't matter. I'm dying, but I don't care.

Finally, I know. I see. Finally.

I remember the apple; I remember being young and stupid and reading aloud from behind an echoing lectern. *For God knows that when you eat from it your eyes will be opened, and you will be like God, knowing good and evil.* It's not true. It's just more lies.

I giggle and it hurts my raw throat. 'Don't ask me, man. I just work here.'

I reluctantly turn from the window and pull myself into the medical module. There's no need to enter my password because I never logged out. I type just two short sentences and I'm still crying, still shaking, still giggling as I do it.

You will never see what I see. You will never know what I know.

I shout them too. I shout them loud enough for the alien still beating its chitinous wings inside the walls to hear – and it does. I know it does because it screams back.

And that's okay. I smile and I close my swollen eyes against the brilliant, unending light.

That's okay.

JIM HAWKINS

SKY LEAP – EARTH FLAME

'Why is sky blue, Mariam?'
'I don't know. Ask Victor.'
'Can you touch it, Mariam?'

THE GRASS AROUND the tanks kept itself a perfect green and at a perfect height of one point five centimetres. There were small hills, rocky outcrops, and sudden patches of sand. Over to the east there was a lake that stretched beyond the horizon, and sometimes she spotted a sailboat with white canvas taut in the breeze.

Axon had given up asking her to walk on the water out to the sailboats, but Axon loved it when Mariam stood beside the lake and squeezed the warm mud between her toes. Or when she stripped off and swam in the clear water, diving sometimes to catch sight of a silver-green fish or the tentacles of an octopus peeping out from a reef crevice.

There was no sensation – hot, cold, warm, rough, slippery, prickly, or smooth – that Axon would not take in and absorb. If Mariam cut herself, Axon was fascinated by the bleeding, the scab, and the scars.

Mariam was twelve years old, with coal-black hair, dark

eyebrows and a slim, athletic body. She liked to keep her hair tied back, but sometimes Axon wanted her to let it blow around her face, and mostly she did, unless she was in a mood, which was usually because Victor had told her she was stupid.

Usually she was forbidden to go near the tanks, but today was Axon's *Layer Day* and she was smart enough to know that they didn't want her there for the fun of it. She walked down the slope over the perfect grass towards the white domes of the tanks, her flip-flops smacking against her heels and the light almost too bright to bear.

'What will it be like, Mariam?' asked the soft voice in her head.

'I don't know. I will be with you.'

'Will it hurt?'

'I don't know. If it hurts you, it will hurt me.'

'Are you afraid?'

'Who taught you afraid?'

'Victor.'

'Is Victor afraid?'

'Yes.'

'I'm not.'

'Is there time for swimming?'

'No.'

'That's a shame.'

'Are you afraid, Axon?'

'I'm trying. I know it, but I can't feel it.'

The gate in the electric fence around the tanks opened, and Mariam walked in, head high, but very scared. Her twin, Victor, was already standing on the concourse beside the nearest of the mushroom-like buildings, shading his eyes from the intense light. Mariam was tanned and lithe. Victor was paler, heavier, disliked physical activity, but they were still clearly identical twins. Axon sometimes jokingly called them Exo and

Endo – she was a child of the wind and the waves, and Victor was a more cerebral cave-dweller.

'Hi,' said Victor. This in itself was unusual. Normally they communicated through a private gateway they shared in the Axon interface. But today was different – very different. It was *Layer Day*.

A door in the mushroom-dome's sixty-foot stem slid open and their foster mother, Julia, beckoned them in.

All the adults they knew were in the conference room, and several they had never seen before. Nobody was smiling as they took their seats. It felt as though they'd failed an exam or been caught stealing.

'Don't worry, Axon,' she thought. Silence. She looked at Victor and thought 'Can you get Axon?' He shook his head.

Director Somerton stood up and came to sit beside them.

'During this phase we have to cut your link to Axon,' he said. 'This is just a precaution.'

'Against what?' Victor asked, in his belligerent way.

Somerton ignored Victor's tone, and went on 'This is a critical stage. I will be honest with you – you're both growing up fast and you have a right to know. There have sometimes been complications. It's better for you if we play safe. So we're going to put you in a light sleep for the next few hours and slowly bring back the link when we think it's safe, which I'm sure it will be.'

Victor started to say something, but Mariam shushed him quiet.

'I refuse,' she said.

Somerton was momentarily shocked, but then recovered and said, 'I'm sorry, Mariam. I don't quite understand you.'

She was quivering, find it hard to breathe, but she forced the words out. 'I will not be cut off from Axon. I will not be put to sleep.'

'Why?'

She stood up and ran out of the room. The outside doors slid aside and she kept on running until she reached the gate through the perimeter fence. It wouldn't open. She stood there, staring out at the grass, with her hands on the grill, suddenly crying, until a hand stroked her back. Finally she turned, expecting to see Julia. Instead, it was Victor.

'I suppose they sent you!' she shouted.

'No,' said Victor. 'I decided I agree.'

Inside, Somerton paced around the room. 'The culture is ready,' he said. 'We must proceed.'

Normally, Julia was silent in meetings. She was tiny, beaky-nosed, like a small bird, but now she stood up and said, 'No.' She marched up to the much taller figure of the Director and faced him.

'They're like triplets. They've been in each other's minds for twelve years. Are you surprised they don't just go along with you chopping them off?'

'They're children.'

'Those two are not *just* children, are they? They are nearly teenagers, and they have a right to be included. If they want to maintain the link, that's their decision. Explain it to them. If they want to refuse an anaesthetic, then it's their decision. They are NOT laboratory rats.'

Somerton turned and faced the science team. 'Well?' he asked.

The Senior Biochemist looked at her watch and said 'We have two hours at most to begin layering. If we have to abort it will take four months to breed and verify another batch. The ship is ready and waiting for our signal. They will not be pleased.'

'This is not a democracy, normally, but in this instance I would like to see a show of hands. Should we proceed with the operation with the links open and the children conscious?'

All present raised their hands. Somerton turned back to

Julia. 'Explain the danger to them, ask them one more time, and then we go ahead either way.'

Mariam and Victor were walking around the inside of the perimeter fence. They had never been to this area before. As they passed the main mushroom building they came to a section of fence with a very big gate that could slide aside on rollers, but now refused to budge when they pulled it. A wide concrete road led back from the gate to a high door in a cube-like building with a cluster of antennae on the roof. The road had parallel metal strips with grooves which ran out under the gate and onto a vast grey road with scorch-marks clearly visible and in the distance a group of white-painted parallel stripes.

'What are they for?' Mariam asked, pointing at the metal strips.

'I think they're tracks. Maybe you could run wheels along them.'

They had never witnessed Julia move fast before, but she came sprinting up to them.

'Please listen to me,' she said. 'I'm very sorry. We never told you everything. You were too young. We don't have much time, but let me explain as quickly as I can.'

The human brain contains something like a hundred billion neurons. Nobody knows the real count. Each neuron may connect with up to seven hundred others, making an incomprehensibly complex network. The brain weighs about one point five kilos and has a volume of something like twelve hundred cubic centimetres.

The volume of the two-metre diameter sphere in the centre of the cube-like building was over four million cubic centimetres – the capacity of more than three hundred human brains. It was supported in an alloy framework connected to hoists above. The lights were dimmed and only a diffuse red glow, like a photographic darkroom, lit the lattice of steel pipes that ran from the titanium sphere, through ducts in the wall, and into a second chamber. Technicians clad in full biohazard suits adjusted settings on a large touch-screen panel to one side.

In the wide-windowed observation room set high in the wall, Julia sat between Mariam and Victor. Somerton stood to one side, nearer the window, blinking more rapidly than usual. 'Begin,' he said.

'Am I looking at myself, Mariam? Victor?'

'I don't know. Think about something nice.'

In the next-door chamber digital read-outs on the breeding tanks were steady. Nano-scale sieves measured the exact structure of the stem cell clusters and trapped any that were less than perfect, and the perfect were fed forward to a holding tank.

Through the observation window, as though watching a silent movie, they saw the red-lit sphere begin to rotate about its vertical axis, apparently hanging from the umbilical tubes that entered the centre of the top. On the far wall a projection lit up showing a three dimensional model of the interior of the sphere. It was like a shell with a nut inside. The nut was smaller than the outer shell – held in place by millions of fine struts, surrounded by the image of a light blue membrane. The sphere was not yet full.

The female voice over the loudspeakers was so sudden and loud that everyone was startled. 'Lowering temperature now,' she said. Unseen, viscous chilled cooling fluids moved through capillaries in the central mass of the sphere. Within a few seconds the temperature read-out on the tank dropped five degrees.

'I have no word for this. Thought slow ... fragments, maybe ... discontinuity ... Sky leap – Earth flame.'

'Start cell delivery.'

In the vat chamber, pumps began to spin up, pushing billions of cells in their nutrient wash slowly through sterile pipes from the final holding tank towards their destiny. The projection showed a steadily rising tide filling the space between the central core and the shell of the containment sphere.

'There's no more room after this,' said Victor. 'Is this the final layer?'

'Yes,' Julia replied. 'This is the OCC – the Outer Cortical Complex. When the barrier dissolves, these cells will evolve billions of links into the earlier layers. '

Mariam shivered. 'Axon is cold,' she said.

'No,' Julia said. 'Axon is not cold. Axon has no sensory feelings itself. You are the feelings. You are Axon's skin, eyes, smell, instinct, arms, and legs. That is your purpose.'

Again, there came the calm voice over the loudspeakers in the observation room. 'The layer is stabilised. Raising the temperature to normal minus one . . . preparing to dissolve the barrier. Permission is required. '

Somerton gripped the handrail in front of the wide window, looked back towards Julia and the children, and said 'Proceed.'

New fluids entered the sphere. The temporary membrane surrounding the original core of the Axon brain – the *dura mater* – thinned and its dead cells were washed way. Very slowly the impenetrable wall between the old cells and the new grew thinner. On the big display the blue was steadily eroded and became patchy. At the same time, internal blocking membranes dissolved, and what was a place of many rooms became one. Tendrils of tailored neuronal fibre spread through the new tissue like a root system growing at an impossibly fast rate. Microscopic tubules carrying oxygen and nutrients followed.

It hit Mariam like a tsunami. The world vanished, and huge

arcs of geodesics, star-fields, vector-diagrams, swiftly-changing complex mathematical functions, planetary systems and galaxies swamped her with colour and deep ringing sounds like a vast tolling of underwater bells. And then, suddenly, she felt a terrible pain, and screamed.

Medics who had been standing near the children with their hands behind their backs, as though merely observing, brought the gas-powered syringes forward and sprayed anaesthetic directly into their carotid arteries.

Inside the building, on the outside of it, around the perimeter fence, and throughout the world, biohazard warnings lit up and flashed.

'Switch the HUD on!' Somerton shouted. A technician on the floor below pressed a finger on a panel and an incomprehensible green text overlay appeared on the window, scrolling fast.

'Interpenetration failure-level rising. Core temperature rising. Re-cooling initiated.'

'Cortical activity symmetry is collapsing.'

As the soothing coolants flowed into the maddened biological brain that was Axon, the medics lifted Mariam and Victor onto wheeled stretchers and pushed them down long white corridors to the hospital suite, Julia walking alongside.

'Prognosis? Assessment?' Somerton snapped at the Senior Biochemist, who was standing next to him. She took a step backwards, ran her fingers through her blonde hair, and said 'I did warn you that this was a dangerously large volume to layer at one time.'

'I didn't ask for a history lesson!'

'This is not just a brainstorm. This is a hurricane. We were prepared and we're doing what we can, but it looks at the moment like total network collapse.'

Axon raged in random fury and fever. The trees of logic

grown over years fell apart. The music of the synapses lost all coherence and was swamped in chaotic noise. The older connections fought the new, and the new knew nothing except their urge to be, to be something, to be a link, or a constant, or a function, or the signature of the scent of a rose. Fractal patterns swept through the complex of tissues. Filaments grew and shrank, touched and embraced or touched and withered, as their electrical charges and biochemical payloads summed or negated.

Evolution can be slow. To build a hawk or a daffodil can take several million years. But it can also be very fast. Axon's brain was a war zone as strategies competed. But eventually, all wars come to an end.

Thirty-seven hours later the anaesthetists turned off the systems which had been keeping Mariam and Victor safe from the storm in their bunker of unconsciousness.

Mariam's first thought was not hers: '*I could do with a swim.*' She smiled as the nurse held the plastic beaker of water to her lips.

Victor opened his eyes and saw a thought that was an equation. '*Sparse search on eleven dimensional vector space in log(n) time. Not bad for a twelve-year old!*'

The ship was two thousand metres long and shaped like an elongated silver ovoid with lattices of filigree golden wire at each end, like a vast insect egg trapped between the centres of two magical spiders' webs that connected to – nothing. The light from the star reflected from its body and drive webs, but here there were no eyes to see its strange beauty. It orbited the star silently, patiently and entirely automatically. Yes – it did contain life: plants, seeds, soil, saplings, mature olive trees, fish, sheep, ravens and cabbages – but they were all frozen and silent in the hold. The control bridge, with its comfortable chairs and wrap-around 3D screens was empty. All was dark; the screens and tell-tale lights were of no use to a room without observers.

Sixteen navigational and systems computers controlled the ship's status constantly and voted on any required action, which, since they had arrived into the vicinity of the star Angelus XI three hundred Earth days ago, had been next to nothing apart from an unanimous decision to send a mining drone to a metal-rich asteroid within easy reach.

It had been a long journey. The silicon-based computers could not manage the complexity of a level three void jump, and they'd coasted here at only near light-speed.

The ship was waiting.

In an orbit perpendicular to the ship a strange object moved around Angelus XI. Take a can of beer and add a cone to one end and half of a transparent ball to the other. Add gigantic light-catching wings radiating from its waist, and colour it a blue so deep it bordered on the ultraviolet. Now, expand the length of the can to fourteen thousand metres, and spin it slowly around the long axis. Add some powerful transmitters that broadcast, on a sweeping frequency band covering most of the electromagnetic spectrum, the following message: *'Bio-containment station Alpha Delta Epsilon Theta Seventeen. Warning. Unauthorised approaches within one million kilometres will trigger lethal and indiscriminate attack. This facility is protected with a network of cloaked military drones with a lot of fire-power and a minimal sense of humour. Have a very nice day.'*

Times passes. That's its job. Sixteen year old Victor was sitting on the beach beside the lake eating something that resembled a hamburger. He refused to go into the water where Mariam floated, flipped and dived.

'Why won't you show me the world?' Victor thought.

'It's not allowed.'

'Why not?'

'Don't be stupid, Victor. If I could tell you why, you would see it. Go for a swim while you can.'

'And if I don't?'

'I won't share some quite cute solutions for quantum gravity. No swim, no tell.'

Victor kicked off his shoes, his tee-shirt and shorts, walked down to the edge of the water, and stuck his toes in. 'It's freezing!' he yelled. Mariam emerged from the lake very close to the shore and splashed water over Victor. He ran back up the beach, swearing.

In the cluster of buildings that housed the Axon development system, Somerton was hosting a five-hour crucial meeting of the full team. 'This,' he said, 'is the decision point. If there are any doubts you must articulate them now.'

One by one the teams voted. Only the Senior Biochemist raised an issue. 'The complexity of Axon is now, as we would expect, far beyond our diagnostics. However, we can see some zones that are constantly changing – changing faster than we would expect. Specifically, these are in the *inferior temporal gyrus* region. We predict that this pattern will eventually stabilise, but I must flag up this slight anomaly. We have no objection to advancement.'

'Very well,' Somerton said. 'Many of you have given the best years of your lives to this project. There have been differences, and quite properly so, but we move towards our goal united in the will to succeed. I hereby authorise advancement to level Sigma.'

Far away, the ship decoded a signal and began to move.

Julia walked down from the Centre towards the lake as the flyer came in low over the beach with a sound like a deep breath. They ran towards her.

'What was that?'

'Get dressed. Then you really can come and see your world.'

The gate to the runway was open. The flyer was parked on

an apron area, gleaming bright blue, its hatch raised and stairs ascended into its interior. Even Victor's constant stream of questions ceased as they walked across the apron following Julia. Axon was also unusually quiet.

Mariam thought 'What is it?'

'I'm too busy to talk,' came the reply.

'Come,' Julia said, and led the way up the stairs into the flyer. Three rows of light blue seats were arranged just behind the wide windscreen. Behind them was a large cargo area. Everything was tastefully colour-coordinated – what might have been harsh edges rounded and softened.

'This is a flyer,' Julia said. 'Sit in the front seats. This is the most important day of your lives. So far, at least.'

As soon as they sat down, shoulder restraints moved gently into place. Julia had taken the control seat. Had Mariam and Victor lived in a different place in a different time they might have been concerned at the lack of any visible controls and any sign of a pilot. Julia inspected the flyer's identification code neatly stencilled onto the bulkhead below the windscreen. Some things, over centuries, slip from languages and cultures, whilst others stick and are still used when their origins are lost in obscurity.

'Charlie Delta Golf,' she said.

'Yes, Julia,' a soft male voice responded.

'Lock my voice only.'

'Yes, Julia.'

'Depart the facility, and then fly a circum-axial route at three thousand meters and just above stall speed.'

'Yes, Julia.'

The cabin door swung downwards and closed with a hiss.

'Performing mandatory biohazard check.'

A stream of almost invisible nano-scale particles issued from a vent in the roof of the flyer and formed tenuous clouds around the three of them.

'What's this?' Victor demanded.

'A routine check to see if we have any infections that might cause problems for other people.'

The nano-clouds swept back into the roof and the flyer said 'Cleared for take-off.' Powerful fan jets wound up to a roar and they began to taxi out to the runway, turning to face a long strip of lights that stretched away into the distance. Then they accelerated quickly, the nose lifted, and the flyer headed for what Mariam and Victor knew as the sky.

Overhead it seemed misty. Below, the buildings of the Facility shrank, and at two thousand feet (aircraft had never gone metric) it was clear that this was a tiny world that was like an undulating disc of green hills and sparkling water. Then, ahead of them, the mist began to move and a circular aperture appeared in what they thought of as the sky, but was really a huge inflated dome of light, biologically impermeable, plastic. When the opening reached a diameter precisely two metres wider than the flyer's wings the expansion stopped. Seconds later the aircraft passed through, and the hole in the dome began to close.

Mariam and Victor gasped as they realised they had been living in a small bubble inside a vast space. The inside of the Bio-Containment station Alpha Delta Epsilon Theta Seventeen was a cylindrical space thirteen thousand metres long and many kilometres in diameter. A white tubular structure ran along the entire axis, and from it service and support spokes radiated down to a curving landscape of farms, villages, workshops, parks, lakes, harbours and roads.

'Did you know this, Axon?' Victor thought – a thought coloured, perhaps, with tints of anger.

'*I did.*'

'Why didn't you tell us?'

'*It was not permitted. Or, to put it another way, it was not possible.*'

'Is there more you can't tell us?'

The flyer descended to a thousand feet and then flew low. The huge cylinder seemed to rotate below them.

Julia received a brief message in her transparent earpiece, and said 'You're talking to Axon. Would you like Axon to explain, or shall I?'

'Both.' Mariam said.

'I'm too busy.' Axon said. Mariam repeated this to Julia, and added 'What's Axon doing?'

'Developing. Growing very fast. Learning interfaces. Testing controls. Now – look over there – you see that white dome? It's another bubble, like the one you were born and brought up in. There are eight domes. Each dome has, or had, a thing like Axon growing inside it. Charlie Delta Golf, fly the axis – close.'

'Yes, Julia.'

The flyer rose and turned from its track inside the circumference of the cylinder, and rotated so that 'down' was now the thirteen kilometre extent of the axial tube. The engine noise reduced to a low hiss as it changed from full to low-gravity mode and the atmospheric pressure reduced to near-nothing. It was now less of an aircraft than a space shuttle, steered and propelled by impulse and correction jets of superheated steam. From the interior it seemed to be flying a straight line along the axial spine, but was in reality moving with a corkscrew movement to compensate for the rotation of the cylindrical worldlet.

Julia spoke to the flyer again, and dipped towards the wall that closed the end of the giant cylinder. At 'ground' level a door slid upwards and closed behind them as soon as they had flown in. They landed silently on a grey steel floor, next to three other flyers, each brightly coloured. The hangar was high and wide, with tool bays, hoists, service pits and gantries. Julia watched Mariam and Victor carefully, prepared to halt this voyage of discovery if they were being mentally overloaded.

But, subliminally, they knew all this because the knowledge had been implanted subtly and appeared only in dreams. They chattered endlessly, pointing things out to each other.

'Come,' Julia said, as the restraining arms slid back into their chairs, the hatch opened, and the stairs touched the floor with a quick clang of metal on metal.

When the human-scale door opened into the next chamber the bright light of Angelus XI flooded the hangar and they squinted at this new shock to the senses. As they entered they saw through the thick glass windows the uncountable splash of the fiery points that made up the Milky Way.

Mariam shivered. 'It's all so – big.' she said 'Too big.'

A huge egg-like shape covered the sky as the ship completed its deceleration phase, and, with machine precision, matched orbits with the rotating worldlet.

'What's that?' Victor asked.

Julia put her arms about their shoulders and said,

'That, my darlings, is your new home.'

Axon's spherical container, with umbilicals connecting to temporary nutrient tanks, pumps, sensory interface cables, all on a metal-wheeled base, rolled slowly and carefully out of the bay doors in the side of the containment, surrounded by a posse of anxious attendants, and an even more anxious Director Somerton. Victor walked beside him, asking an endless stream of questions, until Somerton finally told him to go and pester somebody else.

Mariam swam in the lake, diving for flashing silver fishes, floating on her back looking up at what she once thought was the sky, and now knew to be the canopy of the containment dome lit by the huge artificial sunlight generators arrayed along the axial spine far above.

'*You are sad, Mariam,*' Axon's thought-voice said, gently.

'Am I? Yes, I think perhaps I am. I shall miss the fishes.'

'There are lakes and fishes in the ship.'

'Not these fishes. These are my fish.'

'I understand.'

'Do you, Axon? Can you?'

'I am in you. You are in me. These are my fishes, too.' A long pause, and Axon added, *'They want you to get ready.'*

For one last time she flipped onto her stomach, pointed her heels up at the fake sky and moved down among the fish, the weeds, the crabs in the rocks on the lake bed – staying underwater until she was nearly at the shore.

The rails ran to the base of the nearest spoke connecting the floor of the cylinder to the axis. At the base of the fifty metre wide spoke, inside the wide doors that had hissed aside, a pressurised lift waited. The strange procession of Axon and his attendants rolled slowly into the lift. Clamps secured the sphere and its equipment to the floor, and were checked and double checked. People took to seats around the circumference of the lift, and buckled harnesses. The doors closed, the air pressure increased a little as the lift sealed itself and began to rise within the spoke. A cloud of smart nano filled the air with a fine mist – probing the humans for traces of un-permitted viruses or microbial life, and, where necessary, purging, excising, cleaning.

Somerton's pad beeped as it displayed a message from Axon. It was a crude way of communicating, but only Mariam and Victor had the complex web of sensory fibres and high-speed electromagnetic receivers and transmitters that enabled communication at the most intimate cerebral level. He flicked his finger across the pad to enable voice input.

'Totally impossible,' he said. 'The only biological entities allowed onto the ship are Mariam and Victor, and you know that.'

Alarms at various pitches and volumes shrieked and warning lights lit up the monitoring panels around Axon. The lift's steady point eight G rise stopped as emergency overrides kicked in. Panicking engineers frantically released their harnesses and struggled awkwardly in what was now severely reduced gravity.

As suddenly as it started, the violent noise stopped and the warning lights returned to green. Somerton's pad beeped again.

'We are in command of the ship, not you. It is simple. It is safe. It is necessary. You will help me with this tiny kindness, or the ship is going nowhere. Axon.'

Nearby, Victor laughed. Axon was sharing this with him, but not Mariam. Somerton thumbed his panel and was not amused. At the weightless point where the spoke entered the axial tunnel the lift entered a zone where 'up' and 'down' were meaningless, and changed to what could well be described as 'along', traversing the axis inside a smaller tube within the larger.

At the end of the axial tube airlock doors opened and the lift slid into the lock and stopped. Hatches in the walls of the lift opened, revealing ranks of white pressure suits. They began to pull them on, awkward in the low gravity. Tell-tales flashed amber and then green on each suit. All but Mariam and Victor clipped tethering ropes to cleats on the floor.

'Mariam – Victor – clip your tethers on,' Julia said.

'Axon says not to bother,' they responded as one voice. Somerton frowned and then decided to say nothing. Satisfied that all suits were safe, the lift lit a sign saying 'Depressurising' and the air was sucked out of both the airlock and the lift. The sign changed to 'Vacuum' and the doors opened onto the sight of a cylindrical docking bay the size of a dozen cathedrals. In the distance, shuttles of many kinds and sizes were clamped into bays around the internal circumference. The great circular eye of the dock was open – shutters folded back outside like petals of dark grey radiation-blocking metal and plastic. Hanging in front of them exactly fifty metres away was a box-like silver shape – one of the ship's non-atmosphere cargo transports. Away in the distance the gigantic form of the ship was a brilliant ellipse in the angled light of Angelus XI.

The transport steadily moved closer, robot arms extending ready to grasp Axon and its support tanks.

'No need to wait for me,' Axon said – the tone unusually cheerful. *'Step out of the door – I have you.'*

The two sixteen year olds fought to overcome their fear of falling and stepped slowly out of the lift door. Jets on their suits moved them out into the hangar, and they were turning to face the door of the lift and the figures floating inside and around it on their tethers.

'I think it is customary to wave,' Axon said. So they waved, and the anonymous space suits waved back. And then they were accelerating, out of the hangar, past the incoming transport and into space, racing towards the ship. Victor was not happy, but Axon could feel the smile on Mariam's face.

'I love it.' She said. 'It's like swimming! Star diving!'

So Axon took her in a series of loops, dives, spin-turns and crazy corkscrews around the unwaveringly straight track of Victor, who would have white-knuckle gripped the arm-rests of whatever seat he was riding on, but there was no seat and no arm-rests. Behind them the transport entered the dock; a telescopic arm extended into the lift and, attaching to Axon's support platform pulled the protected, but still fragile, cargo of biology into its hold.

And so the months of training began. The command deck of the ship was in the centre of the egg-like structure, surrounded by layers of decks and parks. The thick outer shell was hollow and filled with its own skins of radiation-damping liquid hydrogen, polyethylene and water. Each of the 'floors' of the one hundred and twenty eight decks was made of a hybrid of concrete and tailored plastic. Not many tissue-damaging particles were going to get through to the yolk at the heart of the ship.

The deck was a sphere of seamless 3D display panels, punctuated by some hatches to the living quarters and the chamber which held Axon and its support systems. Four couches were attached on gimbals to a central column.

'Why four?'

'Did you think they'd build something this big just for you?'

Mariam and Victor had explored many areas of the ship, but most of it was secured and Axon refused to open the whole vastness on the unarguable grounds that many sectors were mothballed, and it would be a waste of energy to open them merely for pleasure trips.

'You have diagrams, schematics, 3D models, images – what more do you want?'

'I like to touch things,' Mariam answered. But on their birthday, when they had been greeted with a tuneless rendition of 'Happy Birthday To You' over a video link to base, Axon summoned them both to the control room and issued some instructions. Victor, he sent to a newly-unlocked Virtual Reality games centre, where he spent eight hours slaying Hell-Spawn with a variety of swords, axes, razor-whips, soul-wands, fire-bolts and other hard and soft weapons, and discovered that a rail-gun is of absolutely no use against Undead Wraiths, although average Zombies could be fragged quite successfully.

Mariam followed her plan and navigated a maze of corridors and jump tubes until she reached a door with an illuminated red sign above it – 'Not Available'. Then, as she was close to the door, the sign changed to a green heart and vanished. The door whispered open. She walked through into a chamber filled with sunlight. Surrounded by low grassy hillocks, a blue lake gleamed and rippled. Dragonflies darted over the water. House martins swooped low over the surface, the blue reflecting on their pale breasts and making them seem exotic and rare.

She followed a narrow path to a strangely familiar rock jutting out over the lake, peeled off her clothes and followed the birds in a graceful dive. Under water she swam strongly and suddenly was in the centre of a host of silver fish, darting and flocking.

'Are these real fish?' she thought at Axon.

'They're not just real fish, Mariam. They're your fish.'

'I don't believe you.'

'Ask Victor. Dr Somerton was most displeased.'

Mariam thought a giant smile, and took only the briefest of breaths before diving again and again amongst the flickering, shining creatures.

After they'd eaten their supper in what was called the Crew Mess, Axon said 'You must both go immediately to level five, corridor seven, room seventeen.'

'Why?' Victor demanded.

'These are not my instructions. I have no idea.'

Twenty minutes later they walked into a dome-like chamber with curiously-textured non-reflective walls. Seats faced a series of display panels. As soon as they entered, the doors closed and the lights dimmed.

The big central 3D display lit up and Julia appeared. 'There's no need to be alarmed,' she said. 'This presentation is pre-recorded and will take one hour. Whilst in this room you will not be able to access Axon and he will have no access to you. You are of age now, and will soon know everything.'

Julia walked away and Somerton stepped into view.

'For over fifty years now,' he began, 'we humans have tried to reach beyond the confines of our galactic arm. All but one attempt has failed, and that exception is not a happy story. Victor, you're fond of asking 'Why?' and that's the easiest of questions to answer. In four hundred years' time a dense ball of dark matter eight light years in diameter will fly through our local systems. The gravitational consequences will be devastating. Stars will collide. Planets will fall into their suns or be flung into the outer darkness. Nothing can survive. Many such catastrophes have happened in the history of the universe, but this will be *our* catastrophe. Our only hope is to escape it, destroy it, or deflect it.

'This information is not known by many. The truth behind it has been systematically discredited for centuries. Scientists have been persuaded into public scepticism, sent into exile, or even killed. Yes – killed.

'Long ago people thought the end of the Earth could be escaped by building ark ships, and we have inhabited planets around seventeen nearby stars. But now, that seems futile. None can evade the invisible destruction which is coming.

'No human mind can control a ship like yours. We cannot build computers complex enough to do so. Consequently, we started to harness the billion-year work of evolution – we began to build larger and larger biological brains. Most of these have failed. One did not – but an error caused it to die of an infection, stranding its ship and crew ninety-seven light years away.

'Your first mission is to rescue that ship and what it contains, which is vital for the survival of the human race. You will be briefed in more detail on that later. In the meantime, Axon trusts you, but you must be very careful. If you need to discuss things only between yourselves, come into this room.'

Mariam lay awake in her cabin. Sleep refused to come. The simulations had come to an end, and the first real flight, their first defiance of the universe's unfeeling indifference, was only twelve hours away. Restlessly, her hand strayed across her breasts, her nipples stiffening under her fingers, and then slid slowly down her stomach.

'*It's nice when you do that.*'

'Go away Axon, This is private.'

'*Victor does it too.*'

'I don't want to know.'

'*I think you do. It's different, but similar. Sometimes he goes very fast, sometimes very slowly. Like you. I know what he thinks about. Shall I tell you?*'

'No.'

'*He thinks about lying beside you, touching and kissing. He thinks about your breasts. He thinks about you opening to him. Don't you, Victor?*'

A long mental pause, and then Victor's thought voice – 'Yes. Yes, I do.'

'*So does Mariam. Don't you, Mariam?*'

Mariam's fingers were wet. 'It is forbidden,' she thought at them. 'We are brother and sister.'

'*That's what they told you. It's not true. You are from different gene pools. They modified a few things to make you look alike. There is no reason why you should not share your sexual feelings with each other. Even if you didn't know it, you have shared them with me. Perhaps that was part of the plan.*'

Mariam rolled off the bed, pulled a shift over her head and left the cabin. Down the corridor, she opened Victor's room without going in, said 'Isolation room. Now!' and continued walking.

'*I don't like it when you go in there. Why do you want to cut me out?*'

'Do you understand the word 'private'?'

'*Of course.*'

'I don't think you do.' She went into the isolation room and the door closed behind her. Soon after, Victor came in, looking flushed and embarrassed.

'Why do you think Axon is suddenly so interested in our sex lives?' she asked. 'Why now?'

'No idea.'

'Control. He's looking for ways to control us. So either Axon's lying or Julia and the others have lied to us. I think we need to find out.'

Ten minutes later a sleepy Julia came on line and gave them the answer. Axon was telling the truth. 'You should have told us!' Victor shouted. 'What else does Axon know that we don't know?'

'We thought it was best for all three of you. I'm sorry if we were wrong.'

As they were about to leave the room Mariam stepped in front of Victor. 'If ever . . . if we ever . . . in here and nowhere else. Agree?' Victor nodded, and she went on 'Okay. Truth time. We have to know if Axon's using us for some hidden reason. So . . . when you . . . do you really think about me?'

He nodded slowly and looked away, whispering 'Sorry.' Mariam smiled and said 'Stop saying sorry. For some reason I'm not surprised. Perhaps I . . . well, to be fair, I should confess too. I often wonder what it would be like to touch you there. It's going to take a bit of getting used to. '

'I know why they did it. They wanted to create a bond we couldn't break.'

'I think those come in several flavours.'

'I still love you, *Siss*.'

'And I still love you, *Brother*.' And then they burst into laughter. 'There's one thing, though. If you're going to be my lover instead of my brother you're going to have to be a whole lot nicer to me.'

Then she kissed him on the cheek, ruffled his hair, and went off to her cabin to sleep.

For twenty-six hours the reaction-mass engines accelerated

the ship away from the containment wordlet and the star Angelus XI, with its rocky planets and settlements. Mariam and Victor took four hour shifts, and Axon 'slept' for the last twelve hours whilst unconscious, massively-parallel processes assessed the constant data from the arsenal of sensors as they probed the space ahead of them at a deep level for a distance of many light-years. Finally, the words they'd heard a thousand times in simulations rang out: 'Impulse engine shutdown in five seconds'. A pause for breath, and then the steady two-G push ceased. 'All ready?' In the strange ordering of things evolved over seventeen years it was necessary for all three consciousnesses to agree before radical action could be taken. Three thought yesses committed them.

Outside the ship the mesh sails expanded, thinning to a web of mono-atomic threads. Power surged through the web. Axon sensed the multi-dimensional space around the ship, almost tasted the seething point-events in the quantum foam. Under Axon's control, the web twisted into planes and interlinked toroids, into cylinders with spheres, into spikes of filigree fronds, focusing, concentrating. Suddenly, the point-particles of the foam could not annihilate each other as they wished. The forces of annihilation were cancelling out. Unwilling to accept this breach of fundamental laws, space shifted, moving the ship into an absolute vacuum, falling down the front of a huge energy wave.

Right across the galactic arm, a burst of high-energy neutrinos signalled ignition. The entire ship's mass, its hull, its plants, fishes and tiny human population experienced no acceleration forces. The bubble of modified quantum events simply translated itself elsewhere, although *where* is a complex concept in eleven-dimensional space-time. You might say that at the moment Axon released the field it had travelled twenty-seven light years – but *year* and *travel* didn't apply in any meaningful sense. It just was where it was not, and the universe repaired its minor injury. From ignition to shutdown had taken thirty-six seconds of ship time.

Displays which had blanked during the space-time shift began to light up.

'*I'm sorry,*' Axon thought at them. '*I missed the target.*'

'By how much?'

'*Eight point five three metres. I'll try to do better next time!*'

Mariam and Victor slapped their restraining harnesses off, whooped and high-fived.

'Ship's status?'

'*Checks are still running. So far, only trivial damage to a couple of X-ray sensors and a slightly higher level of radiation in the outer skin than expected. We appear to be stable. May I signal the damaged ship* Iron Lady?'

'Agreed.'

Multi-frequency lasers aimed at a point four hundred thousand kilometres ahead and pumped a dense burst of information down the beam. They sat calmly and waited. After seven minutes a screen lit up, showing a white-haired gaunt woman.

'That was quite a spectacular arrival. It's pretty dark out here, but you sure lit it up. Thank you. The *Iron Lady* is not in good shape. We have your ship identified as *Zbeta97gamma*. Do you have a friendlier name?'

Victor held down the 'Mute' button his chair arm and said 'We never got around to naming the ship. Any ideas?'

'Oh yes,' said Mariam. 'Axon came up with the name a long time ago.'

'*Did I?*'

'We'll have the champagne later. I name this ship *Sky Leap*. May she and all who travel in her be safe and happy!'

Others were steadily crowding in behind the woman – Renata – on the display. 'We need to know, ' she said, 'if your imploders are intact. Ours are, but we have no motive power of any sort.'

'What imploders?' Victor and Mariam asked in unison.

Axon broke the link and the screen went dark.

'The forward halves of this ship and Iron Lady *contain devices to collapse local space into super-massive black holes. The intention is to put these in place so that their immense gravity will slingshot the dark matter object heading for the Orion-Cygnus arm of the Milky Way out of the ecliptic and off to who cares where?'*

'Why weren't we told? There seem to be a lot of things we weren't told!'

'There are consequences.'

'Oh,' said Victor,' I think I see. Unless the ships jump at exactly the right time we're going to get a close-up view of some very nasty event horizons.'

'Correct.'

'Oh, shit! It's a suicide mission.'

'Look on the bright side,' Axon said. '*Iron Lady's central brain is totally dead. Without that the operation becomes almost impossible.'*

'I don't think *almost* is that bright a side,' Mariam said. 'I would prefer *totally impossible.*'

The impulse engines powered up and Sky Leap accelerated towards Iron Lady; estimated journey time fifty-seven hours. As the adrenalin-rush faded, Mariam and Victor were suddenly hungry and thirsty. They dialled the food system in the crew mess to deliver kebabs, salad, and a bottle of champagne. When he'd popped the cork, Victor splashed champagne down the wall.

'What are you doing?'

'Ship-naming.'

'Isn't the champagne supposed to be on the outside?'

'The door's that way. Off you go, Siss.'

'Ex-sis. Remember?'

'Oh yes. I very definitely remember.'

'Good. Looks like we're going to die soon, so we may have to pack the rest of our lives into a couple of days. So don't take too long eating that kebab.'

He was still chewing his last mouthful when she took the champagne bottle in one hand and his arm in the other, kissed him, and led him off towards the isolation chamber.

They were still lying in each other's arms when the alarms went off. Naked, they ran to the door. The second it slid back, blinding pain shot through their heads and they both screamed.

Victor pulled Mariam back inside the containment chamber and hit the manual door-close button. They leaned, panting, against the wall as the pain subsided. 'Axon,' Mariam said. 'Something's seriously wrong.'

Victor went to the control panel and cancelled the alarm. 'System – diagnostics – Axon-specific.' Data streamed down the right of the main screen, and to the left a coloured diagram of Axon's spherical brain pulsed with bright green highlights. 'Analysis,' Victor snapped. After a few seconds a synthesised voice said *'Ninety-four per cent of neurons are firing synchronously.'*

Mariam stared at the data. 'What does that mean?'

'It means,' Victor replied, 'that Axon is having an epileptic fit.'

'What can we do?'

'Wait. The support systems are supplying suppressants.'

A chime sounded, the data shrank away, and Renata appeared. 'Why are you initiating a jump?' she demanded.

'We're not,' Mariam answered.

'Your webs are deploying and charging. Have you kids gone crazy? If you jump now you will annihilate us. You must stop it!'

Victor switched the diagnostics from Axon-specific to

general, and there it was – clear evidence of the first stage of a launch.

'Axon's having a fit. We can't go outside this area without frying our brains.'

'Look,' Mariam said, pointing at the ship's schematic on one of the screens. Slowly, the front section was peeling back.

'Oh, my God!' Renata shouted. 'He's arming the collapsers.'

'I'm going to try to reach the control room,' Victor said. 'It's the only way.'

Mariam grabbed him. 'You won't make it!' she yelled. He shrugged her off, and headed for the door. Intolerable pain. Fire raging behind the eyes. Fear, torture, anguish, blindness. Victor stumbled on along the corridor trying hard to keep moving through the overwhelming horror in his head. He had no idea that Mariam was close behind him. They sensed without senses that they were in the control room, where warning lights were flashing red.

Victor forced himself to shout 'Emergency power-down! All systems.' He scarcely heard the request for multiple confirmation, or Mariam's strained 'Confirmed.'

Circuits disconnected. Pumps ceased to spin. The fierce pain in their heads reduced to the mere level of a bad migraine. Only emergency lights lit the chamber. Outside, the great flaps at the front of the ship stopped moving, at half retraction, arrayed like petals around the bulbous hull.

'You're an idiot,' Mariam said as they lay slumped in their chairs. 'So are you,' he replied.

'I hate to ask, but now what?'

The emergency power supply kept the control panels alight. Victor touched and swiped across them. 'If we don't supply power to Axon's nutrient and oxygen supplies he'll be dead in ten minutes.'

'Can we disable the link to us, and feed him?'

'No idea.'

'Well start thinking.'

'We need to talk to *Iron Lady*, so I'm restarting power to the isolation area, our life-support, and Axon's vital supplies. Done.'

The lights in the control room came back on, and speech recognition systems re-booted.

'Power to the central brain – monitoring only.'

The image of Axon's neurons still pulsed with abnormal regularity.

'Power to external telemetry and comms links.'

After a pause, the worried face of Renata reappeared, and then she smiled and said 'Fantastic! How did you do it?'

'Victor hit the big *off* switch,' Mariam said. 'We're bringing systems back if they are not controlled by Axon. Victor, send the brain imaging to *Iron Lady*, please. Renata, do you have a doctor in your crew?'

'Three.'

'Get them to look at the images. We need suggestions urgently. What's happening is outside the automatic brain control system's programming.'

'Keep transmitting. I'll get to you ASAP.'

Victor was carefully studying the complex diagrams of the ship's electrical systems.

'Apply power to distributors alpha theta nine-seventy and nine-seventy-one. Then close the forward doors.'

'Weapons control is not available to you.'

'Bollocks!' Victor shouted. 'Give us control, now!'

'That cannot be done.'

Mariam put her hand on his shoulder. 'Calm down. There has to be a way around this. They must have planned for central brain malfunction, surely?'

'If they did, it's something else they forgot to tell us.'

Renata reappeared on the screen. 'Can you give us control of the brain support systems? The medics want to send instructions to produce some drugs that should halt the seizure.'

'OK, but I doubt if the ship will let you.' Victor said.

'Oh – it will.'

Shortly they watched the brain read-out as it was flooded with anaesthetics and seizure-suppressants. Slowly the storm calmed and normal sleep patterns emerged. And then the brain went dark. Warning signals flared on the control panel. Axon's support system went into overdrive, injecting adrenalin, administering electric shocks. But still, the mighty brain remained inert.

Axon was dead, and with him any hope of going anywhere. They stood silently for a moment, and then Victor turned towards the image of Renata.

'To put it in the vernacular,' he said, 'it looks as though you fucked up.' Before she could reply he reached over and cut the comms link.

'Look,' Mariam said. 'The forward doors are closing. System – explain.'

'Fallback condition assigns full command to Victor and Mariam.'

'Restore the quantum webs to the rest position.'

The webs slowly retreated.

'Restore full power. Correct the course alignment to previous targeting schedule.'

'Deceleration will begin in three hundred and twenty minutes. Alignment with Iron Lady *in seventeen hours.'*

'Victor,' Mariam said, 'I can *feel* your thoughts. Something's happening to us. And by the way, it's bad luck for men to baptise ships. Just thought I'd tell you.'

They ate and then slept for a while, curled up together, exhausted, mourning the loss of Axon, their triplet. Then they were summoned to the isolation chamber, where a pre-recorded message from Somerton gave them a new briefing.

Silently, *Sky Leap* slipped into position parallel with *Iron Lady*. When they reopened the comms link to the other ship, Renata was furious. 'You cannot cut communications like that. You will come over to *Iron Lady* in your shuttle immediately.'

'On the contrary,' Mariam said, perhaps too sweetly, 'You will use your shuttles. All personnel on *Iron Lady* will be transferred to *Sky Leap* in the next eight hours.'

'Impossible.'

'Check the authorisation codes we've just sent you. Both ships are now under our command.'

Mariam and Victor had never seen so many people before. Areas of the ship that had been mothballed were opened up: kitchens came to life and remembered how to cook; previously dark corridors were full of life; laboratories span up centrifuges and forged new and complex molecules.

During the next twenty-four hours, six hundred injections of newly-manufactured nano began to work on six hundred terrified human brains.

Renata and the other senior members of the *Iron Lady*'s crew were not taking kindly to having their power usurped by a couple of teenagers. Arguments raged in the control centre, until Victor banned the dissenters. Mariam was better at empathy, and went to great lengths over coffee and cakes to reduce the tension. 'Look,' she said time after time, 'if you have a better idea, let's discuss it. Otherwise, the choices are, stay here and run out of everything, or take the risk that we can complete the task we came to perform.' At last, if they didn't see reason, they saw inevitability; and they saw the truth that the supposed twins had more abilities than even they themselves knew.

At midnight, ship's time, the nano-injections had diffused through grey-matter. Every human was strapped securely into an inertia-damping chair. *Sky Leap* and *Iron Lady* began to accelerate in perfect synchronisation. For the first time in their lives, over six hundred souls heard a voice, not through their ears, but in their minds – the calm voice of Mariam. 'Dear friends,' she said, '*Iron Lady* is now slaved to this ship. We have begun the launch sequence. Our great brains failed us, so now we must link our small brains together and hope that we can succeed.'

Outside petal-like doors folded back from the noses of the ships, and the gossamer webs unfolded and expanded.

'Immediately after the collapsers have been launched,' she went on, 'we will turn and attempt to ignite the main drives. You may find it disturbing, possibly frightening, but you must not fight it. Victor and I were bred for this task, but we need each of you, and all of you, if we are to have any chance. Let us wish ourselves well.'

In the control centre the one-time twins looked at each other, 'This could be a rough ride,' Victor said, and blew Mariam a kiss. 'Let's do it.' He issued the final command.

Missiles streamed from the nose of the ships. The impulse drives shut down, and the bay doors were closing even as the great vessels changed course, turning away from the missile tracks. And then Victor and Mariam locked their brains with all the other brains and began the impossible calculus which could subject the quantum foam to their bidding. Strange fire crackled through the webs. Slowly, much too slowly, flickering erratically, the ships began their uncertain leap into the void.

To one side of the projected path of the massive cluster of dark matter that hurtled towards the Milky Way, the collapsers fired. Matter turned on matter, dimensions distorted, and eight massive black holes erupted into terrible being. Gravity waves wracked the heavens. The gates of Hades were opened and the Furies unleashed. The pathways of the skies were remapping themselves.

At last, one lonely ship emerged from the roiling energies, its quantum webs destroyed, its outer shields ablated, stripped of sensors, black, inert, rock-like. It was impossible to detect the name painted on the hull, or whether there ever had been a name.

But deep inside, a shoal of silver fish swam to and fro in a blue lake bordered with perfect grass and gently waving trees.

GUY HALEY

IROBOT

THERE IS NOTHING but the desert, a landscape of dust and ceaseless wind. Dunes of dust creep across the land, dust sheets from their scimitar peaks. Ribbons of dust undulate swiftly up and down their sides. The dust makes the sky brown, the rising sun pale and dirty. Shrouds of dust chase each other through the air, tangling daylight in their umber strands. The sun retaliates, flaring a little brighter, calling shadows from the desert; hard and straight, traces of something beneath the sand.

There was a city here once.

Wind blows harder. Brick and worn concrete rise from the desert, grains of dust carried from them in torrents. The walls have lost their edges, worn smooth by the scouring sands. They are as cracked as ancient teeth, and yet in procession, taken from afar, unwavering. The lines and cells the walls describe are echoes of lost angles and cast geometry, straight where the dust is rippled and curled. In their simple precision the walls defy the fractal whorls of the dust, although they cannot win the battle, and have lost it many times before.

These are secret marks, conjured rarely when the light is just so, legible only to archaeology. Their testimony goes unread. There are no archaeologists any more.

Nor are there doctors, nor policemen. No bums, no vendors,

no consumers, no mothers or fathers or children, no dogs or cats or bees or ants or trees. There is no one and nothing at all; nothing but brown dust and the ruins they suffocate, uncover, and suffocate again.

Something terrible happened here. When or what, nobody knows, because there is nobody left to know. Only the wind has a voice, but it says little; it does not care or remember.

In the lee of a broken wall two figures are revealed. One, huddled within the remains of long coat that flaps in the freezing wind, was once a man. Desiccated black flesh, hard as plastic, clings to yellow bones. Hair is still attached to his shrivelled scalp. His eyes are raisins in his sockets. His mouth is as wide as only the mouths of the dead can be, his tongue hard and sharp inside his jaw. He lies on one arm. The other is flung out. The bones of his fingers are outstretched toward the second figure, as if in supplication, or in revelation; the hand of an apostle reaching out to say 'See! Here is the son of God'.

There are no gods now.

The second figure is not human. It is blocky and broken and its torso is pitted by the actions of the elements. Of its four limbs, one arm remains. Two of the fingers on the hand of this arm have broken away. It remains cloaked to its waist in the sand, coyly hiding the stumps of its legs. The wind pushes grains of sand from globules of melted plastic and metal scattered around the machine like dropped pearls. The ground they rest on is fused to glass.

For much of the year the machine is hidden. Summer storms periodically uncover the city, and then it and its companion. Shifting ramparts build themselves up to the shattered chest plate and fall away to the whim of the wind. The sports of dust are relentless, and have no winner.

The robot still has a head, a cartoonish facsimile of a human being. Its eyes are broken. Those parts of its solar array that are whole are scrubbed opaque, as is the screen upon its chest.

The machine has been dying a long time, but it is not yet dead.

As the veiled sun strikes the machine, something sparks inside. Images, as indistinct through the robot's ruined screen as the sun is indistinct in the ruined sky, flicker and dance.

'Good morning,' the robot's voice speaks. It does not matter in which language, it knows them all in any case, and the speakers of languages are all dead and gone from the Earth. 'Good morning. I have four thousand and five reminders!' Without preamble, it begins. Music, the choice of a person whose dust is at one with all the other dust, crackles in the background. 'Parminder is 1723 years old today!' The reminders are the longest part of its liturgy, reminders of things that were missed. Birthdays in the main, where cards were not sent. Others are appointments never kept and prompts to attend regular meetings that ceased to be regular long ago. The machine recites them all with equanimity. Its voice is faint but cheerful, although a buzz mars it. At its sound the wind seems cowed, as if offended. The recitation takes a long time. Finally, it is done.

'Last twittles: Moshe Horowitz is having palm-steamed yam for breakfast. Liam's train is late again, but he is enjoying a bacon sandwich, Melinda is very tired, but last night was fun! Rodrigo Anamate says you must check out this link. Link unavailable. No further messages. These messages are 619,423 days old. Delete? Please repeat. Voice command only. My touch screen is damaged. Please have me serviced at your earliest convenience. I am not connected to the internet. Searching for wifi connection.'

For a long minute the silence is given back to the wind, to break or not as it chooses.

'No wifi detected.'

Silence again. The silence lasts the rest of the day. Today is a bright day by the standards of the era, and at times almost warm. The passage of time is uncertain. Noon is a blur in a different part of the sky, afternoon a smear near the horizon. Brown day makes way for grey dusk. Night comes swiftly. There are no stars.

The glow from the robot's screen is a lonely light. The world retreats within it, becoming a square patch of sand with sloping sides, framing a dead man's outstretched hand. His bones gleam like gold.

The robot is limited. It is programmed to show concern, yet not to be intrusive. In its mind, flickering so erratically now, a facsimile of compassion gives rise to a need to reassure. 'I am afraid I cannot answer your last queries,' it says. 'I am not equipped to make fire. I do not know how to make fire. I do not know the location of water. I cannot make water. This information is not available to me. I am not connected to the internet. I am sorry.

'You are quiet,' it says. 'Are you sad?

Again the machine falls silent as its worn brain searches for something to cheer this last master.

'I have some amusing footage of kittens, if you would like to see it.'

The night wears on. The machine's solar charge runs out, the light dies.

The wind tucks the city back in, into its blankets of dust.

CHRIS BUTLER

THE ANIMATOR

Mr Jackson's studio nestled in the northwest sector of Autumn City, in an area known for its jewellers and clothing emporiums. The streets outside buzzed with hectic activity, the clatter of cycles and rickshaws, street sellers calling, all through the daylight hours, while we laboured quietly inside.

Eleanor had called in to see me while Mr Jackson was out at lunch. 'Powell,' she said abruptly, 'I think I'll introduce you to my uncle.'

I almost spat my drink across the workbench, but managed to gulp down the hot tea.

She laughed, and her spores were almost giddily effervescent.

'Oh don't worry about it,' she said. 'He's got to meet you sometime.'

'He does?'

She leant forward again, gazing into the phenakistoscope, which was mounted on a spinning plate on the bench. I pushed alternately on the pedals under the workbench to keep the plate turning.

'It really is a marvel,' she said again. 'You're so clever, Powell.'

In reality the machine was very simple. And clever or not, I was merely an apprentice at Mr Jackson's studio. Nevertheless, I *had* taken great care with the photographs of Mr and Mrs Stevenson. Looking through the slats into the spinning barrel, their images appeared to come alive so that the couple danced around and around.

'I'll arrange everything,' Eleanor said. I looked at her blankly for a moment. With an exasperated burst of spores she said, 'With my uncle, the Duke!'

She was serious; she planned to introduce me to the Autumn Duke. 'Are you sure it's not, well, a bit premature?' I was probably mumbling, I realised. As an afterthought I added the word 'Darling' in an all-too-transparent attempt to stay in her good books. Assuming I was in them in the first place.

'You have prospects,' she said, referring either to our relationship or my career, I wasn't sure which.

She made her way around the bench, leant over and kissed me on the cheek, whispering in my ear, 'See you later.'

My fellow apprentice, Ivy, gave me a withering look as Eleanor flounced out of the door.

'It'll end in tears,' she said, 'mark my words.'

She tucked her hair behind her ear and looked wistfully in the direction of the door.

Before I could comment, Mr Jackson came back from lunch. He removed his coat and hung it on the stand. Our main business was clocks, making and repairs, but phenakistoscopes were a profitable sideline. He cast an appraising eye over my work.

'Set it spinning,' he said, waving his finger in a circular motion. 'Let's have a look.'

I pushed on the pedals again, sending the plate turning.

He peered in at the animation, then gave me a big smile. 'It's good work, Powell,' he said. 'You better get it delivered to the Stevensons.'

'Yes, sir.'

Ivy helped me to box it up. 'It really is a beauty,' she said. She smiled, relaxed and happy. Her eyes were bright blue.

I nodded. 'I hope they like it.'

'Of course they will,' she said. 'How could they not?'

After work I headed through the town square on my way to meet Eleanor, but my route was blocked by a crowd. Above the crowd, I could see men being brought up onto the platform for public hanging.

'Bear witness!' the Autumn Guard called out.

I would have preferred to pass by, but the Duke's men were stationed throughout the crowd, and they pulled me in. Their spores were strong and dominating. I found myself wanting to see the men dead for their crimes, even before I knew what they were.

'These men are guilty of conspiracy,' the clerk called out from the platform. 'They consorted to spread lies about the Autumn Duke. By this action they have made themselves unclean. Their punishment shall be swift and without mercy.'

The ropes were tightened around their necks, and the traps went from under them. At that moment I knew it was good and proper. It was only later, after I walked away from that place, that I felt bad about it.

I met Eleanor at the Café Soleil. It was a favourite spot of mine after work, on the corner just round from my lodgings, with good sunlight in the early evening through the wide glass windows. Two teas there, then I snuck her back to my room.

'Albert, my landlord, he knows I bring someone back,' I said. I rolled up a towel and jammed it against the bottom edge of the door to stop our spores drifting under and out into the hall. 'I don't think he minds, though.'

'I bet he doesn't. The smell of us probably puts his wife in the mood.'

'That's so rude!'

I didn't have much stuff, and I liked to keep the place tidy. Maybe that was the clockmaker in me. Precision in all things. Eleanor wandered over to the edge of the window and peeked down into the street. Carefully she pulled the pins from her hair and set them aside. Her hair fell straight and long, and dark as molasses.

'Some people say that's the whole point of spores,' she said. 'It's reproductive.'

I didn't think so, even though spores were a part of what made someone attractive to you, or not, and gave you a strong sense of whether that attraction was mutual. 'But that's like saying the whole point of your eyes is reproductive. If you see something you like . . .'

She laughed. 'Maybe that's true too.'

I wasn't sure what the point of this conversation was, but she was reluctant to let it drop.

'It's the biggest turn on there is, though,' she said, 'when you know for sure that someone wants you. Don't you think?'

She had slipped off her skirt and unbuttoned her blouse. I certainly wanted her and there was absolutely no doubt about it.

We spent a delirious hour in bed together, taking precautions not to get her pregnant, because actual reproduction has very little to do with spores. Although, lying there in the cloudy haze of our lust could easily inspire recklessness, so maybe I was wrong.

It occurred to me that the only reason we were together was because she knew I wanted her. My mind clouded with doubt. Was that enough in the long run? These thoughts were careless and too easily noticed. Eleanor climbed from the bed and began to get dressed.

I didn't want to end the night with an argument, and thankfully nor did she. She couldn't stay the night and it was getting dark out, so I had to let her go. She seemed strangely smug about something as she left. I could taste it from her but she wouldn't explain.

I pulled on my jacket, straightened my tie, and headed down the stairs, trying to be careful not to draw the attention of the landlord, whose spores were present only faintly in the front hall. As usual I spared no more than a glance at the morning's letters arranged neatly on the table by the front door. And drew to an abrupt halt. There was a letter with my name on it. I picked it up, cautiously, turned it over. And saw the state seal stamped in red wax.

The landlord bellowed my name down the hall. 'Powell!'

Blast.

'Albert, I have a letter,' I said, and waved it in the air like a waiter casting a napkin back and forth. 'I wasn't expecting a letter.'

'I'm thrilled for you,' Albert said, his tone and the impact of his spores heavy with sarcasm.

'You're worrying about the rent again, aren't you? Worry not, you'll have it, I assure you.'

The burly landlord huffed. 'I wouldn't need to worry, if you had the slightest confidence in your own words.'

I sighed. My own spores always betrayed me. 'Well, in any case, I must go to my work.'

Albert folded his arms across his chest, but then another tenant came down the stairs and started complaining about a dripping tap in his room. I took advantage of the distraction, tucked the envelope into my pocket, and headed down the hall to the rear exit.

In the back yard my cycle was stored under a rickety shelter. I pulled it free and set off down the street at pace, heading towards work.

The sun was lifting above the level of the tenements,

sending glittering shards of light over the rooftops to fall into the street like arrows. Autumn City came awake in the glare of the new day.

A state seal meant only one thing: a summons from the Duke, or someone close to him. Now I knew why Eleanor had been so smug the night before. Good as her word, she had arranged a meeting. I felt butterflies in my stomach. This was all wrong. She had no idea what she was doing. And nor did I.

Autumn City is crowded and sprawling in the northern region, tapering down to a sparsely populated area in the south. The Autumn Duke was not a town person. He had a palace in the countryside, set in acres of land maintained meticulously by his staff. I rode out most of the way, then hid my cycle and walked the last bit.

A footman showed me in to a room where the Duke appeared to be working with clerical staff. I could have spent hours studying the decorations around the room, but the Duke suddenly dismissed the staff and I found myself alone under his scrutiny.

He was a stocky man, but hard like steel. His hair had been shaved close to his scalp. His attire was formal, in seasonal russet colours. I could feel my heartbeat accelerating as we exchanged pleasantries. A surly dissatisfaction with me was unmistakable in his spores. He indicated a chair so I sat down, but he himself remained standing.

'My niece speaks very highly of you,' he said. 'She is, of course, an impressionable young girl.'

'Your Grace?'

'Do you really think these phenakistoscopes will lead you to the kind of wealth that is expected?'

'I –'

'I have seen other similar designs, from other inventors.

To my eye it is a child's toy. And you, just an apprentice. No, it won't do, it won't do at all. You agree, I'm sure.'

The word *spore* is derived from the Greek, meaning the act of sowing. It is meant metaphorically rather than literally, for the sowing of understanding between us. But at that moment I was quite sure the Duke and I did not understand each other at all. In his presence I could not argue with him, the power of his spores so overwhelming. I wondered how a man like him could ever engage meaningfully with anyone.

'I am sure you are correct, Your Grace,' was all I could say.

'Yes, I feel sure I am. But – prove me wrong, if you like. Find other work. Improve your fortunes, if you can.'

A glimmer of hope, then. Not a complete and utter dismissal. Or was I just fooling myself? Surely he had no real expectation that I would somehow reinvent myself and earn my fortune.

The truth was, I loved my work at Mr Jackson's studio and I didn't want to leave. All I could think of to improve my standing was perhaps to invent some new kind of clock or animation device.

'You can do it,' Eleanor said, when I next met her in the café. 'Invent something new, make a name for yourself.'

She brushed her hand across her forehead, tidying some wayward strands of her hair. I looked past her at the way the sunlight cast the design of the glass café door onto the floor.

'I've tried but I can't think of a single thing,' I said. 'Maybe I could ask Mr Jackson. Perhaps between us we might come up with something.'

A burst of sourness from her told me she was less than impressed with this suggestion. 'If Jackson had any ideas he'd have come up with them by now.'

Behind the counter I could see the waitress lift the kettle off the stove. I wished she would hurry up and bring the drinks. Any distraction would be welcome at this point.

'He's made a success of his business, though,' I said.

'Yes, by taking advantage of two young apprentices and paying them hardly anything. Just what does this apprenticeship of yours lead to, anyway?'

'Er, well, a permanent position, I suppose.'

'With more money?'

'Undoubtedly,' I said, but as ever my spores betrayed me.

'You're hopeless,' she said.

When the drinks came we mostly sat with them in silence, and the spores drifting between us were clingy and sombre. Eleanor wouldn't come back to my place, and I had no idea when I might see her again. No idea at all.

'Do you know what the problem with the phenakistoscope is, Ivy?' I asked her, still maddened by my inability to invent something.

She looked up from her work. 'Problem?'

'Yes, the problem.'

'I wasn't aware there was one, Powell.'

'There are no spores. The device doesn't generate any spores. So no matter how appealing the illusion, it just doesn't *feel* real.'

I was aware of a flicker of something complex from Ivy then, as if the notion troubled her. Her mood could cloud over in a second sometimes. 'I suppose that's true,' she said, brightening again, 'but people do like them, even so.'

'Maybe we could bottle them, the spores, and somehow release them. Later.'

She burst out laughing. Apparently I had now invented hysterical laughter.

'Oh you are funny,' she said, when at last she could speak again. 'You might as well try to bottle the ripples in a pond after a stone has been thrown into it! I think you'd be better off sticking closer to the basic idea of the phenakistoscope. Only bigger and better, somehow.'

I nodded. Perhaps she was right.

'How about a camera obscura?' I said. 'I've been reading about those. They sound entertaining.'

Ivy looked at me, her face blank. 'A camera what?'

'You build a hut with a hole in the wall. Light comes through the hole and falls onto a screen.'

'And?'

'And you can see what's happening outside. On the screen.'

'You go into a hut to see what's happening outside?'

'Yes.'

'Why wouldn't you just go outside?'

I laughed. 'You have a point.'

We laughed a lot, Ivy and me. She was good fun, most of the time.

'What do you – ' I found myself changing the subject without really meaning to. 'What do you hope for, in life, Ivy?'

'Gosh, Powell, I don't know. A nice place to live. Someone who treats me kind. And to be good at my work, of course.'

Ivy worked with meticulous care at all times, I thought. She might have been a better choice for me than Eleanor, except for the fact that Ivy would also have preferred Eleanor, for herself.

'So you want to earn the good things in life through your own endeavours?'

'Oh yes,' she said. 'No one's going to just give it all to me, are they! Oh, and there's one other thing I want. I want to invent something better than whatever you invent.'

I smiled. Quite right too. 'Some people do have everything just given to them,' I said.

'They probably don't appreciate it all, though, do they?'

'No,' I said, 'I don't think they do.'

~

I sat in the Café Soleil on my own after work. I found myself gazing at the way the light shone through the door of the café, casting the coloured design onto the floor. Maybe somehow that projection could be harnessed to greater effect.

The beginning of an idea was coming to me. The Café Soleil must have the best light in all of Autumn City. But come to think of it, the place hadn't been very busy at all, for a while now.

'How's business?' I said to the old guy who brought me my drink.

'Slow.' He shook his head sadly. 'Very slow.'

'Who owns this place?'

'I do,' he said. 'I just had to let my best waitress go.' He held out his hand. 'Name's Bigbury,' he told me.

I shook his hand. 'Powell.'

'I see you in here a lot,' he said. 'Wish we had more like you.'

My idea was crystallising quickly in my mind. I mulled a few last details before speaking. 'What would you say, Mr Bigbury, if I said I could double your business?'

'I'd say, "Who do I have to kill?"'

'Ha ha. Good one. Your takings have been steady the last few weeks?' He nodded. 'Let's say I double it, I get thirty per cent of the extra. Deal?'

'Thirty per cent of half?'

'Thirty per cent of the extra. Maybe I'll do better than double your income.'

'All right, it's a deal. What do you need, kid?'

I pointed in the direction of the window. 'I just need permission to do whatever I want with your window.'

Mr Jackson was a decent man, and he said I could use the

workshop in the evenings as long as it was all in my own time and I paid for any materials I used.

The clockwork mechanism was quite straightforward, though I wanted it to be sturdy enough to drive a selection of plates around. I figured it wasn't much use to have the image projected onto the floor, but there was a lot of white wall space in the Café Soleil. A careful arrangement of mirrors and lenses would lift the image up to fill that space.

'Understand, sir,' I told Mr Bigbury, 'this is just the first prototype. I'll build something more elaborate. I just wanted to get us up and running. See what response we get.'

'Right you are, Powell.'

The prototype cast simple abstract colour designs across the walls of the Café Soleil. A modest start but it seemed to impress the few customers who were in when I set it up. I showed Mr Bigbury how to wind the mechanism, which at regular intervals moved a new image in front of the lens.

We'd see how that went, and in the meantime I'd develop some more elaborate animations. I had in mind a kind of picture book, using coloured images or silhouettes to tell a story.

I carried out my normal work for Mr Jackson during the day, and worked on my own project in the evenings. For some reason I couldn't quite decipher, Ivy was being rather cold and distant with me. It was something to do with the mechanism I was developing, but I thought it unlikely this was any kind of professional jealousy. She refused to discuss it.

I could prepare the plates in Mr Jackson's workshop, and fit them to a duplicate mechanism, but we didn't have the Café Soleil's light. So I had only a sense of how well my first shadow mechanism would work once installed. Nevertheless as I sat in the workshop and watched the plates shifting around as the cogs turned, I had high hopes for it. The plates were intended to illustrate the story of Sholla, the warrior woman who single-handedly defended her King against an invading army. Silhouettes of enemy warriors with swords or bows, on foot or on horseback, rose and fell. Each came forward and was struck down by Sholla, while the sun and the moon and the stars rotated around and around.

When I went back to the Café Soleil, a week after first installing the prototype mechanism, there had already been an increase in trade. Mr Bigbury shook my hand and said he was delighted. 'It's working, Powell, it's working!' he told me enthusiastically. The spores in the room communicated a palpable sense of happiness and excitement.

I unfastened the device from its mountings against the window and took it down. There was a murmur of disapproval from the café patrons as I did so. It appeared people really were coming here to experience the display. I set about removing the older colour plates quickly, and fitted the new ones. I wound the mechanism, feeling a little nervous. Perhaps I should have tested it while the café was closed, but I could not do so in the dark, and the Café Soleil had always opened from daybreak till dusk.

I managed to find one unoccupied chair and sat down to watch. The scenes were projected onto the café walls exactly as I hoped. Whether or not the display proved popular remained to be seen, but I rejoiced in having achieved what I set out to. I was so captivated by my work that I forgot to take notice of how the other patrons were receiving it. When I did think at last to consider them, I saw they had become perfectly still and seemed entranced.

The display reached its end, the silhouette plates withdrawn into the mechanism's housing for a minute or two till it would start over. A quiet hush had descended on the café – the spores in the room were unlike anything I had experienced before.

'Wonderful,' someone said, breaking the silence.

Others said the same. They came to me and shook my hand; congratulated me. Asked me questions about how it was done. Had I made the machine or only installed it? How marvellous it was!

I went home that night feeling elated, completely unable to sleep, planning what to do next.

'I've been thinking about what you said.' I'd thought Ivy was engrossed in her work, but obviously not. 'About images not seeming real because of the absence of spores.'

She had my interest. 'Yes?'

'Suppose you put a group of people together in a room and show them an image that makes them laugh.'

'Yes?'

'Well, they're going to supply the spores, aren't they? Because they're amused. Once they get started they will supply the missing spores themselves. It'll be self-fulfilling.'

Was she right? 'I'm not sure,' I said.

She cast a glance around to make sure we were alone. In a hushed voice she said, 'What you're doing at the café, you realise it's – '

'What?'

'It's *theatre*, Powell.'

I blinked. 'No it isn't,' I said, 'it's just a light show.'

Ivy looked very thoughtful. 'Made from sunlight, yes. But in essence it's theatre.'

'But . . .' I floundered, uncomfortable. 'This isn't people gathering in secret in dark rooms. It's nothing like it.'

I remembered clearly when I'd first heard of the idea of theatre. I was just a child. One of the carers in the orphanage had whispered to me about it. There had been a brief attempt to legitimise the theatre, with performances held openly.

This woman, she made it sound exciting but, soon after, she changed and never spoke of it again.

No one spoke of it except in hushed whispers. It was a perverse activity in which people allowed their mood to be manipulated, till they wallowed in a haze of their own sordid spores. 'It's not the kind of thing that goes on in Autumn City,' I said.

'Are you sure about that?' Ivy asked pointedly.

I couldn't believe what I was hearing. Was she implying she knew it *did* go on? She looked lost, her spores vague and cold, like she was clouded in a fog of sad weariness.

'Maybe you're right and what you're doing is something different,' she said at last. 'But I think your café idea is going to work brilliantly, and I think the reason why it will work is that the people in there are going to feed off each others' spores.'

I didn't know what to say.

She shook her head, then went back to focusing on her work. She didn't look at me for a long time after that.

The next time I saw Eleanor she arrived with a minder at her side. He said he would leave us alone while we took a walk through the park, but in fact he followed discreetly some distance behind us; I couldn't help glancing back at him from time to time. His presence was unusual and unnerved me.

'Is something wrong?' I asked her.

'I don't know,' she said. She leant down and picked a flower and held it to her nose. 'Things are impossible lately. I just want to be my own person, to be with the people I like. Is that so wrong?'

'People?'

'Artists, craftsmen, talented people.'

I smiled. 'Is there none of that in your – '

'No,' she said, cutting me off. 'In my world they all believe so fervently in our traditions that you have no choice but to fall in line with them. I feel completely stifled, for days on end. But then when I escape for a while, to sit with a painter at work, or a sculptor, or a poet, then I feel . . . something more.'

'Was that what you saw in me, the night we met?'

She laughed gently. 'You were very drunk!'

That was true. I had gone out drinking with my friend Patrice, who was originally from Winter City and had decided to go back there to try to find work. We drank far too much and then went to eat. Patrice managed somehow to persuade Eleanor and her friend Catherine to join their restaurant table with ours. Neither of them knew us before that night, but we talked easily with each other. By the end of it I knew I had to see Eleanor again. I sometimes wonder if Patrice and Catherine might have . . . But anyway, the next day he left as planned.

'It might be more difficult to see you for a while,' Eleanor said. She cast aside the flower she'd been holding.

'What? Why do you say that?'

She seemed so unhappy suddenly. I reached out and took her hand, half-expecting she would snatch it away. But she held mine tightly and leant against me as we walked.

'No one explains anything to me,' she said. 'I'll just have to hope these restrictions won't last. Be patient, Powell.'

'Of course,' I said, 'but you'll see me when you can, won't you?'

She nodded, and held my hand more tightly. After that the conversation turned to the latest gossip from her circle of friends, and she seemed happier.

I spent a lot of time in the City Library, looking for new ideas for my mechanism. What stories or illuminations might it show? In the southern reaches of Winter City there were feral cats clothed in fur the colour of snow. It might be amusing to imagine them as fierce tribes warring with each other.

Frequently I found myself pondering what kind of entertainment I was seeking to provide. I just wanted to tell stories, like those in books. What was wrong with that? At what point did this cross over into something forbidden?

Eventually I put aside the books I had been studying and instead directed my attention to some older newspapers. These were all filed meticulously, and surely if I hit upon the right date I would find journalistic coverage of the theatre performances I recalled from my childhood. I remembered it was in the Riverside area, perhaps ten years earlier?

I soon found a paper containing an advertisement for the opening of a theatre. That led me to the week of the opening itself and a report on the event. Fascinated, I read that the first night had been hailed as a compelling new experience. But weeks later an entirely different story was being told: lack of interest, financial losses. Eventually, just a small notice that the theatre had closed.

I made a note of the significant names: the owner of the theatre, the play's leading performers, the name of the newspaper reporter. I left the library and set off in the direction of the Riverside district where the theatre had stood. Was it even there now, I wondered?

The sun shone brightly, as if determined to project this story before me. But I couldn't see it clearly. Not yet.

It took some days of asking around and further delving into archives before I made much progress. The Autumn Theatre, as it was known, still occupied its original location in the northeast part of the city, near to the river, but it was completely derelict now. There was no sign bearing its name, no clue now as to its former purpose.

The owner denied any knowledge of the building's use as a theatre, saying only that he had acquired it around the time in question; he would not say from whom. This would be a matter of public record, however, so I knew I could uncover that if I wanted. Was it relevant? It was hard to imagine that detail would turn out to be important. Why had he allowed it to fall into dereliction? He had lost money in other ventures, he said, and could not afford repairs.

The performers had common names and, since no further theatre performances had ever occurred openly in Autumn City, I struggled to trace any of them.

Only the name of the reporter, James Knox, stirred some recognition when I asked around the neighbourhood bars. The man was apparently not well regarded. Often dishevelled and rumoured to be untrustworthy. Nevertheless I traced him to a small flat in a less appealing neighbourhood a little further south.

'Might I speak to you?' I asked the man who answered the door. He had not shaved, had untidy hair, and his ragged clothing hung loosely on his thin frame.

'Who are you?'

'I am an apprentice clockmaker,' I said. This seemed a wholly inappropriate answer given my recent activity, so I added, 'amongst other things.'

'Got no use for clocks,' he said, and began to push the door closed again.

'I'm also interested in theatre,' I said, the words tumbling out as quickly as I could manage.

This stopped him completely for a moment, but then he recovered and pulled the door open. The stench of his spores was not pleasant, and I suppose the reaction in me must have been apparent to him.

'Yeah, I'm not much these days, am I?' he said.

I became acutely aware of the power dynamic between us. I was in a position of relative strength, which was new to me. In theory he should defer to me in most matters, within reason.

'Let me in,' I said. 'I'd like to talk to you about what happened with the Autumn Theatre.'

He wavered for just a moment, then nodded and let me follow him back into the flat.

He slumped down into a sofa, scattering a cloud of dust as he did so. There was a chair opposite so I took that, reluctantly because of the general state of filth.

'I guess what I really want to know is why people didn't like it, why it failed.'

He snorted, like I had just said something incredibly stupid.

'Didn't like it,' he mumbled. 'Kid, people loved that show.'

'They did?'

He nodded and smiled, like just the memory of it felt good to him.

'Then why did it close? What went wrong?'

He paused a moment, then said, 'Think carefully about why you're asking me this. Look at what's happened to me. Maybe this is what's waiting for you, if you go down a certain path.'

'I don't understand.'

'All I'm saying is, maybe it would be better for you if you walked out of here right now and didn't look back.'

I thought about what he was saying, trying to imagine what dire consequences might befall me. I felt sure that I would be better off knowing the nature of his concerns rather than not knowing.

'If you'd just tell me what happened,' I said.

'All right then. You know what a theatre's like, right? Big audience of people all looking at the same thing, following what's happening on the stage. You ever experience anything like that?'

I thought back to what had happened in the Café Soleil. The show I had created there, and the appreciation I'd received.

'Yes, Mr Knox. In a small way.'

'Suppose in the play something amusing happens, or something sad perhaps. What happens to the audience do you think?'

'Well, they would react to it.'

'In the same way, or each in different ways?'

'In the same way, I suppose.'

'Now, let's for a moment look instead at this situation here, with you and me. You're a respectable, intelligent young man, making your way in the world, I'm sure. Full of optimism, you are. You stink of it. Whereas I've gone down in the world, lost my standing, lost confidence in myself. That being the case you can dominate this situation, this dynamic between us, as in fact you have already demonstrated from the moment you got here.'

'I didn't mean – '

He waved away my objection.

'It doesn't matter. But imagine there were ten people like me sat here, all ten feeling the same identical things as me, but still only one of you. Imagine a hundred of me, and one of you. Imagine a theatre full of me, and one of you. Well, do you see that the dynamic would be a little different?'

I did see. I saw it clearly.

'Maybe I wouldn't care about you,' he said, 'maybe I wouldn't even notice you. Maybe the power you have over me would just melt away.'

'In which case – '

'You're starting to get it, aren't you? Now, suppose a powerful man, like, say, the Autumn Duke, were to attend the theatre production one night. How do you think he would feel? The man who normally dictates and controls everything? Rendered powerless in comparison with the strength of everyone else combined? Powerless before the strength of the message conveyed by the play.'

'Was the message of the play controversial?'

'Not in our case, no, not at all. But the point is, it could have been. The point is, we were one step away from a mechanism for revolution.'

'And the Duke understood this?'

'I believe he did. In any case pressures were brought to bear on everyone involved. The theatre soon closed, and very few people ever spoke of it again. Most everyone involved drifted away, supposedly moved to other cities. I don't know if that's really what happened to them. They're gone from Autumn City anyway.'

'But surely,' I struggled to grasp all the implications, 'it's not unheard of for crowds of people to gather together.'

'It's rarer than you think. And when it does happen, who do the people gather to listen to?'

'The Duke,' I said.

'Yes – or his officials. And who does he place throughout the crowd?'

I thought back to the public hangings I had seen not long before. People were gathered in the square. The Autumn Guard had been placed strategically among the crowd. They were all strong men and fiercely loyal to the Duke. They set the tone for such gatherings, always.

He smiled. 'You might think the Duke is always going to parties, always surrounded by many people. In a modestly sized room with not too many people, he can still dominate. He is, after all, one of the most powerful men in the city, a popular man. So long as the people admire him, he has nothing to fear.'

'Every public appearance is carefully managed?'

'The mores of our society have been meticulously orchestrated for generations. The room is never too big, the crowd too large, unless the situation is controlled.'

I sat in silence for a while, considering what he had said.

He was the one to break that silence. 'I'm wondering what you've got yourself into, kid.'

I stood up and headed for the door. 'Thank you for your time, Mr Knox.'

As I was leaving he said, 'Whatever it is, if I were you I would put a stop to it, before they notice you.' He grabbed my arm. 'And one other thing. Whatever you do, don't mention *my* name.'

I stared at him, then pulled my arm free. 'One other question,' I said. 'I've heard rumours of secret theatres, secret performances.' In truth I had heard only the slightest hint of this, from Ivy. 'Know anything about that?'

He shook his head, so I turned and walked away.

He called after me. 'Promise me you won't mention my name.'

I walked along the river for a while, going over what Knox had said, then decided to head back to the Café Soleil. The place was full when I went in, and there was an intoxicating taste of joy in the spores in the air. Mr Bigbury spotted me, came over and shook my hand warmly.

'It's incredible,' he said, 'I've had people queuing to come in.'

The Sholla silhouette play was running. I could see Bigbury had already employed new serving staff to cope with the upturn in his fortunes. I glanced around the café. Over by the window there were two men who looked out of place. They were dressed sombrely and seemed to be more interested in us than in the play. I couldn't sense their spores, beneath the strength of the others in the café. One of them had a notebook and wrote something down in it. As he began to look up in my direction I turned away.

'Mr Bigbury, can I speak to you in private?'

'Very busy here,' he said, waving me away.

I wanted to insist but what would I say to him now? Did I

really expect him to let me just pack up the mechanism and take it away? Was that even what I wanted?

It was getting late and I needed to think. I left the café and headed for my lodgings.

I lay on my bed, my mind a whirl. Would my little silhouette display in a small café really cause concern amongst the city's rich and powerful?

Then there was a knock on the door, and the fact that I almost jumped out of my skin told me how on edge I'd become. To my surprise, the person standing there when I opened the door was Eleanor. She looked almost as nervous as I felt.

'Powell,' she said. She threw her arms around me and kissed me.

Her spores insinuated themselves into me, dark and heavy like anchor weights dragging me down into darkness and uncertainty. She was on the verge of tears, and all I could think of then was that I wanted to make things right with her. She kissed me again, so fiercely I couldn't help but respond. She pulled me over to the bed and brought me down with her. She pulled her skirt up and grappled with my belt. The sex was desperate and brief, and she left the bed almost immediately afterwards.

'I can't stay,' she said simply, 'and I can't see you again.'

'What?'

'You're being watched. I've taken a risk by being here.'

'You can't just, do what we just did, then leave.'

'I have to. If you care anything for me, don't try to speak to me again. Go back to clocks and phenakistoscopes, Powell. Do it now, while maybe you still can.'

She came close, kissed me again, then left before I could argue any more.

I hardly slept that night. In the morning I forced myself to get dressed and head out to work. I moved down the stairs. In the front hall I looked for the morning's letters on the table by the door. There was a letter with my name on it. I picked it up, cautiously, turned it over. And saw the state seal stamped in red wax.

I opened the letter at once. I had been summoned to meet with the Duke again, that afternoon. A carriage would be sent for me this time.

At work I explained to Mr Jackson that I would have to go out in the afternoon, and showed him the letter. I struggled through the morning, unable to focus on my work.

'Whatever is the matter with you?' Ivy asked me.

'It's nothing,' I said.

She frowned at me, knowing I had lied but not knowing why.

The carriage arrived at the appointed hour. I was ushered into the room and left alone with the Duke.

'Take a seat, Powell,' he said.

I sat down.

He paused, then took a quick breath. When he spoke, it was a grave sound at the lower end of his register. 'Last year, over in Summer City, the Summer Duke was replaced. Did you hear of that?'

'It was reported,' I said, 'in the newspapers, Your Grace.'

'Yes. The Summer Duke developed a kind of illness. He no longer commanded the respect of others. It emerged that while in office he had committed certain acts that were illegal, and he was brought to justice for his crimes. It was all quite shocking.'

I tried to remain calm. I thought it best not to comment unless comment was requested.

'Those of us in positions of power, we have a certain responsibility to maintain order. Don't you agree? Events cannot be allowed to fall out of control. That would embarrass us all.'

'I agree,' I said, automatically without any conscious

thought. I could not do otherwise in the presence of a man whose spores were so dominant.

'I feel in a way that I am responsible for the situation you find yourself in. I encouraged you to take action. But to improve your prospects, not to cast them to the wind. Unfortunately you have chosen a very unwise path.' He picked up a piece of paper that was on his desk, then placed it back again. 'This café owner, Mr Bigbury, is in a very precarious position, though I daresay he is unaware of it.'

'I would like to assure you – '

The Duke held up a hand to silence me, and fixed me with an icy stare. 'Should things return to normal quickly, there will be no need for any action against *him*.'

'His business had declined of late, Your Grace,' I said. I don't know what I hoped to achieve by this.

'Should things not return to normal he shall have no business at all. Are we clear?'

'Yes, Your Grace.'

'I am being lenient with you, Powell,' he said. 'As a kindness to my niece, I am taking the view that your actions were unthinking and careless, and that you did not intend this . . .' He hesitated, then said, '*Perversion*.'

The force of his contempt struck me like a fist.

'I could easily take a different view,' he said. 'You can leave now. I hope for your sake I have no cause to speak to you again. Live a *quiet* life, Powell.'

A footman escorted me from the building. A carriage took me to the Café Soleil, rather than to Mr Jackson's studio. It seemed I was to waste no time in removing my mechanism.

Mr Bigbury had seen the carriage drop me off outside.

'Was that a state carriage?'

'It was,' I told him. 'There is something I have to discuss with you.'

'Can't you see I'm busy?'

'You need to make time for this,' I said. 'I'm taking the mechanism.'

His expression changed from impatience to confusion. 'What are you talking about?'

'Please, can we go somewhere and talk?'

He relented, gave some instructions to his staff and went with me to an upstairs room. I followed him up the stairs with a heavy heart, readying myself for another difficult discussion. With Knox I had been in charge. With the Autumn Duke I had been powerless. What was my relationship with Mr Bigbury? I realised I had not given this any thought till now.

Before we'd even sat down in the small sitting room he said, 'You can't have it.'

'It seems I've infringed someone else's copyright,' I said. 'The machine is illegal. I've been ordered to dismantle it.'

'Who has the copyright, then? I will deal with them instead of you.'

My heart fell, caught out immediately in a deception conceived in too much haste and told with too little conviction. He caught the crestfallen stench in my spores and his eyes narrowed.

'You're lying.'

I nodded, admitted it, and told him the truth at length. Slowly he came to accept that the machine would have to come down. In the course of this he seemed to age before my eyes, the spark of new life I had ignited in him cruelly snuffed out.

We sat in silence for a while, not knowing what more to say. At last he looked at me and shook his head sadly.

'We'll take the machine down after I close up for the day. If we try to do it with customers in we'll have a riot on our hands.'

I nodded.

'I'll take no money from you,' I said. 'Perhaps what you've made will tide you over for a while.'

'That's not necessary,' he said, 'we made a deal.'

But I insisted.

'If only we were warriors like Sholla,' he said.

'She defended her King,' I said, 'but I wonder if perhaps she had no more choice than us.'

I tried to go back to my former life. Weeks passed. I assembled clock mechanisms, and always in my head I imagined they would drive a play of light and shadow through mirrors and lenses. I took photographs and installed them within phenakistoscopes. How joyously the images danced before my eyes as I gazed through the slats as the drum turned.

Sometimes I would look up from my work and catch Ivy watching me. She would sigh and shake her head, and swear that she did not know what to do with me. I felt some kind of mistrust from her, or disappointment, which I could not understand.

I went back to the Café Soleil from time to time, and was relieved to see the business had not gone completely back to its former state of ruin. For now at least, many customers were continuing to visit there. I came to recognise a certain look in the eye of the people there, the scent of nostalgia lingering in their spores. They had found something wonderful for a time, and they would remember it always.

I thought often of Sholla, the warrior woman who defended her King. How I wished that she could have been free to follow her own destiny, to live a life of her own choosing.

One day I saw Eleanor again. She was on the opposite side of a busy square, almost masked by street stalls, but we saw each other and she came over to speak to me.

'Powell,' she said, 'it's been a while.'

'How are you?'

She sighed and glanced behind her. People were bustling around us and our voices could barely be heard with the rattle of barrows and cycles moving past. 'I don't have the same freedom I once did,' she said.

'What can I do?' I asked.

'Can you change the world for me?'

At the time, I didn't know how to answer. She smiled sadly, then said goodbye and vanished back into the crowd.

It struck me then that the danger had not passed. If I stayed in Autumn City I would always be watched, for years to come. I would have to live my life within the narrowest of margins or suffer the consequences.

That would be no way to live.

'I have to leave,' I said.

Ivy and I were alone in the workshop. I had already spoken to Mr Jackson.

She said, 'I think that will be for the best.'

There was suddenly a striking openness in the taste of her spores, like a flower opening up in the morning sun. I was quite taken aback by it, hadn't realised until that moment how very closed off she had been with me.

'This episode,' she said, 'has put many people in danger. Those of us who love theatre so very much.'

'Ivy?'

'Oh Powell, you really have been crashing around. Your research in the library was noticed, of course. Then asking questions down in the old Riverside district. Fortunately you never did track down anyone really important. If you had, I don't know what we would have done with you.'

'Done with me?'

She reached out a hand across the workbench and placed it tenderly on mine. 'I wish I could take you to a performance, let you see for yourself, but the risk is too great now. I could never be sure that we wouldn't be followed.'

I should have been shocked, but somehow I was not surprised by any of this, not at all. Spores may tell you that someone is being evasive, but they do not always tell you why. Now I knew.

'The best I can say to you, Powell, is that you were almost there, with what you did at the Café Soleil. If you really want to know what it is, what's so very special about theatre, you have the means to discover it for yourself.'

I smiled, and she did too.

She rose to her feet, withdrawing her hand from mine. 'But,' she said, 'you will be very wise to discover it somewhere far away from here.'

She pressed her hat into place, paused for a moment by the entrance. It was late and it looked dark outside.

When she had gone I sat alone for a while in the quiet stillness of the workshop, then locked up for the last time, posting my keys through the letterbox as I left.

The difficult part was figuring out how to travel lightly with the gear we needed. A quadricycle with a storage compartment at the back met our needs perfectly. It meant we had to follow well-worn routes, but that suited us. After all, we needed to come into contact with people.

We'd spend the morning setting up the tent, and putting up signs advertising our show. If we chose our spot well we could easily get a dozen customers, several times over each afternoon, enough to fill our small tent. We sold drinks too, at a little profit per bottle. We got by.

Knox really took to this kind of life. It came naturally and easily to him. He was hardly recognisable as the dishevelled, beaten down man I first met in a hovel in Autumn City.

'Roll up,' he called out. 'See something you've never seen before!'

I wound up the mechanism and let it go, casting light and shadow inside the tent. Over time we created new plates for the mechanism, some of them a little more political than others. Someday, perhaps, things could change. But for now we concentrated on putting on a good show. We got a real sense of satisfaction from that, and we always had happy customers.

We travelled far from Autumn City. A small show like this could go unnoticed, we hoped, so long as we kept moving and never stayed in one place too long. It's a very small kind of revolution, I know, but maybe that is the only way it can be done. Knox and Powell took each day as it came, and served no Duke or King.

V. H. LESLIE

THE CLOUD CARTOGRAPHER

THE PLAIN STRETCHED boundlessly into the distance, an uninterrupted path of white. Frontier land as untouched as virgin snow. The wind at this height blew unrestrained, buffeting the terrain, shaping it, creating a rolling appearance like the crests of waves ebbing and flowing against the horizon. It looked pure, solid from afar, but when up close, in the midst of it, you could see how insubstantial it was. Not even white but a medley of misty colours, grey or blue or pink. In a certain light, you could almost see the particles, the ground grainy underfoot as if you were seeing it drunk. If you looked at it too hard, at the hazy floor beneath your feet, your body would become conscious of the laws it defied and it was easy to imagine yourself plummeting back to earth. So you kept your eyes level with a point at the horizon and kept on walking.

Ahren had been cloudwalking for ninety days. He knew exactly as he recorded each day in his journal. It was more of a log really, containing details about the expedition so far, the terrain he'd covered and the distance he made each day, along with any meteorological data of significance. But he'd always conclude with a line or two of his personal musings, fragments of half-remembered poetry, his memories and regrets. In such a lonely land, his thoughts were his only company.

Ahren looked up. Above, cirrostratus clouds had appeared like floating cotton and he squinted into the halo they'd formed around the sun. He was happy for the reprieve; the last fortnight had been especially fine and the lack of cloud cover above had left him terribly exposed. But though he was thankful, he watched the sky cautiously for if the halo began to shrink, it would bring rain. And rain was the worst variable on this cloudface.

Ahren needed to get further inland, where the terrain was more solid. He pulled the compass from his pocket and watched as the needle settled. He wrote the coordinates in his journal and began the slight ascent west.

Ahren had always been fascinated with the contours of the sky. He wanted to go up, up where the air was cleaner and purer, up where you could see stars, a mere myth to the people below his feet: the sky forever obscured by smog and dense cloudscapes of pollutants. The clouds that floated above Ahren – cirrus, altostratus, cumulonimbus – were the only reminders of what had existed before, and he was one of only a few privileged enough to see them.

Ahren had never known a time before the cloudstraits. They hung low and heavy, enormous masses clinging to the world like parasites, brushing the tips of mountain ranges, obscuring the sun. They lingered like floating tectonic plates constantly settling into new positions, the atmosphere shifting just like the ground below it. For Ahren they were platforms above the earth, a delicate bridge over the world below. But it was a rope bridge at best. You had to know where to step.

Ahren carted his equipment on a small sledge. He didn't have much, just the essentials: his ration pack, a small portable stove, a first aid kit (including an oxy-pack and a couple of back up canisters) and a change of clothes. His outgear was state of the art, all-weather terrain, thermal lined, with the Company's name brandished across the front in illuminous lettering. Not that anyone could see it up here. It was his cartographical equipment that weighed the most though. Especially the density sensors and various mapping devices but they were crucial to his task. His task was relatively simple: he measured this undiscovered landscape and mapped it.

Ahren reached a reasonably safe spot and took some preliminary readings. When he was satisfied that the ground was stable, he sat down and opened his ration pack. Inside were a few protein bars and a selection of the Company's brand of liquefied meals. He selected one, opened, and drank without pleasure. There was a time when he studied the list of ingredients on each container in an attempt to determine what the pulp was, but the chemical names were always too obscure and despite whatever food it tried to resemble, it was always orange. Ahren pretended it was something else, some great feast, some culinary delight, and he would enter it later in his journal as pad thai or a cheeseburger and fries in the hope of wilfully deceiving his memory.

Often, if he was near the edge of a cloudface, he'd chuck the carton over when he was done. It somehow appeased a strange rebelliousness inside of him. If he wasn't near an edge, he sometimes chucked it anyway; the force of his throw could sometimes penetrate the surface of the cloud if it was a weak spot. Sometimes it could unsettle a whole cloudmass.

Ahren tried it now and it whistled through the air before thumping against the surface. He sighed and hauled himself to his feet to retrieve it. He wasn't going to litter the only unpolluted space on the planet. Below was different. Below was already messed up.

Ahren walked the rest of the day, only stopping when darkness began to descend. He took some more readings and pitched his tent, activating the synthetic cloudbase. He started the stove, warming his hands above it, and ate some more food from his ration pack.

It was very cold at night. Despite his thermal outgear and the stove, it was colder than anything Ahren had ever known. After his meagre meal, ham and eggs he decided, he retreated to his tent to record the day's activity.

Ahren was a creature of habit and he approached his task as mapmaker the same way every night. He began by entering all his data into the cartographical programme and watched as it constructed a topographical relief of the area he'd covered. Then, because he was slightly distrustful of technology, he unrolled a large sheet of paper and drew the map by hand. His drawing was much more topological, omitting many of the details of the computer projection in favour of aesthetics. This map was his backup, sketchily drawn like the ones leading to pirate treasure and included only the most significant features of the cloudmass – the valleys and peaks, the areas prone to flux and the places that were unstable. He always carried this on his person, folded into the inside pocket of his outgear. Then he'd write a brief summation of his day in his journal and pack his equipment away.

It wasn't all work. Before he slept, Ahren would pour himself a scotch, a fine mature malt he'd told the Company was a medicinal necessity. Then he'd crawl out of the tent, his insulated sleeping bag wrapped around him, and watch the spectacle above. He loved the stars. They illuminated the otherwise absolute black, as no artificial light from below could penetrate the cloudstraits, and Ahren thought he could feel their light shining on him. He was comforted, enjoying the exclusive proximity to the heavens. Sometimes he traced patterns in their constellations and at other times he just let his mind drift, meditating on the composition of the universe or remembering snatches of poetry he'd read so avidly as a child.

I know that I shall meet my fate somewhere among the clouds above. Before he became too drowsy he always retreated back inside his tent. He couldn't fall asleep outside where he could roll off in the night and plunge back down to earth. He had to stay grounded. So he finished the dregs of his whisky and went back inside.

'Do you think if there was a tree tall enough we could climb all the way to the clouds?' Lucy asked. They were perched in the highest branches of an old oak tree, looking up at the cloud-straits above.

'Like Jack and the Beanstalk?' Ahren replied, trying not to look down.

'Yeah.'

'You'd need some magic beans.'

'I've got some magic acorns.' Lucy dug deep into her pocket and withdrew a handful.

'They're not magic.'

'Yes they are. A fairy cast a spell on them.'

Ahren sighed. It was pointless arguing with her.

'One day you won't need magic to go to the clouds,' Ahren said with the certainty of a twelve year old boy, 'we'll all be able to go. And live up there, and build cities up there in the sky.'

Lucy smiled a partially toothless grin. 'I'd like to go up to the clouds.'

'Why?'

'To see what the angels see.'

Ahren woke with a start. He lay still until the disorientation subsided and remembered where he was. Most days began like this, as if not only his body but his mind gravitated towards the world below. He unzipped the tent and stepped out into the clouds and began the day as any other – with a carton of Company-endorsed baby food (that he pretended were eggs and bacon) and a strong coffee. Imitation or not, he savoured his caffeine fix and packed up his belongings with no great speed. The cirrostratus clouds from the day before had grown in size and darkened in colour. If it was going to rain, it was better that he was here, in the middle of a fairly stable cloudmass, than walking on unpredictable terrain.

The problem with rain was that it rendered all terrain unpredictable. The cloudslide at the start of his journey had taught him that. He'd thought his position pretty secure – the readings were mostly stable – when the cloudmass below gave way and Ahren found himself running on a surface that seemed to collapse with every footfall. The Company had to send him more equipment to compensate for the kit that he lost to gravity.

Ahren called them aerial avalanches and they happened fairly frequently. Mostly near the edge of a cloudface but sometimes in the middle as precipitation and air pressures collided or mingled. Sometimes these air parcels became gaps or holes and often once they'd formed they released pressure, making the surface more stable. It was the forming of them that was precarious, marked by a distant rumble and the sudden appearance of a vacuum, sucking the ground out from under you. But much of the terrain was fairly solid, and after three months of cloudwalking, Ahren knew which straits were safe. That was what he was paid to discover. But there was always a level of unpredictability up here; it was what had attracted him to the job in the first place.

Ahren wasn't planning to go very far today with such ominous clouds nearby. He unrolled the map of the clouds he'd drawn and studied it for patterns. He saw the strait that he might recommend to the developers. With the world below crumbling, the Company could charge a fortune up here for unspoilt, virgin land. But Ahren wanted to be sure before he made any proposals; the clouds were in constant flux and he had to understand more about their extraordinary nature. Besides, he wasn't ready to share this land with anyone else yet. Or worse, to go back below.

When Ahren was a boy he had an atlas which he studied everyday. He'd make his sister Lucy test his knowledge of it, deriving boundless pleasure in accurately pointing out the source of the Nile or the location of Everest. Sometimes he asked Lucy questions, assuming that she'd assimilated some understanding of the world during these hours of play, but her responses were always a disappointment. He'd ask her easier questions but she found them just as hard. Lucy couldn't imagine the world like Ahren. She couldn't see it in a map. She tried but she found the visualising of it difficult. She understood what surrounded her, she could read the individual components – the trees, the warrens, the pond – but she couldn't see the bigger picture.

'If you ever get lost,' Ahren had told her, 'just climb up high and look down. Then you can see the way home.'

Lucy had liked that answer and she'd begun to scale the nearby oaks. She knew the treetops like Ahren knew the ground. Ahren waited at the bottom, reading a collection of poetry from his father's study. He was clumsy in the trees and not too fond of heights.

Ahren and Lucy were fortunate to grow up knowing the natural world. Their father owned a vast quantity of woodland, an area coveted by developers and businessmen eager to accommodate ever-expanding population demands. It was only when Ahren and his father moved to the city and into one of a hundred tower-blocks that he realised just how rare and fortunate a childhood it was. The city towers attained impossible heights, people stacked on top of one another as in some delicate card trick. It was a forest of concrete stretching up, up, up, brushing the cloudmass above.

Their father was a rarity too, though Ahren hadn't known it at the time. He was a landowner and would have rather died than give up that right. His forest was Lucy's and Ahren's playground. They had no idea how much others wanted it.

'Who's that?' Lucy called from her position in the boughs, pointing. But by the time Ahren had climbed up, whoever she'd seen was gone.

Ahren was walking again. He had a lot of ground to cover due to the delay of the previous day. In the end the cirrostratus clouds had dispersed after little more than a light drizzle and Ahren was reminded again of how powerless he was against the capriciousness of the sky.

He hadn't slept well. He had dreamt of Lucy again and woke up thrashing and flailing in his sleeping bag. When his breathing calmed, he thought he could discern a rustle outside his tent. He'd listened hard, surprised when he'd heard the sound again. Footsteps. The whispered hush of footsteps. Someone was circling his tent, he was sure of it. He grabbed his torch, fumbling for the switch. The inside of the tent was suddenly illuminated and he waited a moment, hoping that the light would scare whatever it was away. Then he stumbled to his feet and hesitantly unzipped the tent opening.

There was nothing there, of course. Absurd to think there would be. He must have imagined it, he told himself. Some sort of dream haze leftover.

But it had felt so real.

Ahren shined the torch over the cloudface a few times more before returning inside. The plains were empty. He was alone.

Walking now, he was annoyed that not only did he have to make up a day but that he had to do it on only a few hours sleep. It could have been an animal scavenging about, maybe.

It was rare for them to be up this high but he'd sighted the occasional bird; sometimes they'd burst through weaker spots in the clouds beneath him. He was always impressed by their conviction, flying into a cloudmass at such speed with no certainty that the cloud was weak enough for them to pass through. It was either an incredible act of faith, or some suicidal impulse. Perhaps they could just read the clouds better than he could. Another time, Ahren had spotted a mountain fox on the edge of a cloudface, forced higher and higher in its search for food. They'd eyed each other for a moment before the fox disappeared into the cloudfog.

But the prowling around his tent hadn't sounded like an animal. It sounded more like human footsteps. Besides he thought he heard the soft ringing of a bell.

Irritable and tired, Ahren eventually settled down for the evening, pitching his tent perfunctorily. He was ravenous, but hungry for real food. The daily exertion and brutal temperatures cultivated an appetite that the contents of the ration pack were just not fit to satisfy. He wanted some meat, something with flavour and texture.

He was being punished, he thought, suffering the tasteless contents of another carton. This was his purgatory.

As if in confirmation, he heard a gentle ringing, far off in the distance.

Ahren paused mid mouthful, straining to hear the sound again. Was his mind playing tricks? Yet there it was again. A ringing, almost too low to hear, but it was there. He was sure of it. He listened hard and squinted into the distance. Was it possible something else occupied the clouds with him?

He put his food aside. 'Hello?' Months of silence had rendered his voice hoarse and alien. He cleared his throat. 'Is anyone there?' He felt instantly foolish. How could anyone be up here? This was frontier land, undiscovered territory. There was more probability that he'd encounter Gabriel and a host of angels, and for an atheist that was something.

He had to be the only one.

Ahren resumed eating, pausing occasionally to listen. Nothing.

He withdrew into the tent, taking one last tentative look around. If he were being tracked, he'd have no way of knowing: there are no footprints in the clouds.

Ahren woke to the sound of rain. Inside his tent it always sounded much louder like horses galloping, but despite its volume it still possessed a strange soothing lullaby quality. The rain always took him back to Lucy. Of endless play days inside when the weather was too wild to go out. Lucy would watch her breath cloud the glass, tracing the journey of wayward raindrops on the windowpane, while Ahren spun his globe faster and faster until he thought it would spin off its axis.

He wondered what she would make of this strange landscape, a world without words. Ahren tried not to adapt the language of below, te*rrain, landscape, plain*. This new world demanded its own vocabulary, a more elevated language, and Ahren recorded his own coinages in the back of his journal. Perhaps, when the clouds were civilised, his words would define this new world.

When the rain subsided, Ahren spread the equipment over the sledge in the hope that it would dry. The ground was wet with the rain that would now descend on the people below, this time carrying the pollutants and poisons of the cloud-straits with it. The wind had not relented, whipping the cloud-face into rolling vaporous peaks. Visibility was poor. He'd have to take it slow if he decided to trek today.

Ahren wrapped his scarf around his face and pressed on. He preferred to be on the move. It felt like progress, though he knew in these conditions he could easily get turned around or lost in a cloudmist. He checked his compass often, preferring it to his more technical software. It felt like a more honest way to navigate the clouds. Ahren followed the quivering needle, aware that he was heading in the direction of the sound of bells he'd heard the previous night.

Ahren kept his head down, concentrating on the cloudsurface and compass. Cloud vapour streamed past him, wrapping him up in a blanket of white. He would have probably walked past it had he not lifted his head at that particular moment, thinking he heard the bells.

A line of prayer flags stretched into the distance, suspended on a length of rope that led into the cloudmist. The colours were so bright they hurt Ahren's eyes. Ahren had seen them before on his way up to the clouds. They were comprised of five colours: blue, white, red, green and yellow. Each colour represented a different element and the order was important. He knew it started with the sky (blue) and ended with the earth (yellow) but he couldn't quite remember the significance of the colours in between, except for white. He knew what that stood for. The white flags were only discernible in the cloudmist because of the printed image on their surface, otherwise they would have disappeared into what they revered – the clouds.

The closest one to him was yellow and blown by the wind it looked like diamond or like the crude stars Lucy made out of tissue paper and glitter. As a whole they looked like a strange rainbow, stretching across the clouds like an absurd paper chain.

Ahren had never seen prayer flags in the clouds, though he'd seen many on his way up. They populated the mountains as abundantly as the people. Ahren hadn't expected so many people on this particular massif, though he knew that all the mountain ranges were prone to overpopulation – being the only pockets of affordable land left. It was his father's fault for telling him legends about the unspoilt mountains here. He'd read him and Lucy tales of Shangri-La. Tales of a mythical place, an impossible place hidden somewhere in the Himalayas. Ahren had imagined it nestled among snow-capped mountains, a beautiful lamasery amid a desert of ice and emptiness. An earthly paradise.

As a boy Ahren had tried to find it on his map and now that he was older he'd trekked the plains seeking it, before he finally came up here to the clouds.

Ahren had seen first-hand how densely populated the mountains were now, sprawling cities replacing green plateaus and paddy fields, tower-blocks upon tower-blocks stacked precariously on cliff faces, not like the images in his father's books.

Ahren was resigned to the fact that the landscape of Shangri-La existed only in his imagination. If it had ever existed at all there was no room for it now.

Ahren looked with dismay at the flags flapping above him in the wind and wondered whether he should take them down. They were not a welcome sight, despite their intentions of good will. Prayer flags were not offered to any higher being, they were a prayer to land. They were here to bless the cloudstraits.

And that could only mean that Ahren was not alone.

That evening was damp. The mist hadn't completely dispersed and it lingered in the air like guilt. Ahren warmed his hands by the stove, conscious that the light was a beacon for whatever or whoever stalked him. Clouds above obscured the stars. He scanned the cloudsurface, staring into the darkness. He wasn't afraid of the dark but the unknown was a different matter. Terra incognita. Unknown land. Terror incognito.

He thought of how cartographers of the past had drawn maps to the edge of the world, a flat earth, before philosophers and astronomers said it was round. Then, if you sailed too far you would fall off the edge and into Hades or Hell or whatever underworld you subscribed to.

They'd said mapping the clouds would be impossible, but here Ahren was, sitting at the top of the world, the vast unknown stretched before him. He'd been in uncharted territory before, but armed with the tools of his trade he didn't need to fear it. But how could he possibly know what the clouds contained? For all he knew monsters could be lurking in the cloudfog.

Ahren stared into the light of the stove. It was far better to draw out whatever it was and face it, than let the unknown haunt him.

Ahren was pitched beneath the prayer flags. He'd thought about tearing them down, of getting rid of all signs that someone had been here first, but he was reluctant to pull out the pole they were connected to. It disappeared deep beneath the cloud surface. It was the fact it could possibly upset a cloudmass, he told himself, rather than his fear of disturbing some kind of spiritual balance.

Ahren tried to stay vigilant but the prayer flags soothed him. They flapped rhythmically in the wind, lulling him to sleep, spreading their blessings like a blanket around his shoulders. Ahren stared at the colours. Each of the flags were decorated with images of different sacred animals but the one that he was drawn to most was the horse. A wind horse: *lung ta.*

Lucy liked horses. Lots of little girls did. He imagined her now – how old would she be? – and the image his mind conjured was a grown woman with flowing charcoal hair. She was riding a wind horse through the clouds, dipping in and out of the swelling peaks, racing along the cloudstraits towards the sky with its stars shining like tiny diamonds. He could almost see her face, her eyes narrowed in concentration as she guided the horse toward a burgeoning cloudmass, so sure she could penetrate the surface of the cloud just like the birds. A rallying cry, the sound of hooves, the jingling of bells, and then she was bursting through, breaking against the cloudface like an enormous wave, an explosion of particles, foaming and frothing, filling the air with billowing clouddust as insubstantial as breath.

Ahren woke to a blurred world. He lay against the entrance of the tent in his outgear, the sleeping bag a nest underneath him. He was annoyed at himself; it was dangerous to fall asleep outside.

Snow was drifting from the underbelly of the clouds above. The suffocating grey – blue colour of cold. Ahren moved, his body stinging with pins and needles.

Something darted up ahead.

Ahren paused, unsure if he'd seen anything. His mind was fuzzy like the landscape as he waited for the cloudmist to pass. He strained his eyes.

There was nothing there.

Though he desperately wanted a coffee, he decided to forgo breakfast and began packing up. He'd tarried here under the auspicious prayer flags long enough. Maybe it had been a mistake to stay here at all.

Again, a darting motion up ahead drew Ahren's attention. He shone his torch into the white haze, hoping it would penetrate the mist. He caught something running between the clouds.

He stood on weak legs, edging forwards but pushed back by the wind.

'Lucy?'

He waited a long time for a response but none came. When the cloudfog began to disperse he moved hastily on.

Ahren wished he were still dreaming when he discovered the

body. He'd been alerted to it by a host of carrion birds, Himalayan vultures with white necks and tawny feathers making the cloudsurface ahead look dirty. They clung to their feast like a moving mantle, relinquishing their meal only when Ahren deliberately chased them away. Even then they took to the air lazily, unperturbed, and Ahren could still sense them above, circling him and the girl.

It was definitely a girl. Ahren could tell that much. A young woman, actually, by her size and shape. He stared down at the body; it was repellent to see so much of what made up a person but still he stared. The flesh of the face was entirely gone, as were the skin on the torso and the tops of the legs. What was left resembled the crude carvings of an unskilled butcher. Red and wet with glimpses of white bone gleaming beneath muscle and sinew.

'Jesus,' Ahren said to the wind.

Around the hollow of her face was a mass of dark bloodied hair, blown into a halo by the wind.

Ahren put a hand to his forehead. How had she gotten up here? Perhaps she'd put up the prayer flags. If so, it hadn't proven lucky for her. He couldn't see any traces of clothing. She wouldn't have been wearing outgear, that stuff was pretty costly. He touched the material he wore for reassurance and cast a glimpse up at the vultures above. Had she been stripped and left here?

Ahren didn't know what to do. It wasn't right for a body to be destroyed by scavengers. It needed a burial. But there were limitations in the clouds. He couldn't bury her up here. He thought about dragging her to the edge of a cloudmass and pushing her over the edge. But he didn't like the thought of her body hurtling toward earth, landing more broken than it was now, and who knew where she would end up? Yet while the body remained here it would only pollute the clouds. It would draw scavengers, and eventually maybe people, with questions. He wished she would just disappear.

The birds circling above waited for him to make a decision. They watched him move on before swooping down to resume their feast. There was nothing Ahren could do. He hoped the birds were swift about it.

I wandered lonely as a cloud.

Ahren walked the rest of the day in no discernable direction. His footsteps were not buoyed by the clouds as usual, but heavy and concrete. He couldn't get the image of the women from his mind. He wondered who she was. Her identity along with her flesh, were being picked clean by the vultures.

But more depressing was the fact the clouds didn't belong to just him anymore. Someone else had been here first. And though he had not known of her existence until that afternoon, the notion that he'd been alone all those months was a myth.

He should have been glad perhaps, had he ever really wanted to be alone?

In response he heard the tintinnabulation of bells.

And in the distance he saw a girl.

It had been a long time since he'd seen a child, a *real* child, not just the one that inhabited his dreams. It had been a long time since he'd seen *anyone* for that matter, besides the corpse a few miles back. Ahren sighed. When had the clouds become so populated?

He hoped she was a hallucination; that he had conjured a strange mirage out of cloudmist, but then the girl addressed him.

'What are you doing up here?'

Ahren was somewhat taken aback. He wanted to ask the same question but worried it would sound childish.

'Lucy?' he asked instead. The girl moved closer, out of the blur and shook her head.

'Are you the one whose been following me?'

She nodded.

'Why?'

'To see if you were real.'

Ahren looked down at himself, half expecting his body to be grainy and blurred, made of the same transient substance as the clouds. He looked real enough.

'Are you satisfied?'

The girl nodded again, retreating back into the fog.

'Wait!' Ahren called, 'Wait!'

He followed the ringing of bells, chasing behind like he was playing hide and seek. Except the girl was too swift and light-footed in the clouds. She disappeared ghost-like, only to reappear a few moments later with a smile and a wave of encouragement. She seemed to want Ahren to follow, though he had no idea where they were going. She was his only guide.

He considered turning around and finding his way back through the cloudmist to his equipment but this was the first person he'd seen on the clouds, apart from the dead young woman. Perhaps they were related? Still it had been impulsive and potentially dangerous abandoning all of his stuff and running after her. Maybe he'd been up on this cloudface too long. Maybe the altitude was affecting his sanity.

Out of the cloudmist came the façade of some kind of construction.

'What the . . .'

It was a cabin. It was comprised entirely of wood and had an aged look as if it had been there for a long time, though Ahren knew that was impossible. It appeared to be built on the clouds though Ahren couldn't see a cloudbase. Above the rafters hung the limp bodies of rabbits. A rocking chair on the porch was covered in the hide of some animal.

Suddenly the little girl was in front of him again. Closer

than before. Ahren noticed she was wearing a fur coat with toggles at the front, a woollen hat on her head.

'Do you wanna come inside?'

What kind of strange fantasy world had he stumbled into? Ahren could see a wind turbine attached to the roof. It appeared to be a perfectly self-sufficient homestead and infinitely more comfortably than his tent. He stood dumbfounded.

The girl shrugged and went inside. Now that she had led him here she seemed disinterested in him. Ahren wondered why she had brought him. More alarmingly, Ahren wondered if she was alone, like him. He couldn't bear the idea of a child alone in such an unremitting land. He climbed the steps and opened the door.

A cloud emerged. Ahren took it to be cloud vapour at first until he smelt tobacco. It was an aroma Ahren hadn't smelt for a long time. It surrounded a man drawing on a pipe. The lips that held it were entirely obscured by a heavy, yellowing white moustache. He had a long fur coat like the girl's. Ahren had the impression of some colonel from some long ago war.

The man stepped out of the smoke. He didn't say a word. Ahren was not one for words either, having exhausted them in his conversation with the girl. They stared at each other for a long time, both painfully sorry at discovering the other's existence. Their fantasy of isolation shattered.

'You'd better make yourself at home,' the man said at last.

Ahren followed him into a warm interior. The smell of stew, mingled with tobacco suffused the room, which was aglow with candles. It was a basic room, though comfortably furnished. In the corner a bird sat on its perch. A bird of prey, maybe a falcon or a kite, though Ahren wasn't sure. It was tethered and hooded, though it hopped in agitation sensing an intruder. A bell tied around its leg rang with its every movement.

'I see you're a Company man.' The man pointed at the branding across Ahren's outgear.

'I'm a cartographer. I work for whoever pays.'

The man nodded and gestured towards the stove. Ahren sat down, removing his gloves and holding his hands to the flames.

'Been up here long?' Ahren asked.

'Since last November.'

'Last November? But what about the cloudslide?'

'We were lucky. It passed us by.'

Ahren made some calculations and began altering the contours of the map in his mind.

'If you don't mind me saying,' the man began, pulling up a chair, 'these clouds can't be mapped.'

Ahren remembered all the people below who'd said the same thing. Only the Company believed it could be done. When you had enough money you were allowed to believe anything.

'Nearly mapped this entire cloudstrait,' Ahren said, feeling a pride he hadn't felt in a long time.

'Not what I meant. It can be done, I'm sure. You're proof of that. But doesn't mean that it should.' The man drew heavily on his pipe. 'Too much change. Clouds don't want it.'

How did this man know what the clouds wanted? Ahren remembered the prayer flags, the way they blessed the land. Were they to appease the clouds?

'Can't have too many folk coming up here,' he continued. 'Only room for a few. Best that this land stays undiscovered, if you ask me.'

Ahren could understand why he wouldn't want to share this world with anyone else. Ahren didn't want to share it either. Maps brought developers, and developers meant people.

'I'm just doing my job.'

'I'm sure you are.'

Ahren sized up the man. Would this be something he thought worth fighting over? He was conscious of the map folded into the pocket of his outgear, close to his chest. He regretted leaving his equipment, anything he could use as a weapon. No-one knew he was here.

'Do you wanna see my pictures?' the girl said. She thrust a series of crayon drawings under Ahren's nose. Pictures of constellations, the stars connected like dot to dots.

The man pulled her back protectively, though she still held her arm out at Ahren.

Ahren took the pictures. They were drawn well, though not to scale.

'These are really good.'

The girl beamed.

'Sally, the man's going to be on his way.'

Ahren returned the pictures.

'I have more if you wanna look?'

Ahren looked towards the man and back at the girl.

'Sure.'

The little girl grabbed Ahren's hand and led him to the other side of the room. Dozens of pictures crammed the walls, the constellations forming elaborate patterns.

'Don't you ever look down?' he asked

Sally shook her head. 'Never.'

Ahren tried to remember how long it had been since he had looked. It was always accompanied by an overwhelming feeling of vertigo. He felt it now. Here in this room, with these strange people, his eyes full of stars, he felt as if he were plummeting back down to earth.

'I draw pictures too,' Ahren said at last.

'Will you draw me one?' Sally asked. Ahren remembered the map he'd drawn for Lucy. Nothing good had come of his drawings.

'Maybe.'

Sally smiled and Ahren was reminded of how long it had been since he'd felt the warmth of another's company.'

'Sally, time for bed,' said the man.

Sally looked disappointed that her time with a stranger was at an end, but she conceded.

'You can keep this one,' she said, handing Ahren's one of her drawings before withdrawing to her bedroom.

The man poured Ahren a measure of whisky and busied himself at the stove. He dished up a bowlful of stew for Ahren. It smelt incredible. Ahren took the bowl gratefully, trying to dismiss images of carrion birds devouring the woman's corpse.

'How'd you come to be up here?' he asked between mouthfuls.

'Some folks need a little more space.'

Ahren looked at the man again. It was likely he was a fugitive. Ahren wished again that he had some kind of weapon on him.

'How do you survive?'

'We have our own means,' the man said, pointing toward the bird. It appeared asleep now, clutching its perch with strong talons. It was easily capable of hunting rabbits, maybe even bigger prey.

'And I have my nets.'

'Nets?'

'Cast 'em over and see what I can catch.'

Ahren couldn't help but be impressed with the ingenuity. They'd made a homestead in the most inhospitable place on earth. But it was built on insecure foundations; Ahren had done the calculations, the cloudslide could have unsettled more than they knew. But Ahren sensed that this man would rather be swept away into oblivion for a few good years in peace, than go back down below.

'Where's Sally mother?' Ahren asked, tipping the bowl and fishing the dregs.

The man tapped his pipe against the table. He looked right

at Ahren. 'The only reason I've been hospitable,' he said, 'is because of that little girl. If it were up to me I'd have thrown you off the edge of this cloudface to see if you'd fly. I don't like Company men, and I'm sure as hell not going to share everything personal with a stranger.'

Ahren found he couldn't make eye contact. 'I found a body a few miles back. A young woman, from what I can tell.'

'What are you implying?'

'How did she die?'

The man shrugged. 'We all die.'

'If a crime's been committed the authorities need to know.'

'We're not on earth now, Company man. The law doesn't apply in the clouds. There's only one authority here. '

Ahren shifted uncomfortably. It sounded like a threat. 'I thought I was alone up here,' he said.

'We ain't never alone.'

'There's more?'

He nodded.

Ahren's head hurt. The cabin felt too warm, too crowded, almost suffocating.

'Well thank you for your kindness,' he said, standing. 'I'll be on my way now.'

The man nodded. He seemed relieved.

'Say thank you to Sally,' Ahren gestured with the picture in his hand.

He walked out into the night, the sky decorated with real stars. The man stood in the doorway within a cloud of his own making.

'Sky burial,' the man said.

'What?'

'It's how we dispose of the dead. Give them to the sky.'

'You knew her, didn't you?' Ahren pressed.

'There'll be nothing left in a few days,' the man said, retreating inside. 'She'll be part of the clouds then.'

Ahren's father wasn't a particularly religious man, yet in his study, above the bookcase filled with Ahren's favourites poets – Yeats, Wordsworth, Dickinson – hung a huge map of the Garden of Eden. It didn't just depict the Garden of Eden but many other significant biblical locations as well: Mount Ararat, the resting place of Noah's Ark, the kingdom of the Queen of Sheba. Ahren had memorised the outline, drawn to the Tower of Babel, reaching higher and higher to the heavens. The architects then had not been driven by the need for space, but for the desire to touch the divine. At the time, Ahren couldn't understand it, though he marvelled at the enterprise.

Ahren had thought it was ridiculous to map a myth, yet here he was in the clouds. It was the only place Lucy could be. He recalled the prayer flags flapping in the wind and his own prayers scattered amongst the clouds. This was the only place left for him to find salvation.

The last time he had seen Lucy was the day of her eighth birthday. He should have known that she wouldn't find the treasure he'd hidden, though he'd drawn a map. The map that led her into the woods and away from the house. She didn't like maps but she was a willing playmate and wanted to please her brother. Ahren had waited at the trail's conclusion – land's end, with the locket he'd bought for her wrapped in a box with a blue ribbon. He waited until the sunlight was gone and returned home to the flashing lights of a parked police car.

They searched the woodland but could find no trace of her. Ahren told them they were looking in the wrong place. They needed to look up.

Ahren's father had sworn never to sell but after Lucy's disappearance, the land had become abhorrent to him, polluted in the way the cities were not. A reminder of innocence stolen – paradise lost.

It was what the developers had wanted all along.

Ahren was lost. He knew on this cloudface, without his equipment, that was tantamount to death. He'd tried following his hand-drawn map but the cloudmist was too thick. He needed to find shelter. He considered making his way back to the cabin, throwing himself at the old man's mercy but then he remembered what he'd told Lucy. If you ever get lost climb up and look down, then you can see the way home.

Ahren made his way to the edge of a cloudmass and lay face down. He tried to peer through the cloud, pressing his face into it. He couldn't see much of the world below, only what the starlight permitted. He remembered all the trees he'd climbed after Lucy's disappearance, despite his aversion for heights. He remembered the one where he'd found a torn piece of her white blouse. She'd tried to climb up and away as well. He'd always thought if he just climbed high enough he'd be able to see her. He'd moved into the highest tower-blocks, scaled mountains and finally arrived here at the top of the world, but the view below was always a disappointment.

Lucy was gone.

He pictured the prayer flags, the white one representing the clouds, ready to wave it in surrender. He stared down at the emptiness below, feeling gravity's pull. He was at land's end, the edge of the world. His underworld was waiting to greet him. He could easily step off the map.

Instead he pulled out the map from inside his outgear. He unfolded it to look at the white expanse he had covered. This was what other's sought, a blueprint of the unknown. It would be worth a lot to the Company, and to others. It wouldn't be virgin land then, it would be crowded with people and tower-blocks.

The wind played with the paper, curling its edges. Ahren gripped it tighter.

Done with the Compass-
Done with the Chart

He ripped the map along its latitudinal and longitudinal lines. He scattered the pieces into the wind, an offering to the clouds to be blown like prayers above the heads of men.

He lay on his back and unfolded Sally's drawing. It was a mirror image of the constellations above. He traced the lines between the stars, imagining them connected by an enormously long string that spanned the galaxy like the contours on a map. It would take light years to follow the threads, to navigate his way through the cosmos. He could follow the stars as old explorers used to. Maybe the stars would lead him to her.

Above, a single star burst across the sky, shining beautifully bright as it expired. She was up there somewhere, Ahren knew, and once he found her he would finally have a place to rest.

In the distance he heard the sound of hooves and the whinnying of a horse, floating among the clouds.

SARAH BROOKS

TRANS-SIBERIA: AN ACCOUNT OF A JOURNEY

with Added Notes from
The Cautious Traveller's Guide to Greater Siberia
(by L. Girard, Mauriac Publishing, Paris, 1859)

THE SOLE MEANS of passage across the Greater Siberian wastes is by train, for those who can afford the ticket, and the risk.

I left Beijing at seventeen, carrying a box of pencils and a suitcase held together with rope. At the station families sobbed and embraced. I tried not to look. Nor did I let my eyes widen at the size of the train, its wheels as tall as a man's shoulder, the iron bars over the windows as thick as my arm. The green paint was faded, but the gold lettering on the carriages still stood out: Beijing to Moscow.

My breath caught in my chest.

Armed guards checked my Chinese papers and the letter of invitation from the Paris Conservatoire des Arts. I was handed waiver forms by representatives of the Trans-Siberia Company, releasing them from any responsibility for my safety and any guarantee of our eventual arrival in Moscow. I kept my expression blank because I was a man now and I could not be afraid.

But my hand shook as I affixed the seal bearing my name. Red ink smeared the paper.

The great train of the Trans-Siberia Company (est. 1800) crosses the border wall two hundred miles from Beijing. It is three thousand miles to Moscow. The journey takes seven days.

The greater part of the train was the so-called cattle-sheds, carriages partitioned by a dozen thin walls, three bunks clinging to either side. I squeezed onto my top bunk, so close to the carriage roof that I was able to sit only if I hunched my shoulders and lowered my head, for all that I was small and slight. But up there, at least, I was away from all the nervous voices, raised as if to ward off gathering fears.

On the bunks below were loud, quick young men from the south, with sunburnt skin. They splashed sweet-smelling liquor into chipped glasses and rummaged in their bags to produce parcels of nuts, dried fruit, packs of cards. One took out a crumpled photograph and smoothed it on his knee, propping it up against the window, and the others whistled and shouted such things as the aunties at the orphanage would have had the skin off my buttocks for even thinking.

I peered down, to see a grainy picture of a woman, her silk *qipao* slit up to her thigh, her lips full and dark in her pale face. She stared right up at me. I looked away.

'To keep us company through the long nights, my friends!' They laughed and crashed their glasses together.

One glanced up at me. 'She doesn't bite, countryman. Come and join us in a drink to her fine health!'

I muttered my excuses and curled back into my bunk.

'Maybe not to his taste,' came the whisper from below, and a wave of raucous laughter.

A familiar, empty feeling sat heavy in my gut. I will climb down, I told myself. I will pour their liquor down my throat, roar out meaningless, terrible words like a man should do, take up their picture and hold it to my lips. I will not be afraid. Here, on this train, I will make myself new, make myself into a man. Climb down, I said.

I didn't climb down. I lay on my stomach and stared out between the bars of the window as the low, ornate buildings of Beijing gave way to the farmsteads of the borderlands. The train travelled slowly. Slowly enough to see the farmers' faces as they straightened up from their work to watch us pass. Some of them took off their hats.

In Greater Siberia it is believed that the shadows have faces. In the deep forests yellow eyes watch the train.

We crossed the border at night. The carriage slept at last, rattling and snoring along the shuddering rails but I lay wide awake, watching the window for the last lights to blink out. A final settlement, then the lights of the border wall, then nothing at all but the empty lands.

When I closed my eyes there were things in the darkness. Things just outside the window. Things formed out of rumours and half-heard stories. Whispering, creeping things. They crowded closer until I swore I could hear their long fingers at the glass.

I woke, shaking. No sleep for me. Instead, I crept from the cabin and made my way to the dining car with my sketch book. Paper and pencils. Safety in shadows and lines.

But my hopes for solitude were shattered. Every lamp in the dining car burned, every table crowded with travellers, with laughter and music and sweat.

I squeezed myself into the nearest seat. I was good at being small, good at passing unnoticed. Taking out my book, I tried to calm my breathing, to banish the movement and noise and lose myself in the familiar hush that seeing – really seeing – always brought; a gemstone earring as it brushed against a neck, the puckering of skin around a scar, the dark strands of a braid of hair. How the lights caught the gold embroidery on women's dresses, how they lit their reds and purples from within and there in the dark glass of the windows we were all doubled, both within the train and without.

A woman in blue caught my eye. I traced the curve of her neck, the curl of her dark hair. The blue stones around her neck were deep and watery, her skin untouched by rouge. All around her men snatched greedy, stolen glimpses, but no-one approached her. She was more alone than anyone here. I bent my head closer to the page.

A voice in my ear. 'Do we scare you so much?'

My pencil skittered, drawing a line across her cheeks. I looked up into dark blue eyes and I was lost for words, as always, though the aunties beat me and told me *Speak, boy, or are you as foolish as you look?*

She gestured to the page. 'Faces, trinkets, hair. We are more than this, you know.'

Her tone was serious but her eyes merry. She spoke in French, the common tongue of Europe, still unfamiliar on my own tongue, though I had spent many hours over my books. So many words needed, to say so little. I felt the flush deepening on my face.

'I . . . I am a student, only,' I manage. I could not hold her eye but looked down at my paper and twisted my pencil around and around in my fingers, waiting for her to leave.

She didn't leave. She down sat beside me, her elbows on the table, her chin in her hands, and watched me as I began to draw again. She was so close that her hair brushed against my cheek.

'They are beautiful,' she said, 'your sketches.'

I told her, slowly, haltingly, that I would go to study in Paris on a scholarship. I told her that I was lucky, luckier than I could ever have imagined.

'Orphans need to be lucky,' she said. 'They have to make their own luck.'

When I looked up, quickly, she laughed at my expression.

'You can tell,' she said. 'You can tell the ones who travel lightly.'

Orphans have to make their own luck. They have to find their own places. I have always remembered this.

'My name is Elena,' she said.

'I am no-one', I said. 'My family name is Wu, which means 'nothing', and is what all the orphans are called. My given name is Gulou, which means Drum Tower, and is where I was found, before the aunties took me in.'

She looked at me for so long that my skin began to feel tight and funny. Then she smiled, a great big smile, and said, 'Well that is a name to be proud of.'

And I think, for the first time, I was.

I drew. She watched. The train hurtled through the darkness and I forgot all about the things outside.

Some travellers say that the cost of the train is much higher than simply the ticket. They say that there is another price, unique to every traveller.

I slept until the morning was almost over and when I opened my eyes she was my first thought. Elena. Her name was Elena. She thought my sketches were beautiful.

The landscape had moved in closer during the night. Outside the window trees clustered so near that they brushed the glass, and greenish underwater light filtered into the train.

I watched for her all day, half hopeful, half scared, not letting myself look at last night's work, afraid that I would not have captured her as I hoped, that under my pencils she would have faded to a poor shadow of what she was. Instead, I sat in the dining car and ate food I couldn't pronounce, found the observation carriage, all glass and iron bars, where there were ladies in silks and men who talked too loudly. And I looked up at every rustle of skirts and every whispery, sibilant murmur of French.

Once, a thump came from the roof above, and to cries from my fellow passengers I looked up to see through the bars an orange eye amidst feathers and scales, great claws and wings spread wide. A lady beside me swooned, carefully.

But I forgot to be scared. I forgot because all I could think was how beautiful those wings were, pale purple and laced with red veins. How beautiful horror could be.

That night before I slept I turned at last to my book. To Elena and her voice in my head saying, 'You have nothing to be afraid of.'

Yet as my eye fell upon the pages, I could not stop myself from crying out. The book dropped from my hands.

Impossible. Impossible. Perhaps I was more tired than I knew. Perhaps the journey had played on my nerves. Shaking, I picked it up again. I blinked, but the pictures remained. Not the face I remembered but something else entirely. A strange, clawed, twisted thing with dark, inhuman eyes.

I slammed the book shut. When I slept, it was to troubled dreams.

In this region grows an interesting genus of fir tree, identifiable by its red-tipped needles and sap. The tree is said to appear to be bleeding. The remains of human settlements can also still be seen, long deserted.

The aunties told us the world is unkind. They told us to rely on ourselves alone. They said that this would make us strong, that fear was for children.

When I was afraid, I took out my pencils. I drew things to show they couldn't hurt me. I drew the older boys as they slept because in sleep they were gentle. And the aunties, as we studied they would let their faces fall slack, when they thought we weren't looking. They would turn old before my eyes and I would be less afraid.

But here, in the midst of the wastelands, I had lost even this small solace. I feared some twisting of the brain. Something broken. Elena must have seen what I created, she must think me a monster. I tore out the pages of my book, kept them hidden against my skin. I feared my madness could be seen by others.

Outside the window the trees wept red tears. We passed a wooden church, alone on a low hill. The roof was caved in, the whole structure leaning, tilted by the wind. There were no windows.

Never stopping, on and on across the continent. Never stopping, the only way to be safe.

'Safe-ish', the mutters went, the jokes. 'Safer'.

But not yet saved.

On the third day we slowed perilously close to walking pace, the track winding past still lakes whose surfaces did not reflect the sky. I stood, nose to the window, rapt and appalled by the non-colour of the water, if that is what it was, and the scuttering, scuttling things, carapaces shining and black.

And in the midst of it all, yellow flowers, a cluster of fragile petals around a central cup, green tendrils creeping upwards. I peered closer, amazed that nature so delicate could exist here, and thrive. But as I watched, something fleshy and red shot out from the flower cup towards a creeping, thorny creature. A flickering tongue; it grasped the creature and pulled it towards those pale petals, faster than I could have believed, and the petals opened, and the teeth were revealed. Row upon row. Sharp and shining.

I stumbled backwards. Other tongues darted out, quick as snakes.

'The flowers are hungry,' said a voice beside me. 'Like everything here is hungry.'

Elena. I had not seen her since that first night. In the daylight she seemed more real, more earthly. How could I have captured so twisted a likeness? The wrongness was within myself. I could not meet her eye.

'Where is your sketchbook?' she asked, standing beside me and watching the terrible, greedy flowers. 'Such rare things deserve preserving, too.'

I shook my head, still unable to look at her. 'I thought . . .' I began.

'That you had found something beautiful?' she said.

'No,' I said. 'Something that I didn't have to be afraid of. But I was wrong.'

We stood in silence for a while, as the train picked up speed again, to its familiar rattling, rolling pace. Finally Elena said, 'Well then, that just confirms my conclusions.'

I turned to her. 'Your conclusions?'

'That you, Monsieur Orphan,' she said, 'may have been found in a drum tower, and may be prone at times to self-pity – ' (this with raised eyebrows) ' – but are nonetheless possessed of common sense, a most under-rated gift.'

I could not resist laughing.

'If you are not afraid of everything outside this train,' she went on, 'then you are a foolish man.'

She put her hand on my arm, and I am happy to tell you that I did not stammer, or blush, or lower my eyes, but stood, contented and unfoolish.

A strange sensation! And strange that it should be here, in this unknown land, with this unknown, blue-eyed woman.

If anything unusual occurs, remain calm. Return to your cabin immediately and lock the door. Stuff your ears with wax, or cloth if no wax is to hand. Make as little sound as possible. Keep an upright position, your back against the wall and your eyes open. Keep your pistol close.

By the fourth day a kind of patient inertia had gripped the train. We became used to waiting our turn for the wash-rooms and trying to keep clean in the one tiny sink in each carriage. We became familiar with the dining car and the same diet of cured meat, bread and olives every day. We learned how best to propel ourselves down the corridors to the swaying rhythm of the train, when best to close the curtains against the approaching night and the shadows outside that moved alongside us with eerie grace. We learned not to look.

On the fifth night the lights went out.

I was in the observation car, my sketchbook open on my lap, no longer afraid of what may appear beneath my pencils. A few other travellers shared the car, talking or playing cards, for the most part. They left me alone. They thought me dull and awkward, unable to joke or boast or flirt.

Elena entered. I knew her by the rustle of her skirts, the way she hesitated in the doorway. She sat down beside me and opened her book. We had taken to sitting like this, in companionable silence. It was a relief, not to need words.

I was about to pick up my pencils again when we were plunged into darkness. We reacted with no more than an intake of breath. No-one spoke. No-one moved. We sat in darkness such that I had never known, with no sound at all but the rails beneath us.

It felt like an age, but could only have been a matter of minutes before the lights came on again and we all looked at each other and burst into nervous laughter.

'Nothing to worry about!' cried someone.

'These things happen,' said someone else, 'Quite normal, I'm sure.'

One of the ladies drew a shuddering breath and began to sob.

Elena stood up. 'Come', she said, 'Quickly.' She took my hand and led me out of the carriage, down corridors where worried faces peered around doors and guards shouted for calm.

Her urgency scared me more than the darkness had.

'Listen.' She stopped. We were alone in the space between two carriages, where a samovar bubbled away and a couch for the guard was tucked up against the wall. A bulb above us flickered.

'There's something here.' She looked around, her eyes midnight blue in the dim light. She took both of my hands in hers. 'You have to trust me,' she said.

I trusted her. The first person I had ever trusted.

She reached up to touch my face, her hands as chilled as if she stood in the snow. She moved closer to me and from somewhere just out of sight I thought I heard a muffled noise, like scuffling footsteps. 'Don't look,' she said, 'Don't look at anything but me.'

I looked in her eyes and saw that the blue was flecked with silver. Her lashes were wet. I had never been so close to another person.

The noise came closer, closer. Elena's arms reached around my neck, her body pressed so close to mine I could feel the beating of her heart. Closer still and I thought I heard a breath and a sound like the licking of lips.

For the briefest of moments Elena's head turned. There was a hiss. A noise like a wet thing hitting the wall and the scrabble of fingernails. Then silence.

She let go, pushed me away, and in the dim light her irises were flooded with waves of dark ink, her hair wet, her fingers, whether reaching for me or warding me off I did not know, long and thin and crabbed. A vein stood out on her forehead, a thread of blue beneath skin stretched tight over bone.

'Monsieur Orphan,' she whispered.

And I stumbled away, stumbled down the rocking carriage, the hissing still in my ears and her hands still reaching like ghosts at my back. Stumbled all the way to the cattle-sheds where the three southerners sat hunched on their bunks.

But if I had hoped to have time to gather my scattered wits, I was sorely mistaken. The men darted towards me.

'There was something here,' one whispered, 'something – '

But I was not listening. I looked at their faces.

'What?' they said, 'What is it?' – scrambling for the cracked mirror on the wall, pushing each other out of the way to be the first to see.

Each of them was missing the colour of their eyes.

It is recommended that you drink two glasses of vodka washed down with milk before bedtime, so that you may have a dreamless sleep.

The next morning it began to snow. Patterns appeared in ice on the window, like the lacquer tracing on the houses of the wealthy in Beijing. When I put my fingers to the glass, the patterns moved.

The southerners stayed huddled in their bunks as other rumours sped around the train. A woman who had lost the little finger on her left hand. Another whose hair had turned into brittle yellow grass. A man who swore he could no longer see the colour red.

'Are we close? Are we close?' whispered someone down the carriage, over and over again. 'Are we there, are we close?'

'Nearly there,' I whispered back. 'Nearly there.'

The last night came. I combed my hair in the mirror and I walked towards the lights of the dining car.

The tables were pushed against the walls and a man sat in the corner with a violin, playing a reel as couples danced, their bodies pressed close together, sweat beading on their foreheads. Through the crowd, I saw her, alone and watchful.

'May I have this dance?' I held out my hand.

She raised her eyes to mine, and I could not tell if she wished to frown or to smile.

'Remember what I said about foolish men.'

'I remember.' I said.

She took my hand. 'You said you trusted me.'

I nodded.

'Then you must do what I say. Tonight especially. You must do what I say.'

'I will,' I said, 'I promise.'

We stepped into the crowd.

'We will pass the dividing line soon,' said Elena.

'And enter Europe.' The word sounded strange on my lips.

'We will dance into a new continent,' she said.

I felt her hair against my neck, her cool hand in mine. The music was unfamiliar, a celebration and a lament all at once.

Faster the violin played, and faster. Elena laughed as stray curls flew in front of her eyes. Couples spun around us, colours turning to dark gold beneath the lights, hair stuck to skin, lips parted, breathless.

I saw my cabin-mates, holding each other's arms, their white eyes stark against their flushed skin. I saw the woman with hair of yellow grass. And Elena, in my arms, her face lined with blue veins, her eyes cloudy, her hand in my hand long-nailed and pale. Water dripped from her hair. As I brushed her skin a few iridescent scales dropped onto her dress.

We danced into a new continent.

I wanted to lean forward and brush my lips against hers. I wanted to stay like this, as close as we were. To imagine we were alone in all the great unknown spaces of Siberia and that nothing could harm us because she would keep all the bad things away.

I felt the tears well up in my eyes, but I was not ashamed.

I looked down and saw that her hair had turned to silvery white. I could feel water trickling over my fingers, down her back, soaking her dress. The tears pooling in my eyes flooded down my cheeks. Heavier and heavier they flowed, over my lips and into my mouth. I struggled to draw a breath. I blinked and blinked but the water had blinded me and I felt something change, felt her stiffen in my arms, felt her try to pull away. She raised her eyes to mine and she spoke words that I could not hear, that I did not want to hear, that were *Let me go.* But I held her tight, though I was weakening, held her as she twisted and twisted in my arms, wet and slippery and icy cold, and her fingernails were in my skin, clawing at me, pushing me away, but I wasn't afraid, I wasn't afraid at all and for a moment she was still and I think I saw her begin to smile, but there was only darkness before my eyes, and the roaring of water.

Those who make the journey make it only once. You can see its traces, if you know how to look. You can see the iron that runs through them, forever.

They told me I was lucky. That I'd had a close escape.

'Stronger than you look!' they said, 'To fight it off like that.' 'To think it had been here all this time. . .' They shook their heads. 'Monster', they said.

They admired me.

And though I searched the train, banged on every cabin door, made myself into a madman, it was all to no end. She had vanished.

We arrived in Moscow in a rainstorm, crossing the border wall into the frontier town. A week later I stood outside the Gare de Lyon in Paris with my suitcase and my box of paints and walked into the city I had travelled thousands of miles to reach.

And here I remain. Paris is filled with sunshine and music. There are roses in bloom in Montmartre. I paint. You may have seen me, I have a spot on Rue Azais, just below Sacre Coeur. I call out to the tourists to come, let me sketch you a portrait! Only a few francs. A memory to treasure, my friends, come, sit, once I studied at the Conservatoire des Arts, I am not just any street pedlar.

And they come, the pleasure-seekers of Paris, and I draw. I like the women the best, I like to draw their dark hair and full lips, the contours of their cheekbones. I have made something of a name for myself – they seek me out, those who are in the bloom of their beauty and youth, because they know I can capture it forever.

And all the time, I look for the face I saw on a train, in the middle of a lost country, many years ago. All the time I hold on to that thin iron thread that links the two halves of my life together, that links me across all those miles, across continents, to what I was, and what I became.

They are here, somewhere. The ones who are like her, who hide behind human faces, who walk amongst us. I have spent my life seeking them out again. This is my price, the price we must all pay, we who ride the train across that terrible, wondrous expanse. Unique to every traveller, it is said, and although the price is high I cannot regret it. I am not afraid.

For I know they are here, and that one day amidst all the many faces I draw I will find one that is twisted and strange and beautiful.

And they will tell me what she was, and what she wanted, and where she has gone.

NINA ALLAN

HIGHER UP

I DIDN'T SEE the twin towers fall.

I heard them, though. I can never quite get that sound out of my head.

I was ten years old when it happened. I was in London with my parents. My father was having lunch with a client in some snazzy restaurant. My mother and I were in a bookshop somewhere in the West End, although the different parts of London all looked the same to me then, we could have been anywhere. What I remember is one of the sales staff, rushing up to the guy on the History counter and asking if he'd heard the news.

'There's been a bomb,' he says. 'A bomb at the World Trade Center.'

It is 3.15 by my wristwatch, 10.15 in New York, although I don't find that out until later. I am browsing through a book of paintings, artists' representations of the Christian saints, and have just reached Tiepolo's painting of St Agatha, gazing skywards with glassy eyes while a pasty pageboy in a yellow dressing gown stands holding her severed breasts on a silver tray like pink blancmanges. I find it ghastly, but fascinating. Only a man could have painted that, I think. This is when I first hear the sales guy mention the bomb. My stomach drops, the way it does in the car when my dad hits a bump in the road. I am terrified of bombs, and kidnappings, and hijackings, all the stuff I see on the news and have nightmares about. My mother is keen for me to watch the news on a regular basis. She thinks it is important for me to know what is going on in the world. I have not told her about my nightmares because I am afraid it would make me seem childish. The guy behind the counter says he hasn't heard anything.

'Has anyone been killed?' he says.

'I don't know,' says the other guy. He shakes his head. 'They didn't say.'

They begin talking together in low voices. I sneak a glance at my mother, who is standing nearby. I see she's gone all stiff and straight, the way she always does when she's eavesdropping. My mother's name is Ruth. She puts down the book she was reading – something about Venice? – and turns round, scouting the area, scanning for my position on her escape-proof radar.

'Elaine,' she says. 'Come on, we're going. What on Earth are you looking at?' I hate my name. The way my mother says it, it has a gilded, princess ring to it that I am embarrassed by. When I am thirteen I start calling myself Laine. If anyone calls me Elaine I refuse to answer.

'Nothing,' I say. I want to ask her if we're leaving because of the bomb, but I don't. I don't want her to know that I've been listening in. I take one last look at poor St Agatha then quickly re-shelve the book, being careful to put it back in the same place I found it.

'Why are we going?' I say. I think that to not make any fuss at all might look suspicious.

'It's getting late,' my mother says. 'Your father will be expecting us back at the hotel.' We go outside and she takes my hand, steering me determinedly through the pedestrians and the hooting traffic. In the tightness of her grip I sense a closely vibrating current of worry, as if she's lost her way but is doing her best to pretend she knows where we are. We enter the Tube at Marylebone. I gaze at the word, signposted above the station entrance and then again against the tiled, curving wall of the tunnel, trying to make the letters that spell it out fit with the name the way my mother has pronounced it.

Mary-le-bone, I say to myself. *Marry*-li-bun. It can be made to fit, after a fashion anyway, so long as you say it quickly enough.

I like the way the word looks written down, a long caterpillar of a word, its four syllables clacking deftly into place like piano keys. I repeat it in my head, over and over in time with the jouncing, rattling rhythm of the speeding Tube train.

When we arrive back at our hotel room my father is there. His jacket is off, flung carelessly across the end of the bed. I think how strange this is – normally my father always hangs things up. The television is on and my father is watching it. There is something odd about this as well, something unsettling. Daytime TV-watching is something my father normally frowns upon.

'Have you seen this, Ruth?' he says. My father's name is Lionel. 'This is incredible.' He barely turns round. It is as if he doesn't want to take his eyes away from the TV screen for even a second.

'I heard something about a bomb,' says my mother. 'What's happening?'

'It's not a bomb,' says my father. 'A plane's crashed into the World Trade Center. Some sort of air accident. No one seems to know what's caused it.'

Neither of them say anything else, not for ages. They stand together, shoulder to shoulder in front of the television set, which is high up on the wall, screwed to some kind of flexible metal bracket. You have to crane your neck to see it. My own view of the screen is blocked almost entirely but then my parents seem to have forgotten I am even there. My mother glances back at me once, just quickly, and I get the feeling she's checking to see if she's remembered to bring me back with her. Once she's sure I am in the room she turns straight back to the TV. I sit down on their bed, a huge double divan with a fitted bedcover, and tug off my trainers. They are red high-top Converse sneakers, the real thing, not some naff Primark rip-off, and I adore them. I sit cross-legged on the bed, staring at my parents' backs in a way I hope approximates to what my gran (that's my mum's mum – my Birmingham nan died three years ago) always refers to as daggers drawn.

My ideas about what is happening are still vague. From what my father said I am able to work out that there has been a plane crash, but I don't know what the World Trade Center is, or even where it is. My first thought is that it is somewhere in London. The idea terrifies me, and it is perhaps for this reason that I don't make more of an effort to see what is happening on the TV screen. I listen instead, trying to piece together a story from sound alone. There are shouts and many sirens, some people screaming, but over and throughout everything there is a kind of uncanny, breathless hush, as if whatever it is isn't over yet, as if people are waiting to see what will happen next.

At some point I realise that all of the voices I can hear have American accents.

'Is it in America, Dad?' I ask quietly. I don't expect an answer – both my parents seem so preoccupied – but my father replies almost at once. It's as if he too has been waiting. Waiting for me to ask him a question so he can explain things.

'Yes, Elaine,' he says. 'It's in New York.' He still doesn't turn round, and all at once I have a funny feeling about why that is.

He can't look at me, I think. He can't look at me because he's scared.

The idea is awful, almost more awful than the thought of a plane crash, which is something that terrifies me even more than bombings and kidnappings.

I have a secret fear that planes are too heavy to fly, that it's only through luck that any of them stay up at all.

If the height of a building is determined by the number of occupied floors it has, the World Trade Center, with 110, held the record for the world's tallest building for nearly four decades.

It was beaten only in 2010, when the Burj Khalifa skyscraper in the United Arab Emirates took over the record with 163. The Burj Khalifa rises out of the ground like a gracefully gleaming rocket in steel and glass. Even in photos it looks impossible, not of this world.

'Come on,' my father says eventually.

It is three hours since my mother and I returned to the hotel. 'We'd better go and get something to eat.'

I am hungry by now but it seems wrong to want to eat, wrong to leave the hotel room, wrong to do anything at all other than stay still and listen. I keep hearing the sound, the 'oomph' that is not quite a boom, not quite a crash, but something that is somehow worse than either of those things, which are both bad, the totally one-off crumping sound that is the sound of the second plane driving its way deep into the south tower.

All the TV stations keep playing that sound, over and over again, as if they can't get enough of it, as if they can't believe it, as if playing it one more time might give them some answers.

I still haven't seen it happen. I have sat still on the bed all this time, just listening. Neither my mother nor my father asks me if I want to look and I do not press them. I don't say anything about not wanting a meal, because I know that whatever I say will sound stupid or wrong. We go down the road to a restaurant. I eat a large portion of chicken with cous cous and a slice of *tarte tatin* with almond pastry. The *tarte tatin* especially is delicious. I chase the last crumbs around my plate, scraping them all together with the edge of my spoon.

'You mustn't be frightened, Elaine,' says my mother at some point during the meal. 'It happened a long way away. They couldn't do that here because none of the buildings in Britain are tall enough.'

I have the feeling that what my mother is saying is some story my parents have agreed on between them, even though they have barely spoken a word to each other since we left our hotel room.

They want to talk though, they are dying to, I can feel it. It's like they're embarrassed to say anything in front of me.

'But they could still crash a plane,' I say. 'Into the ground. Anywhere.'

My outburst is a surprise, even to me.

'The police won't let them,' says my father. He sounds like one of the commentators on the television. I notice we are all saying 'they.' I wonder who exactly 'they' are, when they're at home.

We leave London the following morning, a day early. Everyone on the train seems to be reading the same newspaper. Only gradually do I come to realise that it's not the same paper, just the same picture or versions of it on all the front pages: the south tower, the orange flames shooting out like the breath of a dragon, the hole in its side like a wound, the billowing smoke.

The words '9/11' don't quite exist yet, but I can almost sense them, the need to give a name to what has happened, to give it a shape. I have a book to read on the train, *Gulliver's Travels*, but I can't concentrate on it. I keep looking out the window instead, half expecting to see buildings in flames and people running, to hear that stomach-turning *thrump*, the sound of steel and concrete and human beings being destroyed.

Vaporised, is the word they keep using.

I couldn't stop thinking how September 11th started off normal. It was just a day at first, like any other, until the first plane took off, and even then it still seemed normal for quite a while longer, even though it already wasn't.

The broadcasts mostly happen at night.

I've always depended on the radio for getting to sleep. I've never been a good sleeper, not even in the early years with Willem, when I was happy every minute of every day and before I started going insane. I've always found the radio comforting, those reasoned, measured voices bringing me news. Even if it was bad news the radio made it feel like a solution could still be worked out. Even if the world was going to hell in a handcart at least I could be grateful the world was still there.

Now I'm terrified to turn on the radio because there's a chance, each time I do, that I might hear it, that broadcast, the final communication from the cockpit of United Airlines Flight 259.

Jesus
I think that's done it, I think it's holding
The fuck it is. Merrick, get the nose up, for fuck's sake – we're going down like a –
Your light's on, sir. The carriage release –
I see it. Jeez, give me some space here, won't you?

There's a bumping sound in the background. Once the cockpit tape has played out the studio commentators spend some time speculating over what the bumping sound might be. One of them thinks it's the sound of the cabin door being torn off, the other reckons it's just static. They go on and on about it, as if prolonging their stupid discussion might keep UA 259 from finally slamming into the centre of Istanbul.

The man saying 'jeez' is Captain Willem van Doer. Merrick,

I have discovered, is Willem's co-pilot. The mysterious thumping is the sound of my world, splitting in two.

Willem never swears, at least he never used to.

The sound of his voice saying 'jeez' and 'fuck' is terrifying, because it's the sound of the man I love abandoning hope.

Two seconds after Willem says jeez the jet's cargo bay doors are wrenched off.

A rain of suitcases, mail sacks, industrial grade ball bearings and three Karri-Safe crates containing three pedigree Doberman Pinschers pours down into the streets a thousand feet below. There is something else in the cargo hold as well, something dangerous that should never have been there. It falls with the rest, shedding itself in minute particles all over the city. Moments later the jumbo hits the ground and explodes in a ball of fire.

Night after night they discuss it, those calm voices with their firm and ready opinions.

No one can make up their minds, you see. No one can make up their minds whose fault it is.

The crash of United Airlines 259 has precipitated what is called an *international situation*.

It hasn't happened yet, but I know it will.

I pretended to forget about 9/11.

Actually I did better than that: I pretended not to be interested. Everybody knows that kids have short attention spans. At ten years old, if an adult tells you that what's happening on TV is nothing to worry about you're supposed to believe them. When my mum or dad switched on the news I either made out I wasn't watching or left the room.

It's like running from a bull, or a mad dog. The trick is never to look it in the eye.

Instead of looking it in the eye I collected newspaper clippings about it. I hid the cuttings in a cardboard box under my bed.

Every time I heard a plane going over I would look at the ground. It seemed to me that any plane might be the next one to fall, that if I singled one out with a glance it would somehow mark it down for future destruction.

Willem tells me many pilots see the big jets as a second best.

That pilots who are used to flying thoroughbred fighter aircraft for the military tend to think of the commercial airliners as so many big dumb farm animals. There's fuck all to do except sit there, they say. Once you've handled the take off that's pretty much it. You could spend the whole flight taking a shit and no one would notice.

Willem says the newer planes, the planes that carry fly-by-wire technology, are more or less impossible to crash.

The only way to down a plane like that is to blow it up.

Willem insists that an airline pilot's high salary has nothing to do with the long hours or the night shifts or the disruption to family life caused by jet lag and long absences. An air captain is paid well not as a reward for years of reliable service but for those crucial five minutes when his knowledge and actions will make the difference between life and death.

He says that every pilot will experience such a moment in his career, sooner or later.

'You never know when it will happen, just that it will. And when it does it is your job to be ready for it.'

'Doesn't that freak you out?' I ask him.

He shakes his head. 'It's all about knowing the plane,' he says. 'So long as you know your plane, you'll know what to do.'

I do not ask him about those moments that come to some pilots, when there is nothing that can be done except prepare to die. Instead I ask him what it was that made him want to become a pilot in the first place.

A look comes into his eyes then, a look of such tenderness and longing that it makes my heart clench. His whole mind is bent on remembering, and I can see from his face that he has forgotten, just for a second, that I am there.

I think this is the moment when I fall fully in love with him. In love so there is no way out, in love so that it will hurt me badly if things go wrong.

'I was ten years old,' he says. 'I remember it was night time, we were travelling back upstate, we'd been visiting friends in the city. It was a long drive, some of the country up there was quite isolated. I remember thinking how dark it was, so much darker than night in town. I remember staring out the window of my father's car and seeing this plane go over. The lights of the plane seemed very bright, very beautiful, and I suddenly found myself wondering where it was going. There was something magical about it, the thought of all those people up there, sleeping maybe, or reading quietly in their seats, perhaps looking down into the darkness to where I was, but all of them trusting the captain of the aircraft to bring them safely to where it was they needed to be. I kept thinking it was like the old days, when there were big ships and sea captains, only now we had sky captains instead. Sky captains! I loved even the sound of the words. From that moment on I was lucky, because unlike so many other people in the world I knew exactly what I wanted to do with my life. And it was always the big jets for me. Nothing else would do.'

'That's a beautiful story,' I say to him. I mean it, too. I know already that Willem van Doer is four years older than me, that he became ten years old in 1997, four years before I did, four years before the words 9/11 bore any significance.

For a ten-year-old Willem van Doer the sky was still a place where dreams could unfold.

I do not ask how 9/11 affected him. After what he's just told me the question seems rude.

For my GCSE in physics I chose to do a project on commercial airliners.

At the age of fourteen I still felt vaguely frightened every time I heard a plane go over. The thought of actually having to fly in one made my palms sweat. I thought it might help me feel less afraid if I knew more about them.

I learned everything I could about the air industry, from the early post-war Douglases and Comets to the superjumbo Airbus 380, which came into service right around the time I handed in my project. I learned the difference between piston engines and turbojets, the relative dimensions of a wide-body versus a narrow-body airliner. I knew that the take-off weight for a two-engine aircraft should not exceed fifty tons. I knew that the catastrophic metal fatigue that led to the grounding of the entire fleet of de Havilland Comets in 1953 was ultimately caused by the plane having square windows instead of round windows or oval ones. I could quote chapter and verse on wing angle and runway speeds and what I knew about aerodynamics, Willem later told me, would not have looked out of place on the exam syllabus of a first year undergraduate.

I learned also about air crashes. I learned that the six worst peacetime civilian air disasters by order of their fatalities were Tenerife (1977), Japan Airlines (1985), Haryna (1996), Turkish Airlines (1974), O'Hare (1979) and American Airlines Flight 587, which crashed over New York on November 12th 2001, just two months after the terrorist attacks of September 11th.

Reading about the crashes made me feel small and pointless and terrified. In some strange way I also felt guilty, that I was still alive when the people who'd been on the planes were all dead. That they died horribly made me feel even worse, and yet I could not bring myself to stop obsessing over the facts.

In time I came to realise that I secretly thought of my obsession – my reading about the crashes, my collecting of news clippings and statistics and air accident trivia – as a kind of insurance policy. The more I knew, I reasoned, the less likely it was to happen.

I also came to realise something else: 9/11 hadn't really been an air disaster at all, but a faultlessly staged demonstration in mass murder.

Every source I examined told me that aeroplanes were safe and becoming safer. The statistics insisted I was in less danger inside the cabin of a jumbo jet than I was in my own bedroom. There were fewer air accidents happening year on year, and there had never been all that many in the first place, not in comparison with the number of car crashes, for example, or even bicycle fatalities.

The planes that caused 9/11 had not failed their pilots, they had been misused.

The disaster had been part of the flight plan. The fatal pieces were all in place before the aircraft even taxied down the runway.

The defining tragedy had not taken place in the air, but on the ground.

I did well in my GCSEs, and in my 'A' Levels also.

My parents and teachers took it for granted that I would apply for university. I didn't, though. I could give any number of excuses, but mainly I didn't apply because I didn't know which subjects to choose.

When my mother found out I hadn't sent the forms in she did a mental. She accused me of having a butterfly mind.

'The grass is always greener on the other side with you, isn't it, Elaine?' she said. 'You can never make up your mind, about anything.'

I made all the usual teenage uproar about it being my life

and my choice. It would be better if I took a gap year in any case, I insisted. At least that way I could be earning money while I decided. When the fuss had died down a bit I applied for a job with one of the smaller commercial airlines, working on the helpdesk and check-in at Heathrow Airport. I travelled down to London for the interview and was told more or less then and there that the job was mine if I wanted it.

I accepted on the spot. How weird is that?

In the decade following 9/11, the number of feature films, documentaries and TV programmes about the attacks mounted to a total well in excess of five hundred.

I know, because I've made a list of them. Even so I know I'm bound to have missed some. What surprises me most is the number of films based around 9/11 conspiracy theories.

9/11: In Plane Sight
9/11: Press for Truth
Fahrenheit 9/11
The Man Who Predicted 9/11
The Secret History of 9/11
Loose Change
9/11: the Greatest Lie Ever Sold
9/11 Mysteries
Between the Lies
Core of Corruption
The Elephant in the Room
Great Conspiracy: the 9/11 News Special You Never Saw
9/11: Explosive Evidence
Aftermath: Unanswered Questions from 9/11
'Flight 77': The White Plane
Painful Deceptions
The Truth and Lies of 9/11
The Ultimate Con

The Unofficial Story
September 11: Evidence to the Contrary

The list goes on and on. It's easy to dismiss these films as the work of crackpots and there are plenty that are, but for me at least what's most interesting about the conspiracy theories is not so much the theories themselves (although some of them are so ingenious you can't help but feel a twinge of admiration) but what they indicate: that there are many people, even now, who find the very fact of 9/11 too daunting and too overpowering to accept on trust.

This disaster, they seem to suggest, is a chimera, a group delusion, a conspiracy of the intellect against the imagination.

Many of these films are now available as free downloads. The strange thing is, the more of them you watch, the less certain you become of what actually happened.

The feature films are mostly crap. Oliver Stone's 2006 movie *World Trade Center*, starring Nicholas Cage and Maria Bello, was made for a budget of $65 million with a running time of 129 minutes. For all the time, money and special effects lavished upon it, *World Trade Center*, an unwieldy, overripe fusion of a propaganda newsreel and a 1970s disaster movie, is embarrassingly unsuccessful as cinema. Stephen Daldry's *Extremely Loud and Incredibly Close*, released in 2012 as an adaptation of Jonathan Safran Foer's controversial novel, is more ambitious but equally bad, an attempt, if you can believe it, at 9/11 feelgood.

The best of a bad bunch is Paul Greengrass's 2006 *United 93*. The film plays itself out in real time, and the real air traffic control staff were brought in (wherever possible) to play themselves. There are very few special effects. The film has a tighter focus. It never tries to show more than it can. It succeeds better as a result.

The first 9/11 film I saw was the Oliver Stone. I watched it on DVD as a kind of bet with myself, that I could do it, that I could finally bring myself to watch what happened, even though you could argue that watching a fictional replay of the events was a bit of a cheat. I chose *World Trade Center* as my starting point because I knew it would be shit. I thought that the film being shit might make watching it easier and in a way it did but not in a good way. The script is the worst part. In *World Trade Center*, people say things like 'we're Marines, you *are* our mission,' and 'I don't know if these guys realise it, but this country's at war.' The film ends happily with a barbecue. The glowing figure of Jesus appears from the rubble. For me, Stone's film made the events of 9/11 appear unreal and for the most part survivable. I felt it was an insult, a squirm-making error of taste that should never have happened. In the end it taught me nothing.

United 93 was more difficult because I believed in it. What disturbed me most of all was that a part of me, deep inside, found the film exciting. About half way through I realised I was watching to find out what happened, for God's sake, that I was rooting for the passengers, even though I knew they were dead, that they had all died in terror in spite of their bravery, that was the point.

Part of me still hoped for a happy ending.

Feature films I have trained myself to cope with, after a fashion, but I still haven't watched any more than very brief snatches of actual footage from the actual day. Even worse are those programmes that were put together afterwards, the montages of voicemail recordings and text messages sent by people trapped higher up, in offices above the impact zones, the final phone calls made by passengers on the hijacked aircraft.

I can't watch those at all. I know these programmes are deeply important, living history. But it still feels wrong to me, even so, that they were ever broadcast.

~

My job at the airport granted me a kind of liberty I hadn't expected.

There are people who talk about 'dead end jobs' as if working the supermarket checkout or processing visa applications is the end of the world, just a small step away from hawking *The Big Issue* or cleaning toilets, I say these people don't know what they are talking about.

My work with SwiftAir was physically tiring, mainly because I was on my feet all day, but my mind was free. The money wasn't all that great – it was shit actually, at least to begin with – but at least I hadn't sold out to the banking industry or some multinational food producer that was secretly manufacturing chemical weapons. It was my job to be polite, but I never had to pretend, and so long as I didn't cock up almightily I was mainly left alone to get on with the job.

In a world of limited options, it was an option. It was a job that could buy me the time I needed to work out what I was meant to be doing.

I intended it to last for a year. I didn't like having to wear a uniform and the work was boring, at first it was anyway, an endless stream of dopey customers and their idiot problems, rich bitches moaning about baggage surcharges, trainee Hitlers demanding to know why their flight was delayed. Stuff like that, day after day, can get you down. Added to that my direct supervisor was a complete arsehole, a guy with airport management in his sights and determined to let us all know it. He was a total wanker over *company policy*, although I hardly saw him speak to an actual customer the whole time he was there.

He was a pain but I learned to ignore him, and once he left – promoted, of course, what else? – I began to see things differently. The stand was a much pleasanter place to be, for a start. Added to that I began to take more interest in the job. I got to know all of our most regular flyers and was able to greet them by name. I made up small challenges for myself and felt satisfaction when things went smoothly. The woman who took over from Dorkface, Florence Agyeman, was a bit of a rebel, and I enjoyed the atmosphere of camaraderie that started to develop between us.

You might not believe this, given my plane phobia, but I grew to like the atmosphere of a working airport. I liked the sense of continual movement, of things getting done, of people setting out or coming home, of feeling useful. I also liked it that I could keep my eye on things. I came to know the airport's sounds and routines and rhythms, its ebb and flow. I came to know the air crew and the security guards, their body language and coded signals, their pre-flight banter.

I liked the way they made their jobs seem perfectly normal. I still hadn't stepped on board an aeroplane, but there were times – whole spans of hours – when I genuinely believed that I could do it if I really had to.

A time came when I actually felt safer at the airport than anywhere else.

When my so-called gap year was up I stayed on. Five years later when Florence retired I took over her job.

'I never saw you in management, I must admit, but I suppose it's something,' said my mother. My dad had just started to be unwell – cancer – and so I was travelling up to Birmingham to see him whenever I could. I went by train. When my mother asked me why I didn't fly up I told her the train was cheaper and more convenient. Which was rubbish, of course. SwiftAir flew five flights a day to Birmingham. I could have travelled for free and been there in less than an hour.

Willem van Doer flies for United Airlines, so there was no objective reason why I should have met him.

It happened, as most life-changing events do, completely by chance.

I was buying my morning latte and almond biscotti at Caffe Nero. I was wondering about whether I should do some shopping at the overpriced airport Waitrose when I went off shift, or grab something from the all-night Co-op on my way home. I wasn't concentrating on where I was going, and as I stepped away from the counter I collided with Willem, who had been standing in the queue directly behind me.

My wrist jerked sharply upwards. A penny-sized dollop of boiling latte shot out through the hole in the cup lid and splattered down on my wrist.

Yow, I thought. But what I was mostly thinking was thank fuck it didn't land on that guy's shirt. The shirt was so white it looked newly minted, you know the kind.

I'd already seen the four stripes on his sleeve that meant he was a full captain. I'd been with SwiftAir for almost eight years by then. I knew that pilots were really no different from restaurant managers: some of them were exceptional people, others, to put it frankly, were just a little bit too much in love with themselves. There was no way I was going to get all worked up at the sight of a uniform.

This guy in the shirt though, he looked really nice.

'I am so sorry,' I said to him.

'I reckon you were about a million miles away just then,' said Willem, although of course I don't know him as Willem, not yet. He had an American accent. That ought to have put me off, but it didn't.

'Probably about two,' I said, then stopped, just in time to realise I was blushing like a schoolgirl.

'Don't worry about it,' he said. He laid a hand on my arm, the briefest touch, but I found myself remembering it all afternoon.

Two days later he came to find me on the stand.

'I was just wondering if you fancied a coffee,' he said. 'I promise I won't spill any in retaliation.'

I told him I'd be going on my break at three o'clock.

He said he'd meet me in Gino's then wandered off. He had a long stride, but he didn't strut, not like some of them. He seemed, well, unaware of himself, lost in his thoughts. Unusual.

Chloe – she was new on the stand, she'd just recently started – kept giving me these huge inane grins. The minute there was a lull in the check-ins she was on my case.

'This is your captain speaking,' she said in this ridiculous swoony voice. 'Scrumptastic.'

'I don't even know his name,' I said. 'So you can stop that right there.'

The next second the both of us were cackling like full-on lunatics.

According to statistics, 9/11, with its 2,976 fatalities, is the worst single terrorist incident that has occurred to date.

In fact, this statistic, like so many, is intrinsically flawed. We who have the privilege of electing our governments have the disconcerting habit of accepting government spin. In fact the single most devastating terrorist outrage was perpetrated by the USA upon Japanese civilians in 1945, when an estimated 237,000 people died in the bombing of Hiroshima. A further 100,000 died days later in Nagasaki. We are taught to accept that the ends of our democratic states justify the means, but is this any less of a brainwashing than the indoctrination of impressionable young men by extremist clerics?

The statistics vary considerably, but most sources seem to agree that the number of civilians killed by American bombing in the Iraq war of 2003 – launched as a direct response to 9/11 – was in excess of 100,000.

Most people seem surprised by or even unbelieving of this

statistic. We were told the war was fought mostly with smart-bombs, and that is the version of the story we mostly prefer.

Daniel Pearl, 2002 (1), Yazidi bombings by Al Qaeda in Iraq, 2007 (796), Bloody Sunday, 1920 (31), Bloody Sunday 1972 (14), Coastal Road massacre in Israel, 1978 (38), Beslan school siege, 2004 (396), Madrid train bombings, 2004 (191) Mumbai attacks, 2008 (164), 7/7 London Transport bombings, 2005 (52), Omagh bombing, 1998 (29), Alexandria Hotel siege, 2015 (45), Kabul air attacks, 2017 (5,000) Port Columbus suicide bombing by Meera Chowdri, 2018, (53)

Willem and I have a serious disagreement about Meera Chowdri.

He wants to know why she hadn't been deported from America on account of the contents of her doctoral thesis.

'It's obvious she was anti-America, anti-freedom,' Willem says. 'But that never stops these people taking advantage of our facilities, have you noticed that?'

I am surprised and a little shocked. I have never heard Willem use phrases like 'anti-freedom' or 'these people' before – Willem is the kind of American who tells Romney jokes and reads the New Yorker – but then I try not to react, because I know he's upset. He is upset about the 53 people, all of them ordinary air passengers, men, women and children, who have been killed by Meera Chowdri's suicide bombing of Port Columbus Airport in Ohio. He is also upset, I know, deep down, about Chowdri herself, who had seemed just like an ordinary Asian-American but who turned out not to be.

Meera Chowdri left a clip of video film on her phone, in which she claimed her action was a protest at the indiscriminate bombing of Kabul by American forces.

For Willem, Chowdri's action is like a kick in the teeth.

In the days after the attack on the airport, there is mass

media speculation about whether Chowdri acted alone or whether she was sponsored by Al Qaeda. A growing number of pundits are of the opinion that Meera Chowdri – as well as her family back in Pakistan – was funded by Al Qaeda from day one. A few people seem to think that Chowdri's decision to perpetrate the bombing might be connected with her recent split from her American partner, Duncan Freesland. Duncan Freesland is taken into custody for questioning. The American bombing of Kabul barely gets mentioned.

When I point this out to Willem, he rounds on me angrily. The idea that America should be asked to account for its actions is something he finds incomprehensible.

'Leaving aside Great Britain, can you name a single nation in the world today that prizes freedom more highly? A single political establishment you would trust more than ours? It's not always perfect, but no system can be – that's democracy. You can't blame America for wanting to protect its citizens and its ideals and I'd lay money on it that the victims of Jafari's torture gangs would be the first to agree with me.'

Willem maintains the US had no choice over the bombing of Kabul. He believes it was the only way to make the Islamic government there hand over the Al Qaeda leader Amal Jafari.

No one knows if Jafari is still in Kabul. Some people are saying he never fled to Kabul in the first place. No one knows the truth, or if they do they aren't telling.

'I don't think America should be blamed for having ideals,' I say to Willem. 'I just think it might be better if America kept its nose out of other people's business.'

'And risk another 9/11, or even worse? It's our responsibility as an evolved democracy to stop that from happening.'

I shut up after that. I loathe arguments, which often upset me as much as physical violence, and with Willem most of all. I know he doesn't even mean a lot of what he says, that it has arisen out of his sorrow at the bombing, and from his love of his country, America, which extends, I know already, beyond the rationally explicable.

Willem loves America not only for what it stands for but because of how it physically feels for him to be inside it. He loves its spaces, its colours and textures, its wide horizons. He loves it that it takes a week to drive across, that it carries within one country the dimensions and variations of an entire world.

When Willem thinks of America, I know it is that long-ago jet plane he still thinks of, travelling silently through the night in the blaze of its own lights, the sky captain, bringing his cargo of sleeping passengers safely home.

Who needs heaven, when you have America?

I understand Willem because I know and love him, and it is difficult to condemn the feelings of someone you love.

All the same, deep inside myself I want to tell him that America has got into the habit of behaving like a loud-mouthed playground bully and that it's hardly surprising if the other kids end up wanting to kick the shit out of it.

Meera Chowdri was an intelligent woman, with a small daughter named Rayisa and a first class degree from the University of Karachi. She wasn't mad, not in any sense of the word that makes sense. She had reasons for what she did, even though what she did was totally wrong. Even though it was totally wrong, to dismiss the bombing of Port Columbus as the act of a madwoman is both stupid and dangerous.

I believe we need to try and understand why a woman like Meera Chowdri would do what she did.

I can't say any of that to Willem, though. He would be angry, and he wouldn't get it.

I think Willem has started to think I might be going crazy.

The first time I heard the broadcast I thought it was a dream.

I still get nervous when Willem is flying, but I have learned to hide it. When Willem first learns that I am scared of flying, he is amused. When he realises I'm not joking he is incredulous.

He keeps asking me to go up with him. He says he can get me into the cockpit, no problem.

'Don't you trust me?' he says.

'I trust you,' I assure him. I do my best to convince him that my fear of flying is a form of claustrophobia. In the end he stops asking. I'm not sure if he's accepted that I might never fly with him, but I know the thought makes him sad.

Willem knows to always call me as soon as he lands, whatever the time is. He knows I won't sleep, in any case, until I know he's safely on the ground.

I find airline websites, like airports themselves, reassuring. A live, continually updating data-feed informs you when a plane is ready for boarding, when the flight gates are closed, when the aircraft moves away from the stand to begin its taxi run, how long a flight has been in progress, the ETA, the landing time (both local and portside), the overall flight report. There are minute-by-minute updates on flight delays, industrial action, adverse weather conditions.

It is a choreography of sorts, the choreography of the entirely normal. Hundreds of flights leave from Heathrow Airport every day. The airline websites offer objective evidence of their entirely normal take offs, through flights, and eventual landings. The evidence has a calming effect on me. It is most likely because of this that I find the airline websites a little addictive.

If one of Willem's flights is delayed I will usually know before he has the chance to tell me. Very occasionally a flight is put back with no reason given. When this happens I worry, even though I know a 'no data' tag is of itself an insufficient reason for concern. In almost one hundred percent of cases the cause is banal: a VIP jet has jumped the flight queue, the luggage conveyor belt has broken down, a pilot has gone sick with food poisoning, all the stuff that can upset the schedules but that is too long-winded or too much of a one-off to have its own data sign.

I'm used to it, but I still don't like it. If the unexplained delay goes above one hour I begin to fret. My palms sweat and my mouth goes dry, my heart rate increases. I refresh the site every two minutes, straining towards the moment when it finally updates, revealing to me the source of my own idiocy.

I embrace my idiocy like a secret lover. I bring it treats. If this demon can be assuaged by exciting my foolishness, it seems a small price to pay for Willem's safety to be continued.

On the night of the first broadcast, Willem is on his way back from New York. His flight is due in at 22.45. I am expecting him home by midnight, perhaps a little later. I know that the plane took off on schedule because the United Airlines website has confirmed it.

I clock off from the airport and take the train home. I make supper and watch some TV. I do not check the UA website again until around nine o'clock. The site is down, but I think nothing of it – short outages, usually due to increased traffic, are common. A few minutes later the site is running again but this time when I check Willem's flight it is showing 'no data'.

Quickly I refresh the page. Still no data.

I tell myself it's nothing. I remind myself of all the logical reasons that exist for this to be happening. I know I can call the UA desk if I want to – Jeanne Kreif, who will be on shift now, knows me well – but I have a fear (not as strong as the main one, but up there) of revealing my personal anxieties to other people. It's as if I admit that I am worried, then the fear will come true.

I know how pathetic this sounds, but it doesn't help.

I force myself back to the TV, which is now showing the third part of a crime drama I have been following. After less than five minutes of watching I have only the vaguest idea of what is going on. I am beginning to feel sick. I go upstairs, without checking the site again (a major victory) and run a bath. I lie in the water until it is cold, then put on my dressing gown and come back downstairs to check the site,

The flight's number is still showing, but there is still no data.

I reason that it is just a glitch, a data backlog from the outage earlier, most likely, but I feel weakness spreading throughout my body and my legs are trembling. It is a little before ten o'clock. I put on the news, knowing that a major air crash always hits the headline hot spot, no question. If it isn't there it hasn't happened, full stop.

The lead story is about pension reform. Next up is Meera Chowdri: her doctoral supervisor, Bella Cagill, is refusing to confirm to the US Supreme Court that the content of Chowdri's thesis was 'anti-freedom'. After that there is a story about some footballer being dismissed from the World Cup squad.

I let the rest of the news play out and then prepare for bed. I switch off the coffee machine, switch on the hall light, the way I always do when I know that Willem is going to be late home. I perform these acts as rituals, suddenly convinced – if you are a neurotic then you will know what I mean – that what I have to do is behave exactly as normal. If I act like there's nothing wrong, then nothing will be wrong.

These are the ways we have of exerting control.

I lie in bed, reading the same page – p 238 of Margaret Atwood's *Alias Grace* – over and over again. I am aware of every tiny sound within the flat, every vehicle driving past on the road outside. At some point these sounds recede, then suddenly I can hear the phone ringing. I wrench myself free of the bed covers. My heart is racing. I am terrified that the phone will stop ringing before I can get to it, then I realise it's not ringing at all. Unlikely though it seems, I must have fallen asleep. The ringing phone was a dream-phone, non-existent, except in my head.

I lie there, heart still thumping. My bedside clock-radio says 00.35.

Willem is still not home, but he is not exactly late yet, either. There is still plenty of time for everything to be okay.

I try his mobile, but it is switched off.

I know this means nothing at all, that it is better simply to lie here, to pretend that Willem will come walking through the front door at any moment. I switch on the radio, as I always do when I cannot sleep. I hear the muted, disgruntled rumbling of a parliamentary debate, about the pension thing, most likely, although I am not paying enough attention to know for sure. I wonder about getting up, about perhaps going back downstairs to check the site again, but I refuse to give in, not yet anyway. I let my mind drift, hoping I might fall asleep again, and then suddenly I hear Willem's voice. He is arguing with someone, a man I don't know.

Willem sounds angrily dismissive, completely unlike himself.

I understand at once that there is something wrong.

Jesus
I think that's done it, I think it's holding
The fuck it is. Merrick, get the nose up, for fuck's sake – we're going down like a –
Your light's on, sir. The carriage release –
I see it. Jeez, give me some space here, won't you?

There is a thumping sound, then a moment's silence. The next thing I hear is a studio discussion. Two men are talking with increasing animation. That's when I hear the words 'dirty bomb'.

∼

– So what in fact you are saying in front of the world that United Airlines 259 to Istanbul was actually utilized as a secret conveyance for criminal contraband?
– That's not what I'm saying at all. I'm saying that traces of depleted uranium have been found in the wreckage but that's all we know.
– But you're not denying your previous assertion that the CIA itself was directly involved in this?
– I never said that. What I said was that it was impossible – and I mean impossible – for any unauthorized cargo to have gotten aboard that flight. So we have a duty – a duty in front of the world, as you put it – to ask ourselves who put it there.

I jerk awake. I am trembling, but that is normal when I've had a bad dream. I listen for the voices on the radio but they are gone. I realise that what I am hearing instead is the sound of a key turning in the lock downstairs. A moment later I hear the door opening.

The sound is quiet but it's enough to wake me. Willem always does his best not to disturb me when he gets in late but I'm a light sleeper and I always hear him. There's no way I wouldn't.

I pull on my dressing gown and rush downstairs. Willem is hanging up his coat on one of the hooks by the front door. Often he will change out of his uniform while he's still at the airport but tonight he hasn't. I guess this is because he wanted to get home as quickly as possible.

He looks in my face, the beginnings of his crinkle-eyed smile quickly replaced by a look on concern.

'I did call,' he says. 'I left a message, on the voicemail.'

The phone stands squarely on the hall table. When I look at it I see the red message light blinking rhythmically on and off.

'I heard it ringing, but I thought it was a dream,' I say. I am gritty with sleep and spent anxiety but I hold him close. I breathe in his smells: coffee and Nivea hand lotion, a trace of sweat. The outside air still clings to his clothes.

'You're late,' I say. I rest my head against his chest so I can hear his heartbeat.

'Nothing exciting,' Willem says. 'There was some kind of backlog, that's all. We were stacked above the airport for almost an hour.'

I let it go.

I let the traces of the illusory broadcast drift upwards and out of my mind like threads of spider web. By morning they are gone.

It is a full week before I hear it again. This time it is in the middle of the afternoon. I am on my day off. Willem is on the Frankfurt run. His plane touches down at 18.30, right on schedule.

I have been talking recently about giving up my job with Swift-Air and returning to college.

My mother, Ruth, is all in favour.

'I mean, it's not as if you need the money,' she says. 'Willem's salary is more than enough for you to live on.'

She doesn't quite say so, but I know she thinks I have been wasting my life up till now. She thinks a degree will complete me. When she asks me what I'm thinking of studying I tell her I haven't decided yet. The truth is a touch more calamitous, because in fact I have almost as little idea of what I want to concentrate my efforts on as I did when I left school.

All I know is that I want to make more sense of things. I have ideas I want to explore but I'm not sure where to start. I have been thinking more and more about Meera Chowdri. I wonder what has happened to her daughter, who is taking care of her, what they will tell her about her mother and the way she died. There's a lot of opinion online about Meera Chowdri but not much new information. Most of what's posted ends up being a kind of virtual shouting match between those people who insist that Chowdri was a monster and those who believe she was some kind of hero, some kind of freedom fighter.

It seems there is very little in between.

I wonder if there is something here that I could get interested in. In one of the online articles I discover that Meera Chowdri and I were born just one month apart, that we are more or less exactly the same age. When I tell Willem about this he seems unimpressed.

'Big deal,' he says. 'Just you and several million other people. I don't get why you're so into her. She's just one more loser who thought the world owed her a living. Really not that interesting.'

Willem feels uncomfortable talking about Chowdri because he believes that what terrorists want most of all is to be talked about. He doesn't want to give her the satisfaction, even though she can't be satisfied by anything any more, she's dead, not vaporised but exploded, her remains spread over such a wide area, some forums claim, that they had to be collected in a bin bag. I think about this, because I cannot help it. I also cannot help thinking about how Meera Chowdri and I were both ten years old when 9/11 happened, she would have seen it on TV, just like I did. I wonder what she thought, how she felt. I wonder what happened in her life to make her do what she did. There are parts of our lives that feel almost the same, and yet in so many ways we are worlds apart. *It's taken me so long to know anything.* If I had lived Meera Chowdri's life, lived in her world, might I have ended up doing what she did?

I cannot bring myself to believe it, but it feels important at least to ask the question. I don't know if an answer is possible, or even useful, but I need to find out.

I long to discuss these things with Willem, but it is becoming too difficult.

'Have you ever thought of giving up flying?' I say instead.

'Don't be crazy, Laine,' Willem says. 'Flying is – what I do. I'd be lost without it.' He smiles at me, his crinkle-eyed smile that says he loves me even when I'm weird. It's good to see that smile. I would hate to lose it.

When I try to tell him I think he's in danger he shrugs it off.

'Perhaps you should think about talking to someone,' he says. 'About this flying thing, I mean.'

'You're talking about a psychiatrist,' I say. 'A shrink. You think I'm mad.'

'Not at all,' he says. 'A fear of flying is very common. But I don't like to see it eating into our lives like this. I just thought it might help, you know, to talk about it.'

It is now three months since I first heard the broadcast.

I've heard it six, perhaps eight times since. It catches me off guard each time. I tried to record it once. I hunted out the old tape cassette player I used to have in my bedroom at home and then later, in the Northfields flat, before I moved in with Willem. Amazingly I still have it, and it still works. I know it works, because I tested it out beforehand on the one o'clock news. The news programme recorded perfectly, but when I tried to play back my recording of the broadcast there was nothing, just this dry, scraping sound, like fingernails across a blackboard.

I stopped trying after that. It felt – dangerous.

– The Free-Islam party are saying that some parts of Istanbul may have to be evacuated and sealed off. As a member of the US delegation to the emergency session, can you confirm or deny that there are fears over the contamination of the groundwater supply?

– These allegations about the safety of the water are just rumours put about by Free-Islam to discredit the official

investigations process. If they persist in refusing us access to the main site we may be forced to consider other measures. What's important at this stage is to prevent any kind of security breach.
– Can you say precisely what you mean by 'other measures'?
– As guardians of the free world, we must be prepared to consider any and all measures at our disposal. What's imperative is to put a lid on this situation before it spirals out of control.

I have not been to church in years, not since school.

There is a church nearby, just a couple of streets from our flat. The church is called St Margaret's. It is quite small inside, with plastic chairs instead of pews. There is a smell of damp stone and rotting hymn books. I stand beneath the high arches of St Margaret's church and think about how one day soon all this will be gone, that in another hundred years we'll have forgotten what any of it meant. The thought brings tears to my eyes, but in a way I am glad.

Everything except the chairs feels centuries old and falling apart.

As I pass back towards the entrance I notice a small table towards the rear of the building where there are leaflets describing its history and also a few postcards and a box for donations. I drop a pound coin into the donations box and take one of the postcards. It pictures St Margaret of Antioch, wearing a blue cloak and leading a dragon. The card smells damp, like everything else, but I am glad to have it. I like the image of St Margaret in her blue cloak. Her features are slightly flattened and she has a don't-fuck-with-me look about her that makes me smile.

You know what you know, she seems to say to me. You are not crazy.

Whether she was ever really a saint I don't know, but she's definitely a woman I could admire.

There have been demonstrations in Istanbul.

The Free-Islam opposition have been demanding the closure and dismantling of American missile bases in Turkey. Many of the protestors were carrying placards bearing photographs of Meera Chowdri.

When I ask Chloe what she thinks of Free-Islam's demands, she shrugs and then picks at her nails.

'I don't know about you,' she says, 'but I'm right with them. I wouldn't want a bunch of trigger-happy cowboys keeping their missiles in my back garden, either.'

There's a theory I read somewhere about how time can be folded in two, like a handkerchief.

The next time I hear the broadcast I imagine the handkerchief laid over my face. I can breathe through it, and I can see light through it, but not much else.

I imagine the layers of time laid back to back, chafing against one another softly, like the wings of two angels.

Willem's back on nights at the moment.

When he's on nights I sometimes don't see him for days. I see him this lunchtime, though. He's just come off a flight from Argentina. He looks tired but he's in a good mood. I make us some lunch and we catch up on news. He's not due back at the airport until five o'clock.

I sip my wine. I wonder if I should tell him what came in the post this morning, the prospectus from Birkbeck with the application form. I decide it can wait a while longer.

Willem smiles his crinkle-eyed smile and smoothes the tabletop with his fingers. He has that look on his face, that oddly wistful, boyish expression that comes over him when he remembers something funny.

'What is it?' I say to him. 'Are you going to share that joke with me, or hoard it?'

'It's nothing,' Will says. 'It's just this new co-pilot I've been flying with, Ned Merrick? He's from Texas. Such a funny guy. Used to be a rancher, can you believe it? He's got half the craft in the fleet named after those goddamned prizewinning steers of his.'

He chuckles to himself, smiling his smile. I know he's happy. Happy with his job and with this new colleague, happy to be here with me, sharing his bit of a joke and the rest of his life.

Willem van Doer is lucky, because he has always known what he wanted to do.

For Will the world is a good place, in spite of everything.

Merrick's first name is Ned, I think to myself. I don't think that's ever been mentioned in the broadcast.

I wonder if I am mad, after all. In some ways, I think, that would be easier. Then I wonder how much time I still have left before it happens. Three months? A year? Two days?

It wouldn't make any difference, even if I could convince Willem to give up flying, There are plenty of pilots, after all, there are other sky captains. That plane could still take off.

That plane could still take off at any time.

CONTRIBUTORS' BIOGRAPHIES

PRIYA SHARMA is a doctor in the UK who writes speculative fiction. Her work has appeared in *Interzone, Black Static, Albedo One, Alt Hist* and on *Tor.com*, amongst others. She has been reprinted in various *Best of* anthologies.

JESS HYSLOP currently lives in Cambridge, where she works, writes, and daydreams, but will soon be relocating to Chichester to train as a book conservator. She studied English at the University of Cambridge, and was there awarded the Quiller-Couch prize for creative writing upon her graduation in 2010. Since then, her short fiction has appeared in venues such as *Interzone, Daily Science Fiction,* and *Mirror Dance*.

GEORGINA BRUCE was born in Birmingham and now lives in Edinburgh, where she works as a lecturer in further education. Her fiction has appeared in various anthologies and magazines. 'The Art of Flying' was longlisted for the Bridport Prize 2011 and Mslexia Short Story prize 2012. In 2014, she was shortlisted for the Scottish Book Trust New Writer Award. She is currently working on a novel about mothers, daughters, music and suicide.

TIM MAUGHAN is a British writer currently based in Brooklyn, using both fiction and non-fiction to explore issues around cities, art, class, and technology. His debut short story collection *Paintwork* received critical acclaim when released in 2011, and his story 'Limited Edition' was shortlisted for the 2012 BSFA short fiction award. He sometimes makes films, too.

DAVID TURNBULL is the author of a children's fantasy novel *The Tale Of Euan Redcap*. Born in Edinburgh, but having lived and worked in London for over thirty years, his short fiction has appeared in numerous magazines and anthologies. Recent anthologies include *Dandelions Of Mars*, a Whortleberry Press tribute to Ray Bradbury, *Astrologica* The Alchemy Press and *A Chimerical World Vol 11 – Tales Of The Unseelie Court* Seventh Star Press. He is member of the Clockhouse London group of genre writers.

HELEN JACKSON likes making stuff up and eating cake. She is a short story writer and a Scottish BAFTA-nominated animation director. She's lucky enough to live in Edinburgh, her favourite city. Her stories have been published in various magazines including *Interzone*, and in the anthologies *Rocket Science* and *ImagiNation: Stories Of Scotland's Future*. She was a winner in the 2011 Scottish Wave of Change short story competition with 'Power of Scotland'.

E. J. SWIFT is an English writer who lives and works in London. Her short fiction has previously been published in Interzone magazine. Her debut novel OSIRIS was published by Night Shade Books and Del Rey UK, and is the first in a trilogy, *The Osiris Project*. Book 2 – *Cataveiro* – was also published this year and Book 3 is forthcoming in 2015. Saga's Children was shortlisted for this year's BSFA short fiction award.

CAROLE JOHNSTONE is a Scot living in Essex. Her short stories have appeared in numerous magazines and anthologies. Her work has been reprinted in Ellen Datlow's *Best Of Horror Of The Year* series and Salt Publishing's *Best British Fantasy 2013*. Her debut short story collection, *The Bright Day Is Done*, is forthcoming from Gray Friar Press, and she has two novellas in print: *Frenzy*, published by Damnation Books and *Cold Turkey*, which is part of TTA Press' novella series. She is presently at work on her second novel while seeking fame and fortune with the first – but just can't seem to kick the short story habit.

JIM HAWKINS' first SF story, Play Back, was published in New Worlds in 1969. Since then he has been a teacher, a BBC Producer, a screenwriter with a long list of credits, and software developer. Two of his four novelettes for Interzone have been republished in 'Year's Best' anthologies. His BBC screenplay Thank You Comrades was nominated for a BAFTA award.

After a career writing about science fiction and fantasy on the magazines *SFX*, *Death Ray* and *White Dwarf*, GUY HALEY now writes it. He believes this to be a preferable state of affairs. Guy is the author of *Reality 36*, *Omega Point*, *Champion Of Mars*, *Crash* and numerous titles for the Black Library.

CHRIS BUTLER has published two books, the science fiction novel *Any Time Now* and the fantasy novella *The Flight Of Ravens*, which was shortlisted for the BSFA Award for short fiction in 2013. His short stories have been published in magazines and anthologies including *Asimov's Science Fiction*, *Interzone* and *Nature*. Chris is currently hard at work on new novels and short fiction, including a sequence of stories set in the same world as 'The Animator'.

V. H. LESLIE's stories have appeared in *Black Static*, *Interzone*, *Weird Fiction Review* and *Strange Tales IV*. She has also had fiction and non-fiction published in *Shadows and Tall Trees* and writes a monthly column for *This is Horror*. Her story 'Namesake' was recently selected for *Best British Horror* and 2013 also saw her win a Hawthornden Fellowship and the Lightship First Chapter Prize.

SARAH BROOKS has lived in China, the far south of Italy, and the far north of Japan, but is now settled West Yorkshire. She has recently completed her PhD on classical Chinese ghost stories, and teaches in the East Asian Studies department at the University of Leeds. She's a graduate of the 2012 Clarion West Writers' Workshop, and has had stories published in *Interzone*, *Shimmer* and the *Journal of Unlikely Entomology*.

NINA ALLAN's fiction has featured in numerous magazines and anthologies, including *The Year's Best Fantasy And Science Fiction 2012*, *The Mammoth Book Of British Crime #10* and *Best Horror Of The Year*. Her most recent books include the novella *Spin* (Winner of the this year's BSFA award for Best Short Fiction.) and the story collection *Stardust: The Ruby Castle Stories*. She was the Winner of the Aeon Award (2007) and has been shortlisted for the British Fantasy Award (2006, 2010, 2013) and the British Science Fiction Award (2006, 2010, 2011, 2013). This year, her story, 'The Gateway', has also been nominated for a Shirley Jackson Award in the Best Novella category. Her novel, *The Race*, is forthcoming August 2014 with NewCon Press.

ACKNOWLEDGEMENTS

Steve Haynes would like to thank his wife Jane and their youngest children (Indigo, Dylan and Morris) for putting up with him during the editing process.

'Thesea and Astaurius', copyright © Priya Sharma 2013 was first published in *Interzone* (TTA Press), May – June 2013, and is reprinted by permission of the author.

'Triolet', copyright © Jess Hyslop 2013 was first published in *Interzone* (TTA Press), May – June 2013, and is reprinted by permission of the author.

'Cat World', copyright © Georgina Bruce 2013 was first published in *Interzone* (TTA Press), May – June 2013, and is reprinted by permission of the author.

'Zero Hours', copyright © Tim Maughan 2013 was first published in *Futures Exchange 2013*, and is reprinted by permission of the author.

'Aspects of Aries', copyright © David Turnbull 2013 was first published in *Astrologica: Stories of the Zodiac* (The Alchemy Press), 2013, and is reprinted by permission of the author.

'Build Guide', copyright © Helen Jackson 2013 was first published in *Interzone* (TTA Press), Jan – Feb 2013, and is reprinted by permission of the author.

'Saga's Children', copyright © E. J. Swift 2013 is first published in *The Lowest Heaven* (Jurassic), 2013, and is reprinted here by permission of the author.

'Ad Astra', copyright © Carole Johnstone 2013 was first published in *Interzone* (TTA Press), Sep – Oct 2013, and is reprinted by permission of the author.

'Sky Leap – Earth Flame', copyright © Jim Hawkins 2013 was first published in *Interzone* (TTA Press), Jan – Feb 2013, and is reprinted by permission of the author.

'iRobot', copyright © Guy Haley 2013 was first published in *Interzone* (TTA Press), Jan – Feb 2013, and is reprinted by permission of the author.

'The Animator', copyright © Chris Butler 2013 was first published in *Interzone* (TTA Press), Mar – April 2013, and is reprinted by permission of the author.

'The Cloud Cartographer', copyright © V. H. Leslie 2013 was first published in *Interzone* (TTA Press), Jul – Aug 2013, and is reprinted by permission of the author.

'Trans-Siberia, copyright © Sarah Brooks 2013 was first published in *Interzone* (TTA Press), Nov – Dec 2013, and is reprinted by permission of the author.

'Higher Up', copyright © Nina Allan 2013 was first published in *Microcosmos* (NewCon Press), 2013, and is reprinted by permission of the author.